Lachlan IN A KILT

The Ballachulish Trilogy, Book One

ANNA DURAND

JACOBSVILLE BOOKS · MARIETTA, OHIO

LACHLAN IN A KILT

Copyright © 2021 by Lisa A. Shiel
All rights reserved.

The characters and events in this book are fictional. No portion of this book may be copied, reproduced, or transmitted in any form or by any means, electronic or otherwise, including recording, photocopying, or inclusion in any information storage and retrieval system, without the express written permission of the publisher and author, except for brief excerpts quoted in published reviews.

ISBN: 978-1-949406-61-0 (paperback)
ISBN: 978-1-949406-62-7 (ebook)
ISBN: 978-1-949406-63-4 (audiobook)

Manufactured in the United States.

Jacobsville Books
www.JacobsvilleBooks.com

Publisher's Cataloging-in-Publication Data
provided by Five Rainbows Cataloging Services

Names: Durand, Anna, author.
Title: Lachlan in a kilt / Anna Durand.
Description: Marietta, OH : Jacobsville Books, 2021. | Series: Ballachulish Trilogy, bk. 1.
Identifiers: ISBN 978-1-949406-61-0 (paperback) | ISBN 978-1-949406-62-7 (ebook) | ISBN 978-1-949406-63-4 (audiobook)
Subjects: LCSH: Man-woman relationships--Fiction. | Scots--Fiction. | Americans--Fiction. | Chicago (Ill.)--Fiction. | Romance fiction. | BISAC: FICTION / Romance / Contemporary. | FICTION / Romance / Romantic Comedy. | FICTION / Romance / Later in Life. | GSAFD: Love stories.
Classification: LCC PS3604.U724 L33 2021 (print) | LCC PS3604.U724 (ebook) | DDC 813/.6—dc23.

Other Books by Anna Durand

Aidan in a Kilt (The Ballachulish Trilogy, Book Two)
Rory in a Kilt (The Ballachulish Trilogy, Book Three)
Brit vs. Scot (A Hot Brits/Hot Scots/Au Naturel Crossover Book)
Dangerous in a Kilt (Hot Scots, Book One)
Wicked in a Kilt (Hot Scots, Book Two)
Scandalous in a Kilt (Hot Scots, Book Three)
The MacTaggart Brothers Trilogy (Hot Scots, Books 1-3)
Gift-Wrapped in a Kilt (Hot Scots, Book Four)
Notorious in a Kilt (Hot Scots, Book Five)
Insatiable in a Kilt (Hot Scots, Book Six)
Lethal in a Kilt (Hot Scots, Book Seven)
Irresistible in a Kilt (Hot Scots, Book Eight)
Devastating in a Kilt (Hot Scots, Book Nine)
Spellbound in a Kilt (Hot Scots, Book Ten)
One Hot Chance (Hot Brits, Book One)
One Hot Roomie (Hot Brits, Book Two)
One Hot Crush (Hot Brits, Book Three)
The Dixon Brothers Trilogy (Hot Brits, Books 1-3)
One Hot Escape (Hot Brits, Book Four)
One Hot Rumor (Hot Brits, Book Five)
One Hot Christmas (Hot Brits, Book Six)
Natural Passion (Au Naturel Trilogy, Book One)
Natural Impulse (Au Naturel Trilogy, Book Two)
Natural Satisfaction (Au Naturel Trilogy, Book Three)
Fired Up (a standalone romance)
The Mortal Falls (Undercover Elementals, Book One)
The Mortal Fires (Undercover Elementals, Book Two)
The Mortal Tempest (Undercover Elementals, Book Three)
The Janusite Trilogy (Undercover Elementals, Books 1-3)
Obsidian Hunger (Undercover Elementals, Book Four)
Unbidden Hunger (Undercover Elementals, Book Five)
Willpower (Psychic Crossroads, Book One)
Intuition (Psychic Crossroads, Book Two)
Kinetic (Psychic Crossroads, Book Three)
Passion Never Dies: The Complete Reborn Series

Chapter One

I make my way into the club, down a darkened entryway, following a slender woman dressed in a tartan miniskirt. The plaid crisscrosses her breasts, leaving most of her skin exposed, but the sexy outfit can't rouse my interest. What the bloody hell had I been thinking? I've never liked clubs, and this one calls itself Dance Ardor, of all things. My dancing is of the foot-shuffling sort, not—

Bugger me.

As I step out of the hallway into the main part of the club, I catch sight of the couples on the dance floor. They writhe and thrust their hips, pasted to each other's bodies like cling film on a sausage, and make no attempt to disguise their lustful intentions, evidenced in their hungry gazes and pawing hands. One woman mashes her breasts to her partner's chest and throws her head back, arching her spine so her lover can latch his mouth onto her throat.

I halt at the perimeter, near one of many tables arranged in a semicircle around the dance floor. I'm too old for this shit. A forty-two-year-old Scotsman on the cusp of divorce has no business entering a place like this. It's for the young and unencumbered, not for me.

But the club's advert in a newspaper had caught my attention. "This Friday is Midsummer Kilt Night," the text declared, "step into a fantasy world for one night only."

Maybe I needed a fantasy, because I'd found myself drawn to this place.

The woman who preceded me into the club turns to glance back at me, her wide mouth curling into a sensual smile. She's painted her lips an odd purple shade that glistens like lacquer. The coruscating strobe lights streak shades of violet, crimson, and sapphire across her blonde hair, the tresses cut into one of those short and haphazard styles. A fashion-conscious lass? I hold back a groan, feeling not the slightest inclination to seduce this woman. A casual affair, for one night only, appealed to me until the moment I walked into this place.

The woman sashays up to me. "Hey, babe, wanna hook up?"

Bod a' chac. Are all American women so direct? I'm not sure I like that. Maybe it's my age showing, though forty-two had never seemed old to me until recently. Confronted with this young and attractive woman, I feel like a dirty old man for considering her offer for one bloody second. Half of one second, actually.

"Thank you," I say, "but I'm, ah…meeting someone."

It's bollocks, but I can't think of a better way to dismiss her without causing offense.

She sighs with all the disappointment of a woman whose erotic fantasies have been shattered. "Oh well, it figures a hot British guy is taken."

British? Technically, I suppose I am British—as in a resident of Great Britain—but every American I've met calls me Scottish. This lass seems unaware of the difference, or unable to differentiate a Scots brogue from an English accent.

Another reason this brash woman is not for me, even for a single night.

Her hips sway provocatively as she moves away from me.

I stand frozen in the spot where she left me, watching with tightening brows while the girl I rejected approaches another man. He wears a hip-hugging kilt with a sleeveless shirt that has ragged edges. The woman leans in close—to make another direct offer, no doubt. The man slips his arm around her waist and leads her past the bar toward the dance floor.

For a moment, I consider leaving the club. Spending the night alone in a house that belongs to my American friend, Gil Friedman, sounds better with each passing second. I force myself to scan the club with my gaze, though I hold out little hope I'll spy a woman worthy of my interest. Had I expected to find an intelligent, down-to-earth woman in an underground club? *Bloody eejit ye are, Lachlan.*

Yesterday, I'd spotted a lovely woman tending to her rose bushes in front of the house next door to Gil's, but I hadn't approached her. I want a casual fling, not a relationship. A woman like her, she'd want more. I shake my head at my own arrogance. How can I know a woman's nature based on the way she tends roses? Yet something about her—the way she snipped and trimmed the bushes with exquisite care, her focus entirely on them, her expression soft and almost wistful—made me want to know her.

I do know something about her, aside from her gardening skills. My neighbor for the next month is Erica Teague. Gil told me as much. I can't introduce myself to her, no matter how much the bonnie brunette intrigues me.

A scunner of a man bumps into me, his bleary gaze flashing to me, and mutters a slurred apology before shuffling off.

I frown, but then my gaze travels to the bar—and my pulse accelerates.

There she is. Erica Teague.

She perches on a high stool, her feet dangling above the floor. The thin, dangerously high heels she wears give her slender ankles an enticing curve. Her dress is the color of fresh cherries, ripe for the plucking. The hem must've ridden up when she climbed onto the stool because it reveals most of her thigh, all that creamy skin so appealing that I can't resist admiring the rest of her body. I let my attention wander over those womanly hips and her narrow waist, then higher still to the plunging neckline of her dress. It exposes the inner slopes of her breasts, which are as lush and creamy as the rest of her.

Lust grips me so hard I lose my breath. Erica is a decadent feast for the eyes. I burn to savor her body, from her dainty toes to her flat stomach, even her graceful eyebrows, and everywhere in between.

She lifts a brandy snifter and gulps down a mouthful. Her eyes drift half-closed for a heartbeat, then flutter open as her lips form a delicate smile of satisfaction. Her breasts heave as if she's pulled in a deep breath, completely sated.

Heat rushes through me, shortening my breaths.

Donnae stand here gawping, ye eejit. Get over there and speak to the lass.

I shouldn't. From Gil's description of Erica, she isn't the sort to sign on for a one-night fling, and besides, we'll be neighbors for the month.

My feet have a mind of their own and a different opinion of what I should do. They propel me across the club toward her. My pulse beats faster, harder, every thud of it pulsing through my veins.

Erica hops off her stool.

The dress flounces around her thighs, kissing the tops of her knees. I've never paid much mind to a woman's knees, but hers are…enchanting.

I reach her just as she totters on her impossibly tall heels. With both hands, I grasp her upper arms. The feel of her soft, warm skin has me swallowing hard. The scent of her envelops me, evocative of roses and sweet soap and woman.

"Easy there," I say, steadying her.

She angles her head back, stretching her neck to aim her shimmering hazel eyes at me. The green flecks in them sparkle in the muted white lights at the bar, and even when the strobes splash over her, they can't diminish the striking beauty of her eyes. Her chestnut hair flows down to her shoulders, tumbling over them just far enough to trigger an urge to run my tongue over every millimeter of skin her hair touches.

Erica rakes her gaze over me from head to toe. The pink tip of her tongue pokes out between her lips, moistening them with a quick sweep.

"It's you, Erica," I say like a bloody moron.

Her lips pucker briefly. "And it's you."

She sounds uncertain. Had she seen me watching her yesterday through the living-room window in Gil's house?

Erica brings out a mobile phone and tilts it toward me, tapping one of her wee fingers on the screen. "It's eight thirty-nine."

"Quite the timekeeper, eh?" Maybe she has a fetish about always knowing the time, though Gil hadn't mentioned anything of the sort.

Erica shimmies her shoulders to push my hands off her arms. "I've been here for thirty-nine minutes. Doesn't that mean anything to you?"

Has my luck not changed at all? I find a woman who stirs my desires, but she turns out to be a nutter. A beautiful, disarmingly quirky nutter.

She's staring at me, mouth tight, waiting for my response.

What had she said? Something about the time and didn't I care about it.

"Not really," I say, allowing myself to revel in the vision of her one more time. "Except your bum's oot the windae."

Her mouth falls open. Her hands rise, then fall to her sides again.

"Buckled, are you?" I ask. Drunkenness might explain her odd behavior. I want her to be sane, so I can quench this lust without feeling I've taken advantage of a slightly deranged woman.

Aidan would love this. He enjoys calling me uptight, though I know it's teasing, not a criticism. Among the MacTaggarts, brothers and sisters and cousins alike, Rory is the most uptight by far. Still, the idea of me, the oldest and most serious, drowning in my lust for a woman I've just met would give Aidan a smug satisfaction.

Younger brothers are a trial, for certain.

Erica, the disarming bampot, spreads her arms wide. "Do you see any buckles or belts on this dress?"

I chuckle in spite of myself. "I meant are you drunk, lass?"

"Me?" She snorts, and even that sound makes me hunger to kiss her. She waves a hand, dismissing my question. "No. Never."

My hope for inebriation as the stimulus for her behavior evaporates. Maybe I should double-check.

I slant toward her, and the feminine scent of her envelops me again. My God, this woman is the embodiment of everything I'd wanted in a lover for the night. *Stay with me tonight,* I want to say. *Share my bed, Erica, let me crawl over your body to lick and suckle and nibble your sweet flesh.*

"Your eyes look all right," I tell her.

Despite my every impulse compelling me to do the opposite, I pull away from her.

"What?" she says, her forehead crinkling.

"Pupils get dilated when a person's drunk. Yours look normal, and your breath is fine, so I'm assuming you aren't buckled after all."

"Gee, thanks. Why—"

"Let me buy you a drink." I gesture to the bartender, wondering why the bloody hell I'm suggesting she consume more alcohol. I should walk away and leave the lass alone. Instead, I tell her, "In the name of neighborliness and all."

She stares blankly at me.

I pick up her snifter and swirl the amber liquid inside it.

Erica cants her head, observing me with the confused curiosity of someone who's encountered a strange new species of animal for the first time.

All of her, even her confusion, bewitches me.

I feign disgust at her choice of liquor, wrinkling my nose. "Brandy? That's a bairn's drink." I set the glass on the bar. "You're in a club. Have a real drink with me."

Erica leans that body against the bar, rolling her shoulders back. Her breasts bounce a little, enough to make my breath hitch and my cock jerk.

"Sure," she says. "What did you have in mind?"

If only she knew the real answer, the one I don't dare speak, she would run out the door as fast as her shapely legs can carry her.

Dirty old man, Lachlan, for certain.

Chapter Two

I smile at Erica, fair certain all my inhibitions and good sense have flown oot the windae along with my bum. I may not be speaking nonsense, not just yet, but I seem to have lost my ability to make sound judgment calls. If I were still rational, I'd take us both home in a cab and say good night at her doorstep. Instead, I'm suggesting she drink another cocktail.

The bartender approaches, and I order two glasses of whisky just as the music crescendoes. The man nods and walks away to get our drinks. As the music winds down, it segues into a quieter song with a lulling melody.

Erica rocks her hips to the tempo of the music, her shoulders swaying too, the fabric of her dress shimmying along with her body.

I can't resist sliding my gaze over her from head to toe, admiring her figure from those creamy shoulders down to her slender ankles. Every inch of her is bonnie and sexy and enough to make me want to do things to her I shouldn't be thinking about, much less doing.

She notices my attention and lifts a hand to her throat, as if she's as aroused as I am. Her pupils have enlarged, turning her irises a darker shade of hazel, the green flecks in them seeming more intense. I've never seen anything as beautiful as this woman, and I've never felt such intense lust in my life.

The bartender brings us two glasses of whisky. I toss mine back in one gulp. The burn of the whisky doesn't erase my hunger for her or even dull it, and the fire in my veins has nothing to do with alcohol.

Erica lifts her glass to her lips. She hesitates, sniffing like she's unsure of what she's about to drink. Then the lass takes a deep breath and tosses back the whisky. For a second or two, she freezes as if she's shocked—in a good way or a bad way, I have no idea. She sputters, coughs, and wheezes. Her legs wobble a wee bit, but she locks her knees to stay upright. Her gaze has gone glossy, though I don't think it's from desire.

The whisky has hit her hard.

Erica's lips part, forming a dreamy smile.

"Another," she shouts to the bartender. Within seconds, she's tossing back another finger of whisky, then she slaps her glass down on the bar. "Another."

I should intervene, shouldn't I? Though I don't know Erica, I can't let her get jaked.

When the bartender returns, I wave him away. "The lady's done for the night."

The bartender leaves.

Erica frowns at me. "What'd you do that for?"

She doesn't sound drunk, but she's acting that way.

I pluck the glass from her hand. "Don't drink much, do you?"

"So?"

I grasp her upper arms, her skin soft and cool against my palms, which have grown warm. "Best take it easy, then. Whisky's potent, and one glass has clearly done a number on you."

"I drank whisky?"

"Aye, and that's whisky spelled the Scottish way, without the E." I can't help smiling a wee bit because she is the most adorable, sexiest woman I've ever met. "You Americans don't know how to spell."

"Well, you Scots don't know how to pronounce anything." She slants toward me and tips her head back to look me in the eye. "Are you a Highlander?"

"Matter of fact, I am."

"Got a big sword?"

I capture her chin between my thumb and forefinger, bending my head toward hers. Her lips are close enough to kiss, and I can't keep the lust from coloring my voice. "Matter of fact, I do."

Her attention flicks down to my kilt. "Don't see it."

"Maybe I'll show you later. At home." Why am I saying these things to her? I should see her home and go to bed early, not stand here trying it on with Erica.

She swings her gaze up to mine. "What do Highlanders wear under their kilts?"

Bod an Donais. I'd love to show her what I've got on under my kilt. Love to show her my "sword" too.

I dip my head even closer until my breaths mingle with hers. "I think the whisky's getting to ye."

"Feel fine." She twirls on her high heels without stumbling, as if that proves she isn't intoxicated.

As much as I want this woman, I can't take advantage of her, even if she's only a little tipsy.

She scuffles backward a step and bumps into the bar.

I brace one elbow on the bar, cross my ankles, and let myself devour her body with my eyes one last time before I put her in a taxi.

Erica sidles closer to me.

Tell her to go home, my brain urges. But my cock has other ideas that keep me rooted to this spot.

She hoists herself onto her tiptoes and tilts her chin up. Her mouth hovers so close I could kiss her with only the slightest movement.

"Sure ye didn't have a pint or two before I got here?" I ask.

Why does my voice sound uncertain, almost quivering? I bend toward her an inch, no more, so close I swear I can taste her breaths. Erica leans in too, her heels lifting off the floor and her luscious breasts grazing my chest.

I settle my hands on her elbows, splaying my fingers over her silky bare skin. "Erica, you are exquisite, like a rare orchid plucked from a field of heather."

What a bloody stupid thing to say.

But I can't think anymore or notice anything except her eyes locked on to mine and her mouth so close her chin brushes against mine.

Then she kisses me.

Erica presses her mouth to mine and exhales a whisper of a moan.

My entire body goes rigid, and my cock throbs with a need that's hardening my *slat* more every second. I stop breathing and for certain stop thinking, especially when she flattens her hand on my chest and explores me with her delicate fingers. I don't hear the music anymore, only the pounding of my pulse in my ears as she molds her mouth to mine with more pressure and her tits rub against my chest. I know I shouldn't kiss her back, but the scent of her and the softness of her mouth encourage my muscles to relax—and my lips too.

She tastes like sin and heaven and whisky.

Erica slips her tongue between my lips.

My breath hitches, but despite my body craving her like mad, I know I shouldn't let her kiss me deeply. I'll never be able to say no to her, to what we both want, if I do that. All I can do is keep my teeth locked so she can't steal a deeper taste. And so I can't either.

My resolve lasts a few seconds.

Then I groan and take charge of the kiss, raking my lips over hers, opening to let her steal that deeper taste we've both wanted. She throws her arms around my neck, her body suspended off the floor. I can't stop myself from nibbling on her lower lip, loving the soft noises she makes and the fearless way she plunges deeper. I suck her lip into my mouth, only to release it and reclaim her mouth.

She plows her hand into my hair, the sensation of her fingers teasing my scalp almost too much to bear, then she drags me in for a tongue-thrusting kiss. We consume each other like nothing else in the world can satisfy our hunger, like if we separate our mouths, the world might stop turning.

I want her in my bed. Tonight.

What on earth is wrong with me? I pull away, staring at the lass.

She's staring at me too, her lips parted.

That look does me in, shattering the last thread of my willpower.

I hook an arm around her waist and draw her snug against me. She must feel my stiff cock, but I don't care. My voice comes out raspy and deeper, like I've become a satyr. "Are ye sure ye know what yer doing, lass?"

Her eyes go wide. She shakes her head, all that chestnut hair flinging around her face, and she staggers backward. Her hand flies to her mouth, but her gaze veers down to her free hand. She scrubs her fingers on her dress, though I have no idea why. She seems uncomfortable.

I reach for her hand. "Erica, are ye all right?"

She bolts away from me.

Though I try to run after her, a group of drunken laddies gets in my way, blocking my path to the club's entrance. I glimpse Erica sprinting down that corridor, but by the time I get around the scunners, she's gone.

I race outside. She's not there either. I've lost her.

But I know where she lives. I can check on her tomorrow to make sure she's all right. Her reaction to our kiss seemed…oddly panicked. I should apologize to her, though I can't figure out what I've done wrong.

You're a dunderhead, Lachlan. That's what you've done wrong.

Aye, and I should know better by now.

Chapter Three

After a fitful night's sleep, I wake in the morning feeling like I've committed a crime and need to turn myself in to the authorities. Is it illegal for a forty-two-old man to seduce a young woman? Erica is an adult, but I still feel like I've done something wrong. She kissed me, and I kissed her back. I haven't enjoyed a kiss that much in years.

Erica Teague is the most beautiful woman I've ever seen. According to my mate Gil, she's also clever and sweet. He mentioned she's been quieter lately, and not as "sunny" as usual. I wonder why that is, but it's not my business. I should stay away from Erica.

After having a shower, I get dressed and wander into the living room. Gil Friedman is letting me stay here for a month while he and his bride, Jayne, enjoy the comfort of my Edinburgh flat for a week before they head to my cottage in the Highlands for three weeks. Exchanging houses for a while had seemed like the best way to escape my problems back home, but now I'm wondering if I've made a mistake.

Erica Teague lives next door.

I sit on the sofa while I eat my breakfast, but I try not to gaze out the living-room window. It overlooks Erica's kitchen. So I stare down at my bowl of oatmeal instead. I've eaten half of my breakfast when movement beyond the window catches my eye.

Don't look, ye cacan. Stay away from Erica.

Maybe I should worry for my sanity when I'm calling myself a wee shit in my own thoughts.

I can't resist the siren call of the window, though, and I find my gaze swerving to the view—the one that looks into Erica's kitchen. I see her tossing some kind of food to a golden retriever that hops up on its hind legs in its eagerness to grab the treat. Then Erica washes her hands in the sink. She's bonnie and sexy, even when she's wearing sweatpants and a loose-fitting T-shirt. Her chestnut hair glistens in the morning light that filters through the window into her kitchen. A slight smile tugs at her lips.

Christ, I want her. Even more than I did last night.

Stop looking, you baothair, and stop thinking about her too. Maybe calling myself an idiot in Gaelic will knock some sense into me.

Not bloody likely.

I wolf down the rest of my oatmeal, keeping my head bowed. But when I've finished eating, I stand up and do the last thing I ought to be doing. I glance out the window.

Erica is smiling and saying something to her dog. Based on her expression and the way she puckers her lips when she speaks to the animal, I think she must be cooing silly words, like baby-talk for canines.

Sod it all. I can't pretend I never met the woman and avoid all contact with her for the entire four weeks I'll be here. I could move to a hotel, but I'd been looking forward to staying in a cozy home. I also promised Gil and Jayne I'd look after their house.

I pull on my shoes, grab my mobile, and head for the front door.

My mobile chimes just as I grasp the doorknob. I have a new text message.

Fumbling with the mobile, I open the new text. My brother Rory says, "It's done. Final decree in."

A relieved sigh rushes out of me. Thank God. I'm free of Aisley at last.

With my hand still curled around the doorknob, I stuff the mobile into my pocket. Maybe I should go back into the living room and shut the curtains. Ignore the sexy woman next door. Hide indoors until she leaves for work. She must have a job, right? I could ask her when I go over there to apologize for last night.

I don't need to know anything about her. I don't need to be friends with her. Aisley taught me everything I need to know about the folly of tying my life to a woman's. I will never go down that road again. Never.

But I should apologize to Erica. In the name of neighborliness.

Aye, it has nothing to do with her sensual body.

I march out the door and straight to Erica's house.

The door swings open before I can knock. Erica yelps, jerking in surprise, while she grips the leash of the dog that stands beside her.

I smile. "Morning, neighbor."

The dog flings his entire body at me, his front paws slamming into my thighs.

When was the last time I petted a dog? Or saw a dog? I can't remember, but I do love animals. So I scratch the dog behind his ears, and the pup licks my arm.

I look at Erica, who still seems stunned. "Aren't you happy to see me?"

Erica seizes the dog's collar and drags him backward. "Are you stalking me?"

"Stalking?" I scratch my cheek, wondering how to explain my presence here. I decide the truth is best. "I thought to follow you last night to make sure you were all right, but you took off so bloody fast. Might not believe it, but I am an honorable man."

A panicked laugh hiccups out of her. "Honorable? Stalking is a crime, buddy."

The dog hops up and down on his front feet, his tongue lolling.

Well, at least I've won over the pup. Now, if I can only convince Erica I'm not a stalker…

I shouldn't care what she thinks. I'm making sure she's all right after our encounter last night, nothing more.

"Erica," I begin, but stop when she eyes me with suspicion again. I raise my hands, palms out. "I'm trying to be friendly."

"Go creep out some other random girl you hunted down online." She pushes the dog out of the threshold with her foot and pulls the door halfway closed. "Leave me alone, Cliff."

Erica slams the door in my face. Literally. It misses my nose by an inch at most.

Did she just call me Cliff? That's not my name. Did I ever tell her my name last night? No, I don't think I did. We're having a misunderstanding of some sort.

I clear my throat and shout at the door, "Who the bloody hell is Cliff?"

On the other side of the door, I hear what sounds like a security chain being disengaged, and the door eases open a few inches. Erica peeks out at me through the small gap, still seeming wary—but with a hint of curiosity too.

I lift one brow. "Cliff?"

"Who are you?"

I offer her my hand. "Lachlan MacTaggart. I moved in next door yesterday. Housesitting for my friend, Gil Friedman, as an excuse for a holiday in America. Gil told me about you—your name and how much he and his new bride like you."

She stares at my hand, blinking slowly, like she's trying to make sense of things. Then she clasps my hand, lifting her gaze to mine.

I close my fingers around hers. A strange sensation crackles through me, like electricity, but it vanishes as quickly as it came. I am not excited to touch her again. That would be barmy.

"Erica Teague," she says. "But you know that already."

"Pleasure to meet you, Erica. Officially."

"Uh-huh." She withdraws her hand and folds her arms over her chest. "How did you know what I looked liked?"

"I arrived yesterday while you were out. When you came home, you set about tending to your rose bushes."

She bites her lip, averting her eyes for a moment. "The roses were here when I moved in."

"You care for them with such tenderness, it's wonderful to watch." I smile again, but this time with a touch of guilt. "Suppose I did stalk you, by accident. I truly am sorry about last night, though."

"Wasn't your fault." She studies me with narrowed eyes, pinching her lips into a slight pucker. "How do I know you're really housesitting for Gil and Jayne?"

"Ring him. He's at my place in Scotland and he's got his mobile. Said you knew the number."

I watch her expression, the tiny movements that suggest she's sizing me up as we speak. The lass doesn't trust me, not just yet. I can't blame her for that after the mixup last night. Maybe I should give her some space.

"Ring Gil," I say. "And if you want me, I'll be next door."

I go back to Gil's house and try to forget about Erica, at least for a while. She needs time to adjust to the fact I'll be living next door to her for twenty-eight days. The gentlemanly thing to do is to allow her that time.

And not look out the bloody living-room window.

Chapter Four

Yes, I fully intended to avoid glancing at Erica's house. I meant to leave her alone unless she decided to speak to me, but a few minutes after returning to Gil's house, I wander into the living room. I don't see Erica in her kitchen, and I can't decide if I'm relieved or disappointed. I didn't walk into this room because I hoped to get a glimpse of her. No, I felt like relaxing on the sofa and enjoying the view of…Erica's kitchen.

Bloody hell, I'm a moron. A man of my age should not be spying on his neighbor, no matter how sexy she might be. I wonder how old Erica is. Too young for me, I'm dead certain.

I settle in on the sofa with my laptop and browse the internet for…things. I don't know what I'm looking for because all I'm trying to do is stop thinking about the bonnie American next door.

A flash of movement in Erica's kitchen spurs me to look up from my computer.

Erica has just walked into the kitchen and is fussing with something on the counter while she talks to someone on her mobile phone.

No, I will not spy on her.

I go back to staring at my laptop, though everything on the screen has suddenly blurred. I cannae focus on websites. Cannae focus on anything with that beautiful lass living next door.

My eyes force me to look out the window.

Erica has just ended her call, which I can tell because she slipped the mobile into her jeans pocket.

Since I seem to have developed a fixation with the house next door, I continue peering out the window even after Erica leaves the kitchen. It's good that she left. I do not need to see her again.

Unless she knocks on my door.

"*Mhac na galla*," I hiss. I am a son of a bitch, in English and Gaelic, for even considering the possibility of starting anything with any woman, much less the younger lass next door.

To avoid glancing out the window, I leave my laptop on the living-room table and make my way to the kitchen. I can't see into Erica's house from here, though I can glimpse her porch.

A man saunters up the concrete path and hops up the three steps that lead onto the porch. He fiddles with his clothes as if he's making sure he looks good, then he smooths a hand over his blond hair and knocks on the door.

Erica swings the door open, but I can't see more than a glimpse of her hair. That bonnie, silky chestnut hair. When she sees the man, she retreats from him and seems to be using the door as a shield between them.

The man leans against the outside of the house beside the door and hooks a thumb in the pocket of his posh trousers. I'm no fashion expert, but even I can tell he's wearing expensive clothes. He must have arrived in the yellow Alpha Romeo that's parked at the curb in front of Erica's house. Despite the distance between where I'm standing and where he is, I can see the expression on his face. He gazes at Erica with a lustful slant to his lips.

Cannae blame him. She's stunning.

He tips his head to the side and says something.

I want to open the window above the sink to hear their conversation. More spying? *Bloody hell, man, what's wrong with you?*

Erica's visitor smiles in a way that he must think is endearing, but it makes me want to run over there and punch him. The fact that Erica keeps the door between them suggests she doesn't like the man. Are they former lovers?

The man takes two steps toward Erica and reaches out as if to touch her face, but I can't see that part of her.

My fingers ache. When I look down at them, I realize I'm gripping the sink counter hard enough to cause pain. I cannot stand bullies, and that scunner over there who's speaking to Erica is clearly that sort of man.

Erica's visitor rests one hand on the door and the other on the jamb, leaning into it.

Is that bastard trying to force his way into the house?

Erica tries to shut the door, but the scunner uses his foot to stop her from doing that.

A dog starts barking. Her dog, I assume. It's not friendly barking either, but the sort that means the dog is upset.

And still, the bastard doesn't relent. He keeps his foot jammed in the doorway.

Ye fucking ersehole, treating a woman like that.

I race out the front door, slamming it shut behind me, and run for Erica's house.

The scunner is trying again to stop her from shutting her door. After several attempts, he throws the weight of his body into it, bashing the door into Erica's chin.

I trip over a tree root and need a few seconds to regain my balance and get moving again.

"Quit it!" Erica shouts as she kicks the man's foot. "Stop or I'll call—"

"The police?" the scunner says. He throws his head back and laughs. "You're so funny. Who do you think they'll believe? A filthy little thief, or the Harvard-educated, prized son of the Cichon dynasty?"

"Get away, you twisted son of a bitch!"

I'm on Erica's lawn now, barreling toward the front door of her house.

She yanks the door inward, knocking the *bod ceann* off-balance just enough that she can slam the door on his foot.

He deserves much worse.

The bastard howls, his face wrenching in agony. He stumbles backward, shouting nasty curses, and Erica's dog darts out the door to latch onto the man's calf.

Erica drags the dog back inside the house.

I vault across the concrete walkway and leap onto the porch, landing beside the scunner. But I don't look at him. I aim my gaze at Erica. "Need a hand?"

"Thanks, but this creep was just leaving." She glowers at the cretin, though her lower lip trembles.

Her attacker scrambles to his feet, scowling at me. He's a *bod ceann* without question, though "dickhead" doesn't seem like a strong enough insult for him.

Despite my pulse racing and adrenaline electrifying my blood, I manage to maintain a calm demeanor. Years of working with high-strung clients have taught me that much. But I don't even try to soften the look in my eyes, which must be angry, when I turn my attention to the would-be intruder.

"Your visit is over, laddie," I say in a menacing tone that doesn't sound like me at all. "Take yourself away from here."

The tosser steps away from the door, holding his nose high and tightening his lips into a smirk. "Or what? You'll torture me to death with bagpipe music?"

"I don't take kindly to scunners who try to force their way into a lady's home."

The twat flicks his middle finger at me.

"Okay-okay," Erica says, rushing forward to plant herself between me and the piece of human shit who harassed her. "Let's end this right now. You two walloping each other won't solve anything."

Aye, but it would feel bloody good to do it.

I arch one brow at her. "Sure you don't want me to give him a right skelping with a caber?"

"A caper?" the ersehole says with a snigger. "Ooooh, hitting me with pickled garnish sounds real scary."

I smile at him in a manner sure to convince him I'm not joking. "A caber's a very large wooden pole. Best know what yer on about before ye start bumping yer gums, laddie."

The man's forehead wrinkles as he glances sideways at Erica. "Where'd you find this jerk-wad?"

"He's my new neighbor." She points a finger in the direction of the yellow Alfa Romeo parked at the curb. "You have no place in my life anymore. Go."

How could a lovely woman like Erica get involved with a cretin like this man?

The human shit pile grinds his teeth, his lips working, his gaze nailed to mine.

Does he actually believe he can intimidate me?

The scunner hunches his shoulders and trudges toward his car. As he jerks the driver's door open, he calls out to me, "How ya like my ride, Scotch Tape?"

I give him a big smile. "Quite nice, I must say. Shame I had to leave my Aston Martin back at Inverness, but I've got pictures if you'd like to see."

The bastard dives into the car and yanks the door shut, making the vehicle rock. The Alfa Romeo's engine roars to life. Tires squeal as he tears off down the street.

I sigh. "A right scunner, that one, but a coward at heart."

"He's a lying, cheating asshole too," Erica says. Her entire body seems to be trembling faintly.

I touch her arm. "You're shaking. Let me help you inside."

"I'm fine." She gazes into my eyes, and her posture relaxes a touch. "Thank you, Lachlan. I'm grateful for your help with Presley."

"That'd be the lying, cheating ersehole."

"Yeah."

She looks so exhausted and downtrodden that I can't stop myself from sliding my hand down her arm to take her hand, sandwiching it between both of mine. "Is there someone I could call for you? A relative or friend or…someone."

"I'm fine, I swear. I appreciate your concern, but I have to go."

Erica's dog bounds out the open door to hurl his body at me. His front paws land on my stomach, and I bend down to wrap my arms around the pup, muttering the sort of silly bollocks most people say to dogs.

When I straighten, the pup trots to Erica and sits down.

She scratches the dog's head, looking down at his innocent face. "You're not fooling anybody. Sit and stay, my ass." She looks at me. "Thank you. Again."

I shrug. "I cannot abide bullies. Heard a right rammy going on over here and came to offer my assistance. In the name of neighborliness, of course."

She's twirling a lock of hair with one finger, but then she seems to notice she's doing that and clamps her hand at her nape.

Is that a slight blush on her cheeks? That would mean she wants me.

Christ, I want her. I can't help smiling at the bonnie, sexy, sweet lass.

"Um…" Erica begins, but she can't seem to figure where to go from there. "I could've handled Presley on my own, but I appreciate the save."

"Anytime, lass, anytime. But you can stop thanking me. Three times is plenty."

I should leave her alone now. The lass has been through enough with that scunner ruining her morning. So I turn away, heading toward Gil's house. After a couple of steps, I hesitate and glance back at her. "If you want me—"

"I know where you live." She scratches her neck, suddenly looking sheepish. "Didn't mean that in a creepy way, like I'm planning a home invasion."

My attention flicks down to her breasts, and for a moment, I can do nothing but stare at them and wonder what they look like. What they taste like. *Get a grip, man.* I swerve my focus back to Erica's eyes. "Invade anytime. I'm certain I can take you."

I rush back to Gil's house and slam the door shut behind me.

What am I doing? Flirting with a vibrant young woman, while I'm a forty-two-year-old divorced man with enough scars to keep a plastic surgeon busy for ten years.

I won't see her again. She has problems of her own.

But I need to see her again.

Aye, I'm a dunderhead of the first order.

Chapter Five

For a while after my encounter with Erica and that scunner, Presley, I try everything I can think of to get my mind off what happened. I despise anyone, male or female, who treats others with disdain and hostility. Presley seems like exactly the sort who would bully and cajole someone he views as weaker than himself.

Thinking about all of that makes me tense and slightly nauseous. I need a different distraction, but ringing my brother Rory doesn't help. He isn't answering. Busy with a client, I'm sure. I ring my youngest brother, Aidan, but he also doesn't answer.

Everyone has a life to lead except for me. I'm sitting here in someone else's house, trying to make sense of my world.

The doorbell rings.

Is it Erica?

Bloody hell, man, have your testicles shriveled up and turned you into a woman?

Now I'm insulting myself in my own thoughts. I've turned into a bampot for certain, but I heave my body off the sofa and shuffle to the front door, swinging it inward.

Erica smiles sweetly at me.

All the blood vacates my brain and floods down to my *slat*. I try to seem nonchalant by placing one hand on the door and cocking my hip. And I force myself to look at her face, not her bosom. "You want me, then?"

I want her to say yes, but she ought to say no.

Erica tips her head back to meet my gaze. "I talked to Gil. He sent me a photo of you and him together, so I know you're who you say you are." She points at the bag hooked over her shoulder. The sides are distended as if she's got a large item in there. "Besides, I brought you a housewarming slash thanks-for-scaring-the-bejesus-out-of-my-ex gift."

Heaven above, she is the most adorable woman on earth. Her dog sits beside her, ever the faithful companion.

I duck my head, suddenly feeling like a wee laddie having his first crush on a lassie, and move only my eyes to look up at her. I can't help smiling. "You checked me out, eh? Suppose after last night, I can't blame you for being suspicious. And I must admit, it's rather endearing." I glance at her bag. "You owe me no gifts for lending a hand, but I'll accept it as a housewarming present."

"Deal." She bites her lip. "May I come in?"

"Of course."

The dog jumps up to plant his paws on my stomach, his tail wagging. I can't resist the sweet pup any more than I can resist his owner, so I kneel to scratch behind the dog's ears. He chuffs, clearly enjoying the attention.

I stand up and roll my shoulders back. "Your dog seems to like me."

"His name is Casey, and he's easier than a drunk hooker. He gets just as excited about the mailman and the squirrel in the backyard."

"Careful, with words like those I might get to thinking you fancy me." I shouldn't want her to fancy me, but for some reason, I do.

She smiles. "Then you're easier than Casey. Unfortunately, I'm no longer in the market for romance."

"You did kiss me last night."

"I—well—" Her cheeks turn a bonnie shade of pink as she rocks back on her heels. Her lips are tight, and she won't look at me, seeming to prefer to stare at the doorjamb. "Do you want the damn brownies or what?"

"You are a difficult one, aren't you?" When she finally meets my gaze, I wink. "I love a challenge."

"Oh please." She shakes her head. "I'd have you fleeing back to Scotland in a week, tops."

I swing the door wide, waving for her to come inside.

Casey tumbles over the threshold first, then Erica shuffles past me.

And I pluck the bag from her shoulder as she passes me. "A gentleman never permits a lady to carry a heavy load."

"It's brownies, not iron ore."

The bag isn't heavy, but my mother raised me to be respectful toward women. Sorcha MacTaggart would have my hide if I let Erica carry her own bag.

I shut the door. "Indulge me."

"Fine. But if you try to carry *me*, I'll bite you."

"An intriguing offer."

The confused look on her face makes me want to kiss her, and I can't help grinning at the lass.

Erica straightens, clears her throat, and shoves her hands into her jeans pockets. "It wasn't an offer."

"I know." I bend my head closer to hers. "Thank you for the sweets, Erica."

Since I've invited her into my home—ah, Gil's home—I might as well be neighborly. So I gesture for her to follow me deeper into the house. Erica and her pup trail me down the three steps into the sunken living room where an L-shaped sofa faces two armchairs with a glass-topped coffee table in the middle. Sliding glass doors overlook the backyard, and the sunshine streaming in through the windows and those doors makes Erica look even bonnier, the way the light gives her chestnut hair a golden shine.

She glances at the seating options, then drops down onto the sofa. Casey pounces onto the cushion beside her.

"Casey!" she cries out while trying to push the pup off, but he only snuggles closer to her. "I am so sorry. I let him lie on my sofa, and I don't usually take him to other people's houses."

I can't blame Casey for wanting to get as close as possible to Erica.

"Let the pup have his fun." I settle into an armchair and try not to smirk, but I can't restrain the expression. "Besides, it's not my sofa."

"Gil didn't demand a security deposit?"

"We're friends. He trusts me." I lean back in my chair and brace one ankle on the opposite knee. "Glad as I am to see you, I had the impression you wanted nothing to do with me."

She stares at me for several seconds, not blinking. Finally, she seems to shake off whatever she'd been thinking or feeling. "I thought we should clear the air."

"You mean talk about last night."

She nods, biting her lip. "I've never done anything like that in my life. I didn't intend for it to happen, and it most definitely will not happen again."

"So, you won't be molesting me here in the living room." I wag my eyebrows. Maybe I want her to molest me, but I shouldn't be flirting with her.

Her cheeks turn pink again, and she ducks her head to study the carpeting.

Christ, I've embarrassed her. What an erse I am.

"That was a stupid joke," I say. "I apologize, never meant to embarrass you."

"I humiliated myself quite well." She lifts her gaze to mine. "You must think I'm a total slut."

Tipping my head to the side, I watch her for a moment, wondering why she would say such a thing. Speaking to a stranger, even kissing one, doesn't make her a slag. "May I ask what you were doing in the club?"

"I had a date. He stood me up."

"The infamous Cliff."

"Yes." She clasps her hands on her lap. "When you showed up and knew my name, I assumed you were him."

"That does explain your obsession with the time." I feel my mouth turning down at one corner as I remember what sort of club that place had been. A woman like Erica doesn't belong there. I don't mean to squint at her, but I find I'm doing precisely that. "Did you have any idea what sort of club it was?"

"Yes. I've heard the rumors." Her gaze focused on the carpeting, she grips the sofa's edge. "People go there to find casual sex partners."

"Aye." The word comes out as half sigh and half growl. "You don't belong in that place, Erica."

She rolls her eyes up to scrutinize me. "Why were you there?"

How can I answer her question? I was there for the same reason as everyone in the club.

She keeps watching me, waiting for my response.

Bloody hell. I fidget and make a face that probably looks like I've sat on a sharp rock. "I wanted what the club has to offer."

Her lips crimp briefly, then she flops back against the sofa to wrap her arms around herself.

I wince a touch and scratch my own ear the way I'd scratched Casey's earlier. "It was a mistake. After you left, and I couldn't catch up to you, I went back into the club. Couldn't do it, though."

"Why not?"

"It's simple." I lean forward to trace a fingertip over the coffee table in slow figure-eights, my attention riveted to the movements so I can avoid looking at her. "None of those women measured up to you."

I swear I can feel her gaze on me, and it makes my skin itch. Why did I say that? I have nothing to offer Erica, nothing but pain she won't understand. I will never explain it to her. I want this bonnie, sweet lass to think of me as a strong, virile man, not...what I really am.

Her silence makes my skin itch even more, and I find myself lifting my gaze to hers. "You've enchanted me, Erica."

And it's true. Since the moment I first laid eyes on her yesterday, when she'd been tending her roses, I haven't been able to think about anything else for more than a few minutes at a time, often only a matter of seconds. No woman has ever affected me this way before.

She links her fingers over her belly and presses her knees together, her toes tapping furiously on the carpet.

I wonder if she has the same sort of fears that I battle every day. Might Erica Teague be a kindred spirit? Doesnae matter. I cannot get entangled in a relationship, with her or anyone.

But the anxiety on her face and in her posture makes me need to do something, anything, to soothe her.

I stride around the table, settle onto the sofa beside her, and take her hands in mine. Her palms are surprisingly cool. I raise a hand to cup her cheek and lift her face to mine, keeping my voice soft, though a strange longing creeps into my tone. "You are the loveliest thing I've ever laid eyes on. You're sexy without even trying to be. You made me laugh, and you kiss with all your heart and soul. You've got a passionate heart."

"I shouldn't have kissed you."

"Why not?" I brush my thumb across her bottom lip. "We want each other. No harm in it. We both went there for a fling."

"I couldn't go through with it."

"Not in those circumstances." I raise my free hand to her other cheek, bracketing her face with my palms. When she leans toward me a touch, her eyes shimmering with desire, I exhale a ragged breath. "I still want you. And the circumstances are very different today."

"Yes. Different." Her voice has become hushed and almost dreamy.

"I've tried relationships. Not interested in them anymore." My nose skims across hers while I spread my fingers over her cheeks and glide them down to her throat. I cannae think, not with her body so close to mine and the scent of her overpowering my senses—and my good sense. "I'm here for four weeks. I've nothing more to give. But I do want you, even more today than last night."

"Mmm."

Did I just suggest a casual fling? For four weeks? I shouldn't do it, shouldn't want to do it, but I'm entranced by Erica and her sensual body. What harm could a month of sex do? As long as I make the parameters clear.

No, ye dafty, no.

Erica tips her head back like she's straining to find my lips. Our mouths pass a breath away from each other. The hunger I'd experienced last night erupts inside me again, and any second I'll develop a raging erection. If she didn't smell so good and gaze at me with such longing…

Her tongue sneaks out to tease my lips.

I suck in a sharp breath.

She slides her tongue across my mouth again.

Bod an Donais, I'm not a robot. No man could resist Erica when she's acting this way, and she's even more sensual and desirable today. I should be a gentleman and do what's right. But in the face of her simmering desire, and with blood swiftly filling my cock, I do the exact opposite of the right thing.

"Tonight," I murmur. "Be mine tonight."

Her eyelids flutter closed and then part slightly, her glossy gaze pinned to mine. "What are you suggesting?"

"Spend the night with me."

"What?" She blinks a few times as if she's got grit in her eyes.

And I cannae stop myself. I scrape my lips over hers. "I want you in my bed, for the month. When I leave, we never see each other again."

Her lips fall open, and she stops blinking.

I let my mouth slide into a smile. "Be my American fling."

Chapter Six

*E*rica just stares at me. I can't blame her for being confused, possibly shocked, by what I've suggested. Then again, she did go to that club to meet a stranger and have a fling. Why should my offer sound barmy to her? We want each other, and the more I think about what I suggested, the more sensible it sounds.

Aye, that probably means I'm off my head.

But I need to spend four weeks fucking this woman. I've never had a one-night stand. My marriage had taken up most of my adult life, so I never had the chance to spend a night with a stranger. Not that I would have, even if the opportunity had arisen. It's not in my nature. Everyone thinks my brother Aidan is that sort, but I know he isn't. Aye, he loves to flirt with the lasses, but he would not talk a bonnie, sweet American into a meaningless affair. My brother Rory might do that. We've all had our suspicions that every time he goes on a business trip, he shags a stranger. My uptight younger brother always comes home in a more relaxed state of mind than when he'd left.

Erica leans backward and puckers her lips.

Our gazes remain bound to each other. I couldn't look away if I wanted to, but I don't want to sever the connection. Her eyes entrance me.

Casey bounds off the sofa and nuzzles my hand, then gives it a sloppy lick, his eyes beseeching me in the way only a dog can manage. The pup slathers his tongue over my hand again, and I can't resist Erica's dog any more than I can resist her.

So I pat the pup's head.

Casey glances at his mistress and wags his tail.

While I keep stroking the dog's head, I face Erica. "Think about it, please. We could have an incredible month."

"Then you leave."

"Yes."

She aims a stern look at me. "Let me get this straight. I dash over here every night for a quick roll in the hay? Then I skedaddle back to my place, so we don't accidentally develop a relationship."

My plan sounds bloody ridiculous when she phrases it that way. I open my mouth to tell her that.

She silences me with one raised finger.

Casey lies down at my feet. Well, at least the pup approves of my plan.

Erica scrubs her palms on her thighs. "Look, I realize my behavior last night might've given you the wrong impression of me. I'm sorry. I had no intention of leading you on. But I am not a casual-sex kind of girl."

And I'm not that sort of bloke, but I want her like I've never wanted anything before.

I slide closer to her. "You are a good woman. I can tell, and Gil told me, anyway. Can only imagine what drove you to the club, but it's probably to do with the erse who attacked you earlier." I hook a finger under her chin, lifting gently, easing her head up and backward. With the slender column of her throat exposed to me, I battle the urge to kiss her there and lick a path down her skin. "I'm not asking for one night. What I want from you is four weeks of sex and companionship."

"Would this involve conversation? Or strictly 'wham-bam, thank you, ma'am'?"

I touch my lips to her cheek, near the corner of her mouth. "No wham or bam. Aye, conversation—so long as it doesn't get too personal."

"I see."

She sounds vaguely annoyed, but desire makes her voice huskier.

I skate a hand up and down her soft skin, and when I speak, my lips graze her cheek. "What do ye say, neighbor?"

She licks her lips. "I don't know."

Bod an Donais, I need to taste her again—right now.

I glide my hand up her arm and over her shoulder to cradle her neck. Her breathing has become heavier, as evidenced by the rising and falling of her breasts. I want to shag her right now, here on the sofa, in full view of the windows and the glass doors. Maybe she'd let me have her up against those doors. Christ, I'm off my head for sure, but I donnae care anymore. With the finger I have crooked under her chin, I slant her head up until our gazes lock and our lips almost touch. I'm breathing harder, more excited by the thought of kissing this woman than I ever imagined I could be. I shouldn't do this, but I need to do it.

Erica seizes my shirt. Her breasts heave even more as she tugs me closer. And our lips collide.

I taste the faintest flavor of her, but I need more than that. While a soft wee moan escapes her, I plunge my tongue between her lips, surprised that she opens to me without hesitation and thrusts her tongue into my mouth. The flavor of her… It reminds me of something I cannae quite place, something decadent and arousing, like warm dates and whisky, though not quite like that. I relish the silky warmth of her mouth, and the way she coils her tongue around mine. She releases my shirt and sags into me, her body swaying the slightest bit like she's in a trance. The lass has entranced me for certain. Her hair tickles my cheek, and her breaths tease my lips. The need to possess her overtakes me, and I plunge my tongue in deeper, mash my lips to hers harder, and latch my arms around her so I can run them up and down her back, groping and exploring while I haul her body into mine. Her breasts are crushed to my chest, and I feel the stiff peaks even through my shirt.

I peel my lips away from hers and rub her arms. Bloody hell, that kiss… Are my lips quivering? I cannae be so excited, so desperate to shag her, that my mouth is trembling. I try to smile, but my lips refuse to cooperate.

Erica seems oddly calm when she speaks. "That was nice."

My brows shoot up. "Nice?"

"It's a compliment, Lachlan. Accept it graciously."

"Thank you." I enunciate each syllable with care, baffled by her reaction to our kiss. I must have sounded irritated. Can't help that. I try to quell my annoyance, with little success, and shake my head. "Aye, ye truly are a difficult one."

"You said you liked a challenge." She gestures at her body. "Can you handle this?"

"I can." She can't be about to accept my offer. And I might've sounded slightly annoyed again.

No, I don't believe for one second that she feels nothing after our kiss, despite her composure and her placid expression. She felt that kiss as powerfully as I had, but she must be embarrassed by it, for whatever reason.

Probably because I tried to talk her into a four-week fling. *You sodding ersehole, Lachlan.*

I stifle a groan—because I still want her in my bed for the month.

"Sheesh." Erica sighs. "You are awfully sensitive for a man who threatened to skelp my ex with a caber."

"Maybe I ought to give ye another kiss, full-body this time." I pull her into my arms and splay both hands on her back. "See if ye think that's *nice.*"

She slides her tongue over her bottom lip.

And every time she does that, I want to take her right here on the sofa. I rove my hands over her back. "I need your answer. Please."

She curls her fingers in my hair. "Yes."

<h1 style="text-align:center">Chapter Seven</h1>

y heart is racing. My skin has come alive with electricity that chases over my skin from head to toe, and I'm having trouble catching my breath. This is rubbish. I do not get excited because a woman says she'll have sex with me. But I *am* excited. Because of Erica. I need a bit of space from her. Otherwise, I'll have her naked on the sofa or the floor inside of one minute.

I let go of her body and snatch up her bag. "To the kitchen for a piece."

"A piece of what?"

"Your brownies." I grasp her hand, raising it to my mouth, and brush light kisses over her knuckles. "But I'm open to suggestions."

A few seconds ago, I wanted space. Now, I'm all but seducing her.

"Later," she says, biting the inside of her cheek. "Okay?"

Disappointment floods through me as I rise to help her up. "No rush, lass. No rush at all."

My cock disagrees.

Erica trails behind me as we leave the living room and head down the short hallway that leads into the kitchen. My gaze inevitably keeps flicking to the walls where the man whose house I'm living in displays framed photographs. Gil Friedman took all of those pictures, though not as a hobby. He works as a freelance photographer and does very well at it, which is no surprise considering how good his shots are. The walls in the hallway show off mostly his landscapes and cityscapes but also some of the stunning portraits he's done.

One image catches my eye, and I halt to admire it, tipping my head to the side. In the photo, Erica is laughing and smiling so brightly that I get a pang in my chest just looking at the picture. Sunlight shimmers on her hair while wind whips it across one side of her face. Her cheeks are pink, and her eyes sparkle. She looks so bonnie and happy. I can't remember the last time I felt that way. Maybe I never have.

Erica stops beside me, though she stares at a landscape photo rather than the picture of her.

I point to the portrait. "The loveliest of all Gil's works."

She bows her head, fiddling with her shirt's hem.

"Why don't you look at it?" I ask. "Don't strike me as the shy sort."

Erica shuffles closer to the wall, sucks in a breath, and lifts her gaze to the photograph. Her expression seems pained now, as if the picture portrays something unpleasant.

What about this happy portrait makes her uneasy?

"I hate that picture," she says, then she pushes past me and hurries into the kitchen.

For a few seconds, I just stand here studying the photograph. Something I hadn't noticed before catches my attention now—someone's arm hooked around her shoulders, mostly hidden by her hair. But I can see the other person's hand. It looks like a man's hand. A man's arm.

Could it be the scunner who had harassed her this morning? That would explain her reaction to the beautiful portrait.

I walk into the kitchen only a few paces behind Erica, since she's shuffling along, and Casey gambols in behind me. Erica sits on one side of the small table, so I take a seat on the opposite side. When I deposit her bag on the tabletop, she reaches inside to pull out a glass cake dish. She sets it down on the table. The brownies must still be warm since the sinfully dark treats have steamed up the cling film covering them.

The aroma of the sweet chocolate wafts around me, stimulating my appetite, but the hungry look on Erica's face as she gazes at the brownies makes me want to devour more than food. I strip off the cling film, though my mind insists on torturing me with fantasies of stripping Erica's clothes off and crumbling brownies on her skin so I can lick the crumbs off.

She folds her hands on the tabletop, her thumbs rotating in restless movements. "Lachlan, I know I agreed to the sex thing but, um…"

I freeze, focused on the cling film dangling from my hand. "You've changed your mind?"

Christ, I pray she says no. Why do I care? I met this woman last night, and I do not want to get entangled in a relationship again, not so soon after my divorce. Maybe never. Yet I need to have Erica in my bed for the month.

Aye, I'm a hypocrite and an erse.

I lift my gaze to Erica.

She spreads her hands over the wood tabletop, seeming to study the pattern of the grain. "I haven't changed my mind. But I don't think I'm ready to get started tonight."

My shoulders sag. I'm disappointed she wants to wait, but I understand her reluctance to jump straight into a meaningless fling with me. How long will she need until she feels comfortable with the idea? Maybe I can do something to lessen her anxiety.

What, I've got no bloody idea.

I crumple the cling film and give her a closed-mouth smile. "I understand. We could spend time together, so you'll be comfortable with me before we have a poke."

Her lips pucker briefly, then her brows lift. "Doesn't spending time together count as a relationship?"

"Not if we don't discuss anything too personal." Aye, I'm grasping at straws to explain why I want to be with her when we're not having sex. Should I tell her I'm trying to be a gentleman about this? Giving her time to get used to the idea?

No, I think I shouldn't say that. She might get the wrong idea.

And do what? Decide I'm in love with her? It's rubbish.

I collect two plates from a cupboard and then ease open a drawer full of silverware.

Erica clears her throat. "May I ask what you do for a living? Or is that too personal?"

Grabbing two forks and a knife, I shove the drawer shut with my hip. Don't suppose it could hurt to tell her about my job. "Financial consulting."

She gazes at me without expression.

I set the plates and silverware on the table. "Not exciting enough?"

Her lips almost form a smile. "I'm an accountant. No judgment here."

An accountant? I'd thought she was clever, but now I know for certain.

Erica's gaze flits around the room, and her thumbs start moving again. "Gil said you have an apartment in Edinburgh. Is that where you've always lived?"

"No, I'm a Highland lad by birth and in my heart." I take one large step to reach the refrigerator. "Spent four years in London after university, working at the stock exchange. Hated it. The traffic, the crime, the frantic pace of everything." I pull the refrigerator door open and survey the contents. "I quit my job and moved to Inverness to start my own business."

"Wow, I'm impressed. Starting a business is scary."

I shrug. "Starting it up was the easy part. Fought tooth and nail to win clients, but after a few years, things got rolling. Now I earn enough to live quite comfortably. I've got fifty employees and three offices—Inverness, Glasgow, and Edinburgh."

Should I not have told her that? She might think I'm… I don't know. Up myself, maybe. I'm not arrogant about the fact I've done very well for myself, but I don't want Erica to think I'll be judging her based on my past.

Not that I want to know about her past. I don't.

"Alas," I say, "all I can offer you to drink is water or whisky. Haven't got the messages yet."

"Are you from Inverness?"

Her question seems to come out of nowhere, and she didn't tell me what she prefers to drink with our food. But I answer anyway. "No, I was born and raised in a little village way up in the Highlands called Ballachulish."

"Is that where Gil and Jayne are going? He said you have a place in the Highlands."

"Aye, they'll be staying at my castle."

Glancing over my shoulder, I watch her expression shift from uncertainty to shock in the space of two seconds. All right, I did that on purpose. Strangely, I enjoy teasing Erica.

I chuckle. "I'm joking. My house is modest. I don't care for the trappings of wealth, and my needs are simple."

Unlike my brother Rory. But that's a story I never need to tell Erica.

My attention returns to the refrigerator's contents.

"Does that go for sex too?" Erica asks.

I glance over my shoulder again and notice the pinkness in her cheeks. "You'll find out soon enough."

"I'm not interested in kinky stuff. No whips or chains or anything like that."

"Don't crave excitement?" I pray she says she doesn't because I've had enough of that bollocks.

"Not that much, no," she says. "My needs are simple too."

"Have you tried it? The kinky stuff."

"Ick." She shudders, but I think she's doing that on purpose. "Absolutely not."

Despite her statement, I need to be completely sure of her feelings on the matter. "Then how can you be certain—"

"How many times do I have to say it?" She emphasizes each word by slapping her palms on the table. "I do not want kink."

My lips tick upward of their own volition. She really is adorable.

"Sorry," I say. "We'll drop the subject."

"At last." Her gaze lifts heavenward, and she sighs.

I want to kiss her and shag her and do all sorts of things a man of my age shouldn't do with a woman her age. I don't know her age, but I suspect she's much younger than I am. Her confirmation that she doesn't want kink makes me relax. I don't want it either, and I don't crave the kind of excitement some women seem to need. Aisley certainly didn't have simple needs.

Erica might be the perfect woman for me.

No, not for me. I cannot get involved with her.

"Give me brownies now," Erica says.

I shut the refrigerator door and bend over to pull out the freezer drawer. "Yes, milady. Any other commands for your humble servant?"

"No. Thank you."

"Here to serve." I rifle through the items in the freezer. "Ah-ha! We may not have much in the way of messages, but we do have one essential item."

I pull out a carton of ice cream and toss it onto the table. The carton lands on its bottom and slides into the brownie dish.

"Perfect," she says, rubbing her hands together. Then she looks at me. "I have to ask. What are messages?"

"Groceries." I kick the freezer drawer shut. Sometimes I forget I'm in America where people speak differently. "Did you decide on whisky or water?"

She chews the inside of her lip for a moment, then nods once. "I'll have whisky."

I can't help smiling—and infusing that expression with all the lust I feel for her. "My kind of woman."

Not that she will ever be my woman.

From a cupboard, I retrieve two glasses and a bottle of whiskey, slapping all three items down on the table between me and Erica. I settle into my chair and rotate the bottle so she can see the label.

Erica angles her head slightly as if she's studying that label. She skims a finger down the bottle, from the neck to the base. "Scotch?"

"Talisker single-malt Scotch whisky." Maybe I should use whisky as a means to encourage her desire and make her more comfortable with the sort of affair I suggested. I love watching her reactions, and I'd love it even more if she's getting aroused. So I lean forward and speak in a deep, sensual tone. "This is distilled on the Isle of Skye, a mysterious place inhabited by the spirits of the ancestors, forever haunting the cairns and standing stones they left behind. It's said the isle has the darkest skies you'll ever find, filled with stars so bright and ancient they might be the spirits themselves. And from this enchanting land is born a single malt as unique as its birthplace." I trail a finger over the back of her hand. "Talisker is a smoky, seductive whisky."

Did I overdo it? She might think my speech was barmy.

But she does seem to be breathing harder, and her voice is huskier when she speaks. "You sound like an advertisement."

"Setting you up for the tasting is all." I open the bottle and pour us both a dram of whisky. I let my fingers graze hers when I offer her a glass. Even that light sensation makes my *bagais* ache. Soon, my cock will rouse to join my balls in urging me to seduce Erica, but I cannae stop myself.

Erica clears her throat. "Is there a certain way to drink it?"

"For a whisky virgin, I don't recommend guzzling it like you did last night."

"Good advice." She rolls the glass between her palms, seeming to admire the rich, caramel tones revealed by the sunlight glimmering through the whisky. She raises the glass to sniff the contents. The faintest moan escapes her lips, and she shuts her eyes as she inhales a deeper breath through her nostrils.

"Can you smell the sea and mountains?"

"Yes." She draws out the word like she's lost to the aromas. "Mmm, that and so much more."

Aye, now my cock is awake and stiffening. "Have a sip."

She tilts the glass and lets the whisky slide between her lips. The tip of her tongue is just visible. Her eyes fly open for a heartbeat as if the taste surprises her, then they flutter shut. Setting the glass down, she drags her tongue over her lips and moans.

I can imagine what she's experiencing. Talisker tastes fruity and spicy, with an initial burst of pepper followed by a hint of toasted flavor and a touch of honey. I love whisky, but I've never reacted to it the way she does.

"You like it, then?" I ask, my voice suddenly hoarse. The weight of my lust for her does that to me.

She opens her eyes, though only a sliver. "I enjoyed it, yes."

I thread my fingers through hers, stroking her hand while rubbing the heel of her palm with my thumb. "I like the way you enjoy whisky. Makes me imagine that same look on your face when I take your body."

Her breasts rise and fall with every breath as she examines the whisky left in her glass and turns it in lazy circles to swish the amber liquid. "Do you always equate whisky with sex?"

"Only with you." I drag the brownie dish toward me and plunge the knife through the flaky top layer, deep into the tender, dark-chocolate flesh beneath. "The sensuality of whisky begs for a decadent partner."

I cut two pieces and gently lift the warm slices out of the dish, setting one on each plate. The rich scent of the confection invigorates my senses, but it's the ravenous look on Erica's face that sends blood rushing into my *slat*.

But I don't think she's hungry only for brownies.

After I dish out two servings of ice cream, I offer a plate to Erica.

She accepts it, catching her bottom lip between her teeth and releasing it little by little.

My cock jerks.

I impale my brownie with my fork, penetrating it to the hilt, the way I plan on penetrating her body. When her lips part and her eyes drift half-closed, I thrust the loaded tines of my fork into the ice cream, slathering my treat with it. Erica watches me, seeming almost spellbound as I slide the morsel, now dripping with melting ice cream, between my lips. The flavors of sweet, dark chocolate and vanilla cream inundate my mouth. As good as this tastes, I hunger for a different sort of sweet even more than I want the food. So I let my mind conjure a fantasy of me with my head between Erica's thighs while I devour every last drop of her cream.

Her tongue sneaks out to moisten her lower lip, and her gaze is riveted to my mouth.

Once I've consumed my bite of brownie, I lick the crumbs off my lips. "You'll be in my bed tomorrow night at the outside."

She shoves a mouthful of brownie and ice cream between her lips, consuming it so slowly that the movements become erotic.

Or maybe I'm obsessed with thoughts of ravishing her.

I curl my tongue around another mouthful of my treat, chewing as slowly and erotically as she had done. "What are you thinking of?"

"What's to come."

A smirk tightens my lips, though I try to suppress it. "You, lass. You're what's to come. In my bed, at my hand, over and over and over."

Erica thrusts a forkful of brownie into her mouth, eating it before she speaks again. "Don't get cocky, Mr. MacTaggart."

The lass really shouldn't speak in that sultry tone unless she's wanting to turn me into a rutting beast. Since I can't do that yet, I opt for a different, but no less sensual, option.

I surge forward, half my body slanted over the table, and claim her mouth. I coil my tongue around hers, every possessive lash coaxing a moan out of her, and when I can't take it any longer, I plunge deep into her warm, silky mouth. She slumps a little, her body angling toward mine, and begins to nip and lap at my tongue, letting out wee grunts that evince a hunger as deep as mine. She tastes like brownies and ice cream, but the flavor only intensifies my need for her.

Any second, I'll drag her onto the table and tear her clothes off.

I sever the kiss, though it takes all my willpower to peel my lips away from hers.

Erica wilts into her chair, slack-jawed and almost panting.

Aye, I'm feeling the same way—stunned by the passion that single kiss ignited. I drop back into my chair and spear a bite of brownie, twirling my fork while I envision the night when Erica will finally let me lose myself in her body.

It must be soon. My cock won't let me wait much longer.

That means I need to do whatever it takes to seduce her as soon as possible.

Chapter Eight

"You owe me eleven hundred dollars." Erica smiles with an endearing look of playful smugness on her face and shimmies her bonnie erse on the sofa cushion. She holds her hand outstretched, palm up, while wiggling her fingers. "Gimme."

Sitting forward in my armchair, I brace my elbows on my knees and aim an amused smile at the lass. "Do I now."

Aye, she is adorable. I think that word every thirty seconds, at least, though probably more often since I haven't kept count on my watch.

Across the coffee table from me, Erica perches on the sofa with her erse barely on the cushion and her back straight. The Monopoly board lies on the table between us.

"You know you do," she says, tapping her fingernail on the game board. "You landed on Park Place, which I own. And I have three houses on it. Your ass is mine, MacTaggart."

"Anytime you want, my sweet wildflower."

She rolls her eyes at my sarcastically sweet tone. "You have a one-track mind."

"Only when I'm alone with you."

We haven't left Gil's house all day, but all we've done is play board games. After several rounds of Trivial Pursuit and Scrabble, Erica brought out the Monopoly board. Naturally, I suggested we make it strip Monopoly. Aye, I'm desperate to see her naked. Since she needs time to get used to the idea of having a poke with me, I haven't even kissed her since that moment in the kitchen.

Erica called my idea for strip Monopoly "too dang weird" because it's meant to be a family game.

I'll have to keep waiting—and fantasizing.

My thoughts return to the present, and to Erica where she sits on the sofa.

Her hand rises to her throat but doesn't touch her skin, though she curls her index finger around a lock of that lush hair. Her gaze is fixated on mine. She glances down at my groin, then her lips kink like she's trying not to smile, and she swerves her attention away from me.

I'm debating whether to toss her down on the sofa to fuck her or lay her across the coffee table to do it. Maybe I should throw her over my shoulder and carry her into the bedroom. The way she's looking at me, I wonder if she realizes what I'm thinking about. No, she couldn't.

Bloody hell. I will go insane if I don't seduce her soon.

Erica gathers her Monopoly money and shuffles through it.

I glance down at the fake bills I have and scratch my chin. Five-hundred-dollar bills are all I've got. I look at Erica, though she's still studying her own collection of colorful wee banknotes. "Change, please."

Without raising her head, she lifts her gaze to me. "What's wrong with the way I am?"

She flinches the slightest bit.

I stare at her, probably with a blank expression. What is she on about? Her question seems to have come out of the blue since I never criticized her. But I did say, "Change, please." I suppose the lass might've misinterpreted that, though it seems like an odd misunderstanding.

Shaking my head, I wave the wee orange bills at her. "No-no, I said I need change for these five-hundred-dollar bills."

"Right. Of course." She keeps her gaze downcast while she pulls banknotes out from between her fingers while gnawing on her lower lip. She hands me five wee hundred-dollar bills as change. "Here ya go."

I accept the money, though I grimace and scratch my cheek. What has her so fashed? Maybe it's my offer of sex with no discussion of our personal lives. I open my mouth, but shut it again before I utter one syllable. I doubt anything I might say would make her feel better.

Erica rolls the dice, restarting our game.

Since I can't decipher her anxiety, I focus on the game and finding small ways to make her smile while we vie for control of the board. She holds onto Park Place and gains a few railroads and utilities, but I make some headway too. When I buy a hotel, that puts me in a position to win the game with only one more move, but I don't want to beat Erica. I want to make her happy.

Will she notice if I purposely lose? I am a financial adviser, so losing without letting her see it shouldn't be that difficult.

My next two decisions are less than clever, and Erica raises her brows at me, her lips curving up at one corner. Then she returns her attention to the game.

If she has figured out I'm letting her win, she doesn't seem to mind.

Blowing on the dice, I tell her, "When this game is over, I'll be kissing you for a long, long while."

She slumps against the sofa and clamps her teeth down on both her lips, seeming like she's trying not to smile. Then she makes a noise that sounds like "mmm."

After a few more moves, and intentionally bad decisions by me, Erica is in a strong position to win the game. She rolls the dice and moves her playing piece, a wee cat, around the board. When she sees where she has landed, her happy expression disintegrates, and she almost looks ill as she curls her fingers into her palms.

Erica has landed in jail.

But it's only a game. She looks like she thinks real police will burst through the front door to haul her away to prison. Her features pinch as if she's in pain, and she sets about clumsily shuffling and rearranging her colorful money. Tears glisten in her eyes, about to overflow and trickle down her cheeks. She hiccups and wipes them away with the heel of her hand.

"What's wrong?" I ask.

She keeps fiddling with her banknotes.

"I said, what's wrong?"

Erica sniffles but keeps reordering her money, over and over.

"What's the bother?" I nearly shout, trying to break whatever spell the Monopoly money has cast over her.

She jumps, a stronger hiccup jolting her, and finally looks at me.

I tug at the neck of my T-shirt and contort my lips because suddenly I'm uncomfortable too, though I'm not on the verge of crying. I soften my tone and say, "I'm sorry. Didn't mean to shout, but I asked you twice before and you didn't answer."

"Didn't hear you." A solitary tear trickles down her skin.

The need to comfort her becomes too strong to ignore, but I shouldn't do what I want to do—rush over there to hug her. "Must've been lost in thought, if you didn't hear me ask the first time." I reach across the table to touch her knee. "What's fashed you?"

She swallows hard enough I can see the movement in her throat.

I study her, wondering again what could have upset her so much. We were enjoying a silly game, not discussing painful memories. Unless Monopoly has negative connotations for her. But no, she had suggested we play the game. We'd been having a good time until she landed in jail. Imaginary jail. Why would that fash her? Erica can't have been in prison before.

My hand still rests on her knee, so I caress it with gentle strokes. "Erica?"

She clears her throat. "What does 'fashed' mean?"

I curl my fingers around her knee. "Means bothered, which you seem to be at the moment."

"Oh no, not me." Though she smiles, it seems to be forced rather than natural.

My brows tighten, and I resist the urge to frown. She's lying, and we both know it.

Erica pats my hand. "Thanks for the concern, but didn't we agree to no personal questions?"

"Yes." *Mhac na galla.* I pull my hand away, my jaw tensing. "I apologize for violating our agreement."

Is comforting a woman a criminal offense in America?

"No biggie," Erica says.

My confusion probably shows on my face.

She smiles, and this time, it doesn't seem forced. "That means it's okay."

A breath gusts out of me, and the tension in my body softens. "Good."

Erica bites her fingernail and points at my playing piece, a Scottish terrier. "Your turn."

Her gaze falls to her piece where it lies trapped in jail, and she clamps her lips between her teeth again.

I narrow my gaze on her. "What about a game of Monopoly is too personal to discuss? How can a wee metal cat fash you?"

"It's not the cat." She squeezes her eyes shut and pulls in a deep breath, then lets it out slowly as she opens her lids. "I landed in jail."

"I can't see the significance."

She shakes her head. "It's not important. Can we please move on so I can get the hell out of jail?"

If I can't ask her about her problems, maybe I can help her another way. I have an idea, but aye, it's devious. Donnae care. I need to make her feel better.

She might be annoyed that I've ruined our game. Why? She clearly hadn't cared when I started losing on purpose.

I snatch up her piece and plunk the wee cat down one square forward. Grinning, I announce, "There. Problem solved."

Her lips tighten into a closed-mouth smile, and she touches two fingertips to them. "I would've gotten out on the next move anyway, but thank you."

"What's a jailbreak between fr—companions." I'd been about to use the word friends, but this is meant to be a casual acquaintance. *Bollocks.*

She gestures toward the board. "Still your turn."

I keep my gaze nailed to hers while I lean forward, lift the dice near my mouth, and blow on them.

Her tongue darts across her bottom lip.

I toss the dice.

She waves a hand almost as if she's fanning herself, then her eyes flare wide for a split second, and she shoves her hands under her thighs.

The lass wants me as much as I want her. I'd already known that, but I love watching her struggle with her lust. It makes me fantasize about all the ways I can give her pleasure.

We go back to playing the game.

Forty-five minutes later, I raise my hands in surrender. "The wee lassie is victorious."

"I'd think a financial consultant would be better at Monopoly." She angles her head to squint at me. "You let me win, didn't you?"

With a snort, I wave my hand to dismiss the idea.

Springing forward, her expression almost excited, she jabs a finger in my direction. "You did."

"Does it matter?"

She hisses out a breath, but I suspect she's being sarcastic. "Not very satisfying to win because your opponent gave up."

"A gentleman never bankrupts the woman he plans to seduce." I lean forward too, bringing our faces to within inches of each other. "Would a prize heal your wounded dignity?"

"Depends on what the prize is."

I settle back into the armchair, knees spread wide, and lock my hands behind my head. I can't resist roaming my gaze over her luscious body from head to toe and back again. "I can think of one or two rewards we'd both enjoy."

"I bet you can."

Bending forward again, I collect up the paltry bankroll I have left and stretch further across the table to snatch up Erica's much larger pile of winnings. My head has wound up inches away from her lovely knees, and I turn my face up to her. "Time to relinquish your treasure to the banker."

She lays her hand on mine, the warmth and softness of her palm far too enticing, then she scoops up all the toy money. "Not so fast, Scot. Maybe I want a rematch."

"Happy to oblige." My attention veers to the hallway, and my mind torments me with fantasies of tossing her over my shoulder and carrying her into the bedroom. My cock twitches, fancying the idea. I drop the toy money, flip my hand over, and clasp my fingers around her wrist gently. "You're sweeter than Atholl Brose, and I'm aiming to taste ye tonight."

"Uh…" She clamps her knees together. "Um, well, that sounds… What on earth is Atholl Brose? Is that some kind of Gaelic sex slang?"

"No," I chuckle. Then I lift my free hand to cup her cheek. "It's a sweet liqueur made from oatmeal, honey, whisky, and cream."

"Sounds yummy." She's breathing harder now, just like I am.

I drag my fingertips down her cheek, over her jaw, trailing them along her throat to her collarbone.

"Do you speak Gaelic?" she asks.

My mouth drops open. Aye, she's desperate to change the subject, but that felt like a supersonic jet pulling a hard U-turn.

Erica hunches her shoulders.

What else can I do? I give her a gentle smile and skate my thumb across her lower lip. "My mother insisted we all learn."

"We? Do you have brothers or sisters?"

"Both." I collapse back into the armchair, blustering out a resigned breath. "Two brothers, three sisters."

"Thr—You mean you have *five* siblings?" She blinks once, slowly. "Wow, that's amazing. Do you get along with them?"

"Mostly." I shrug one shoulder. "With a clan as big as ours, the occasional barnie's to be expected."

"Barnie?"

"A tussle." I tilt my head to the side, scrutinizing her for clues to what the bloody hell she's doing. We said nothing personal, but here I am indulging her curiosity. And for reasons I can't fathom, I find myself asking her a question. "Do you have brothers or sisters?"

Well, it's only fair I ask since I told her about my family.

"Nope, just me," she says. Erica picks up the Monopoly board and dumps everything off it. Playing pieces, houses, and hotels scrape across the smooth cardboard to clatter into the box in a wee landslide. "Do you see your family often?"

A noise, somewhere between a growl and sigh, rushes out of me.

She tosses the multicolored money into the box and glances up at me.

This won't do. I cannae get to know her because I donnae want to…feel something for this woman. That was our agreement. No strings, nothing personal. I've gone through enough drama in my life, thanks to the woman I shackled myself to for years.

My mouth twists downward, and my shoulder muscles bunch up. "No more talk of family. Agreed?"

She opens her mouth, then shuts it as she claps the Monopoly box shut. "Sure, you got it. No more family talk."

Christ, I hate causing strife between us. But she needs to understand and stick to the rules. So do I. From this moment forward, I will do that.

My shoulders relaxing, I press my palms to my eyes for a moment before I let them fall to my lap. "Don't quite understand why, but we've derailed in somber territory. Time to get back on track."

Chapter Nine

With both hands on the chair's arms, I thrust my body up and straighten to my full height. Then I saunter around the table to settle in beside Erica, half on the cushion where she's sitting. My weight forces it to slope away from her, tilting her body closer to mine, and her shoulder brushes against mine. I love being this close to her, but I need to kiss her right now, not later or tomorrow or anytime that isn't this moment.

I brace one arm on the sofa's back, behind her shoulders.

She draws in a quick breath, her lips parted.

And I slide my hand up her cheek, diving my fingers into all that soft hair. With delicate pressure, I urge her to turn her face toward mine and tip her head back while I lower mine until our lips are aligned, hovering millimeters apart. My lips are tingling with anticipation, which is barmy. Erica excites me more than any woman ever has, and as my breaths reflect off her lips, I tease them with gentle nips and swift grazes of my mouth across hers. Her eyes drift half-closed. I explore her scalp with my fingers, massaging her skin while I struggle to catch my breath. When she exhales a delicate gasp, I flick my tongue out to trace the seam of her mouth, loving that I can still taste the faintest flavors from our snack earlier—chocolate brownies and Talisker.

Erica sags into me, her hands flat on my chest, her throat exposed to me.

"Sweeter than anything," I purr, ducking my head so I can place open-mouth kisses on her throat. I draw her earlobe between my lips and suckle, licking at the lobe until I hear her suck in a shallow breath. My pulse beats so fast I can't think anymore, and I groan against the shell of her ear. "Forget tasting. Devouring ye is what I'll be doing."

I crush my lips to hers, starved for a deeper taste of her, desperate to thrust inside her mouth the way I need to thrust into her body since I cannae do that yet. I've never kissed a woman this way, with our lips mashed together and our breaths blustering over each other's faces. The entire world seems to disappear, and nothing else exists for me in this moment except for her mouth and her body.

She throws her arms around my neck.

And I lash mine around her body, splaying my palms on her back, my fingers crooking just enough to crinkle her shirt. The feel of her breasts mashed to my chest amps up my need until I'm fighting my every impulse to flip her onto her back and drive into her.

Erica moans into my mouth.

Bod an Donais, that sound, and the way it vibrates from her lips into mine. It's the most erotic thing I've ever experienced. I exhale a long, guttural grown and shove one hand under her erse to hoist her up and lay her down on the cushions, on her back, her body spread across the sofa's length with her legs draped over my lap. I take a moment to just look at her, the way her lips have fallen open and they've turned a darker shade of pink, and the way her tits rise and fall with the hard peaks visible under her shirt. My erection grazes her body when I move the slightest bit.

Her hands grasp my shoulders, but I can't tell if she wants to pull me closer or push me away. I angle in to kiss a path across her forehead, down her temple, and lower to the tender spot under her ear.

"Lachlan," she murmurs, her tone almost dazed.

I close a hand over her hip, massaging the hollow with my thumb. Our lips hover inches apart, but somehow, I restrain myself and don't claim them with another punishing kiss, though I want to so much it physically hurts not to do it. I drag my hand over her hip and down to her groin, where I swear I can smell her cream even through her blue jeans. The scent of it makes me feel drugged, stripping away my willpower and my good sense, but I don't care about any of that. I rest the heel of my hand on her mound, moving it in lazy circles over the spot where I know her clitoris lies, keeping my caresses light and relishing the way she writhes beneath me and spreads her legs in a silent invitation. I push my fingers between her thighs, stroking her right where those luscious folds await me, but I can't do what my body wants—tear open her jeans to fondle her there.

No, I won't shag her yet, despite needing to so badly I'm starting to sweat. Instead of undressing her, I keep circling my palm over her clitoris and keep petting her between her thighs while the scent of her lust envelops me. I haul in a deep breath through my nostrils so I can revel in the aroma. It's better than whisky, better than Atholl Brose, better than anything I've ever smelled before.

She bucks her hips, gasping and moaning and whimpering, her eyes squeezed shut.

Then she clasps her hand around my rock-hard *slat.* The fabric between our bodies does nothing to lessen the effect of her fingers gripping me.

"Och!" I shout, pushing her hand away. My eyes flash wide an instant before they slide mostly shut. Christ, this woman is going to drive me insane. "Donnae be touching me like that. Yet."

"What if I do?" She palms my shaft.

The cheeky woman strokes me with those delicate fingers, and when I bat her hand away, she aims a sultry half smirk, half frown at me.

"If ye keep it up," I say, "the train'll derail again."

"Would that be the fun train?"

"Aye." I scrape my lips across hers. "Keep yer wee hand to yerself."

"Or what?"

Has Erica Teague just issued a challenge? Aye, she has. And I never back down without a fight.

I rip open the button on her jeans and yank the zipper down with a loud noise of metal rasping across metal. Erica gasps when I thrust my hand inside her knickers to spread my palm over the flesh between her thighs. Her cream moistens my skin, which makes my cock throb for her.

She knows what she's doing to me. The cheeky lass wouldn't have palmed my dick if she didn't realize exactly how that would affect me. I never would have guessed Erica could become a brazen, lustful wanton.

But I love that about her.

I circle the heel of my hand over her taut nub again, though now nothing separates my skin from hers. I sweep my fingers up and down her cleft, her juices coating my skin, and I keep stroking her while her back bows up and her mouth falls opens on a strangled whimper. She digs her fingers into my shoulder, but the slight pain only makes me want her more. I seal my mouth over hers, and this time, the kiss is brutal and all-consuming. Diving my fingers inside her, I crook them so they press into the erogenous spot I know lies just inside her opening.

A phone rings.

The sound barely registers in my mind. I plunge two fingers inside Erica while our tongues clash and tangle, our mutual hunger too powerful to deny.

The phone rings again.

Bollocks. I pull away from her body. Breathing hard, I snatch my mobile off the table and glance at the caller ID. I can't help letting out a sharp growl. It's Rory ringing me, but the last thing I want to do right now is chat to him. I can't ignore it, though. Rory is my solicitor as well as my brother, so this could be important.

I prop myself up with one straight arm and accept the call.

Before I can speak, Rory starts talking. "Lachlan, I'm sorry to interrupt your holiday in America, but I've just received some disquieting news. It seems there was a clerical error when the divorce papers were filed. Try not to let it fash you, but it does appear that the papers are invalid which means the final decree also is. I don't have confirmation it's true, so I'll need to investigate on my own. It looks like you are, technically, still married to Aisley."

"What?" I shout. Though Rory told me not to let it fash me, I can't stop the anger that's seething inside me. Aisley, that faithless cow, must have connived to make this happen. I wasn't a good enough husband for her, but she refuses to let me go. My knuckles start to ache, probably because I'm clenching the mobile. Spittle sprays from my mouth when I snarl, "Well, bloody find out if it's true, Rory. I want to know now!"

Grinding my teeth, I grip the mobile even tighter.

"I will get an answer on this, Lachlan," Rory says. "You have my word on it. I'll get to the bottom of this mess whatever it takes. If all else fails, I will ring Stephen Beckham at the Home Office. He has contacts everywhere. One way or another, we will settle the matter once and for all."

I force words out between my gritted teeth. "Sort it out. That's what I pay you for, man." Why am I talking to Rory as if he's my solicitor only, not also my brother? Of course I know he'll move heaven and earth to fix this problem. That's the sort of man he is. "It has to be a mistake. I can't abide another fight with that bitch—"

My gaze lands on Erica, whose brows have lifted, and I freeze.

Bloody hell. I'd all but forgotten about her.

"Wait, Rory," I say. Holding the mobile to my chest, I tell Erica, "Personal call."

Her lips pucker, and her eyes narrow.

What must she think of me, snarling and shouting at someone she can't see? I'm behaving like a wild beast, not like a mature adult. Aisley does this to me, always. Aye, it's entirely her fault I took a call while I still had my hand inside another woman's knickers.

I climb over Erica to get up off the sofa. "Och, I'm sorry. Please forgive me."

"Huh?" She seems dazed again, most likely because I've left her on the edge of orgasm.

"Erica—" What can I say? My chin drops to my chest, and with a rough shake of my head, I turn away from the woman I want like mad and stalk down the hallway to discuss the problem of the wife I can't get rid of.

Once I'm well away from the living room, I hold the mobile to my ear again. "I want to know exactly how this happened, Rory. If Aisley cocked up the paperwork on purpose—"

"I'll find out, and she will regret it."

Rory's steely tone assures me he means that, but I would've known he meant it anyway. MacTaggarts stand by each other, no matter what.

"I know anything to do with Aisley gets you up to high doh," Rory says, "but you really should try to relax. You're on holiday, so do something enjoyable that doesn't involve finance."

"Yes, I know I need to relax. And I know I shouldn't let my ex-wife have this effect on me." But no one realizes what that woman has put me through. I never want anyone to know. Cannae believe how much I put up with in my vain attempts to please Aisley. "I promise to do something enjoyable."

"Good. I'll ring you as soon as I know anything."

"Thank you. Cheers, Rory."

"Cheers, Lachlan."

I disconnect the call. Aye, there's one thing I would love to do that will be enjoyable for certain. But I'll need to apologize to Erica first—grovel if necessary—or she'll never let me shag her. Not that I should do that now. She needs more time to get used to the idea, and I've just given her ample reasons to change her mind.

Leaning back against the wall, I take a few minutes to calm down, taking slow, deep breaths until my heartbeat slows. Then I walk back into the living room.

"I'm awfully sorry, Erica," I say as I stop beside her, where she's admiring one of Gil's pictures on the living-room wall. Though I try to smile, it feels strained. "Best take you home."

"Now?"

"I'll get your things."

Though it's the last thing I want to do, I hurry away to retrieve the brownies and the bag she carried the treats in. Once I've stuffed the brownies back into the bag, I offer it to Erica.

She waves it away. "Keep the brownies."

"They're yours."

"No." She pushes the bag away when I thrust it toward her. "I made them for you. Just return the dish when you're done with it."

I set the bag on the coffee table, but I can't meet her gaze when I speak. "Thank you."

"No biggie."

She takes my hand as we leave the house, heading across the lawn to her front door. I can't understand why she wants to hold my hand after the way I behaved, but I seem incapable of releasing her hand. It feels good to have a woman's palm pressed to mine.

No, not just any palm. I love having hers pressed to mine.

The sun has just begun to set, unfurling streamers of pink and purple that lengthen and grow more intense with every passing second. At the instant we step onto Erica's porch, a light clicks on above our heads. It must be the sort that turns on automatically at sunset.

She unlocks the door and, facing me, grasps the knob with her free hand while keeping her other one around mine. "Want to come in?"

I thread my fingers through hers. "Best not."

Yes, I want to go inside with her more than anything. But I won't. Not tonight. I think I'm still in shock about the way she accepted my apology and forgave my horrible behavior.

"Please," she says, "I'd like you to come in."

"Not tonight." I relinquish her hand, brushing a kiss across her forehead. An idea hits me, and I hear myself saying, "We'll have a picnic tomorrow."

Her lips twitch as if she's trying to smile but too knackered to succeed at it. "Sure, sounds great."

Does she sound too cheerful about the prospect? Like she's forcing herself to want to accept my invitation? I'd rather not have her come on a picnic with me because she feels obligated, for whatever reason.

I squint at her. "Erica..."

"It's fine, go." She raises onto her tiptoes to kiss my cheek. "See you tomorrow."

Without looking back, she rushes into the house and slams the door.

She is angry with me, despite the fact she accepted my apology. I should apologize again, this time with the groveling I hadn't done the first time.

So I tap on the door. "Erica? Would you open the door, please?"

Nothing happens for a few seconds, then the door eases open. Erica stands there wearing a neutral expression.

I manage only a shaky smile. My nerves seem to have gotten the better of me because I'm feeling slightly anxious. "Thank you."

She closes her fingers around the doorknob. "You wanted something?"

I nod. "To apologize. I was unkind to you, and I regret it deeply."

"No big—"

I swing both hands up to cradle her face, skimming my thumbs over the corners of her lips, and bend my head until our foreheads touch. "That was no proper goodnight kiss."

She stands there perfectly still, like she's paralyzed, though I have no idea if it's good paralysis brought on by the surprise I've given her or the bad kind that requires a visit to the emergency room. Since she's still blinking and breathing, I decide it's the former.

Erica's breaths tickle my face.

Canine claws click on the bare floor behind her.

I tip her head back slightly, a millimeter away from kissing her.

That's when Casey appears beside her. He pants and chuffs softly.

I reach down with one hand to pat the pup's head. He slathers Erica's hand with his tongue in what I take for canine kisses. I want my tongue on her body, not the pup's.

Then Erica licks her lips in one long, sensuous glide, and I forget all about the ruddy dog.

I sling an arm around her waist, tugging her out of the threshold, and shut the door in Casey's face. My lips descend on hers, pressing into them, though I have no intention of deepening the kiss. I keep it tender and deliberate, exploring her lips without demanding anything in return. Her lips relax, and her mouth opens for me, but I summon all my self-control to stop myself from ravishing her with a searing kiss, simply skating my lips across hers before I raise my head.

Erica blinks up at me, her cheeks pink.

"Sleep well, bonnie Erica." I tuck a wayward strand of hair behind her ear. "And good night."

I push the door open behind her.

She shuffles across the threshold backward, and Casey licks her palm.

I lift her hand to feather my lips over her skin. "Until tomorrow."

Just when I turn to leave, she says, "Apology accepted."

Her statement gives me a strange sensation in my chest and on my skin, almost like fluttering and tingling. Am I overjoyed? That she forgives me? Maybe I am, because I can't resist flashing her a grin over my shoulder.

I hurry back to Gil's house, and already I'm planning the best and most satisfying ways to seduce her.

Tomorrow, Erica. Tomorrow you will be mine.

Chapter Ten

Today, I'm sitting on a blanket on a beach situated along the shores of Lake Michigan, enjoying the bonnie scenery—but mostly enjoying the view of Erica in shorts and a tank top. That shirt clings to her breasts, which makes me want to fondle them, but I restrain the impulse. Spending time together is meant to reassure her that I'm not an ersehole, so I can convince her to let me shag her tonight. Fondling her body wouldn't accomplish that.

I gaze out across the blue waters of the lake, watching gentle swells sweep onto the shore. I haven't seen a lake like this in ages. Scotland has lochs, but they aren't the Caribbean blue of Lake Michigan. I take a deep breath and let the serenity of our surroundings ease the tension in my body. Yes, I've been a wee bit…stressed. Shouting at Rory yesterday hadn't been my finest moment, and I've decided today I will remember how to relax.

Because that's so bloody easy to do.

Admiring Erica's body helps. So aye, the fact that looking at her relaxes me is my excuse for drinking in the sight of her in those shorts and that top.

She eyes me sideways. "You're sure we have permission to be here?"

Erica had seemed dubious when I brought her to this stretch of beach, especially when we strolled past a two-story Tudor house on our way to the shore. She seems to think I'm the sort who trespasses on private property. Well, I suppose I can't blame her. We've known each other for less than two days, and my behavior hasn't given her reason to trust me.

That changes today.

I sigh, infusing the sound with sarcasm. "Yes, for the third time, we're allowed. Gil knows the owner and comes here often. His friend agreed I could take over beach privileges during Gil's absence." When she opens her mouth to speak, I raise a hand to silence her protest. "Relax. We have permission."

To reach this spot, we had driven up a driveway shrouded in trees, then walked across the well-mown lawn to get onto the beach. Trees encircle the house, providing a privacy screen, so I can do whatever I like with Erica and no one will see.

Erica squeezes her eyes shut and begins to rub her wrist. Then she takes a deep breath and opens her eyes.

"Does your wrist hurt?" I ask.

"Huh?"

I nod toward her hand. "You're rubbing it."

She glances down and stops blinking for a few seconds, then rests her hands on the blanket. "It's nothing."

"If you say so." But I'm still not convinced because her shoulders have bunched up. Maybe I can help her relax. This might be nothing more than an excuse to touch her, but I've decided to call it physical therapy. I settle my hands on her shoulders and knead her flesh, working her tight muscles with my knuckles and my fingertips. "Has work got you bunched up?"

"Sort of." She leans back a touch while I glide my hands up to her neck. I spread my fingers over her throat, massaging her nape with my thumbs. Her head falls back, and her hair tickles my skin. "That feels so good."

"Maybe later I can give you my full massage."

"Does it involve a full-body kiss?"

"If you like." I have no clue what a full-body kiss would be, since I invented that term yesterday, but I have ideas.

"I could go for that."

Casey, who has been frolicking nearby, looks at me and wags his tail. Does the pup approve of my full-body-kiss plans? I think the dog likes me, but apparently, his trust doesn't ease Erica's worries. Casey is at the end of his retractable leash, which I've kept hold of by sitting on it. The pup keeps trying to pull the leash out from under me, but I'm stronger than he is.

Erica twists around almost as if she's trying to get a view of my erse, but she can't quite do it. The lass faces forward again, and I keep rubbing her neck. Her head falls forward, like she's finally let go of the tension inside her.

Despite the warm temperature, her nipples have hardened, making the tips visible through her tight shirt.

I lower my lips to her ear. "Are you thinking about me?"

"What?" She jerks her head up, blinking quickly, almost as if she'd been half-asleep. "Of course, you're right here."

"No." I coast my hands down her arms to close my fingers around her wrists and raise her hands to her breasts so that her fingertips tease her nipples. When her tongue slips out to moisten her lips, I press my cheek to hers. Her eyes go half-closed, and I lift her hand to my face. "You're aroused, and I can't help wondering what you're thinking of."

"Keep wondering." She sits forward, separating our bodies, and flutters her lashes at me over her shoulder, though the expression seems sarcastic rather than seductive. "A woman has a right to be mysterious now and then."

I smile and shake my head. "Mystery is your forte."

She bends one knee, bumping the picnic basket that sits beside her, then she stretches her legs out and braces her body with both hands on the blanket behind her. Though her eyes are hooded again, her gaze flicks to me.

The sight of her in that position, with her shapely legs on full display and her torso curved, accentuating her breasts… It has me struggling to control my hunger for her. Did she move into that pose on purpose? To drive me insane with lust? Since the lass has been reluctant to sleep with me, I can't believe she'd do that. She does enjoy teasing me, though. Maybe showing off her body is simply another form of teasing.

Not that I mind in the least.

She rolls her head to the side, and our gazes lock. "Tell me again why you chose a picnic for today's outing. After the whisky interlude, I expected something more…erotic."

I make a derisive noise. "No respectable Highlander beds a woman without proper seduction."

"I didn't realize consuming ant-ridden food while mosquitoes suck us dry counted as seduction."

A chuckle rumbles out of me. "Do you always look for the negative?" I wave at the surroundings. "Sunshine, blue sky, a warm breeze, and sand between our toes." I look straight into her eyes. "And the company of a braw, bonnie lass. I'd say this is a perfect moment."

"You're quite braw yourself."

I move over to sprawl on the blanket beside her, propped up with my left arm, one leg bent and my free hand dangling over my raised knee. When we had discussed what to do today, I suggested a picnic, and Erica agreed. She then suggested I should wear a kilt, but I informed her that's not beach attire.

But I have plans for my kilt—plans that involve Erica's naked body.

What she said a moment ago finally penetrates my brain, and I lift my brows. "You know what 'braw' means?"

"I also know 'skelp' means to slap and 'scunner' means a nuisance, which fits Presley to a tee."

My mouth drops open. Not a manly response, but I can't hide my surprise. "How'd you know all that?"

Erica lets her head tip backward and shuts her eyes. "I did a little Internet search for Scottish slang. By the way, please don't ever again refer to sex with me as having a poke."

"Slip of the tongue."

I trail my fingertips down her arm.

Her breasts are rising and falling more than normal breathing would make them do. "I still have no clue what you said to me in the club the other night. Since I couldn't figure out how to spell it, I couldn't search for it. I was babbling about the time, and you said what sounded like—"

"Your bum's oot the windae."

"Right." She flips onto her side to face me, bending her knee the same way I've done with mine. "What on earth does it mean?"

Her position snares my attention against my will, forcing me to gaze at her groin. My fingers clench around my knee, and I suck in a breath. All right, maybe I'm not forced to stare at that part of her body, but I seem to have no conscious control over my eyes. My thoughts transform into fantasies of Erica naked on a bed while I shove my face between those thighs to feast on her cream.

Erica sinks her fingers into the sand.

Is she imagining the same thing I am? My cock is hardening, and I'm sure she can see that. I tighten my hand on my knee, then slacken it, over and over, while my fantasy replays in my mind.

She straightens her leg, dropping her knee and clamping her thighs together. Then she flaps a hand in front of my face. "Hey, wake up."

I blink once, slowly, and wet my lips. I need a few seconds before I can manage to tear my focus away from her thighs and look into her eyes again.

"What does it mean?" she asks. "The bum-oot-the-whatever thing."

"Your bum's oot the windae." I drape my arm over my belly. "It's an old Scottish saying. Means you're talking nonsense, which you were at the time."

"Not if you had been Cliff. He would've known why I was furious." She inches her fingers across the sand until they bump mine. "Half of what you say sounds like a foreign language."

"You should visit Scotland. It'll be an adventure for you."

"Maybe I will, someday." Her expression turns melancholy, though only for a moment, making me wonder for the thousandth time what fashes her. No strings, nothing personal, that was my clever idea. Her sexy smile returns. "But I'd have to figure out what you're saying first. I wouldn't want to visit a foreign country without learning at least a bit of the language."

I lay my hand over hers. "I can teach ye."

"You're a one-man immersion program already," she says. "Feel like I need a passport just to have a whisky with you."

"No need. My borders are completely open to you." I sling an arm around her waist, hauling that beautiful body into me. Her stiff nipples rub against my chest, and I splay my fingers over the small of her back. "Come on over and map me out."

She nestles against me, wriggling her hips in a blatant attempt to get me even harder. "So tell me, why don't you do relationships?"

I spring into a sitting position, dumping Erica onto her back. While she heaves herself off the blanket, I flip open the picnic basket's lid. "Personal questions are off-limits."

That will shut her up, won't it? Aye, she's too polite to push me for answers I told her I would never give.

"When did your last relationship end?" she asks.

Brilliant idea, Lachlan. She gave up right away, didn't she?

Still, I'm having trouble summoning any anger toward her. She's too adorably bonnie.

Instead of snarling at her, I toss Erica a plastic-wrapped sandwich and throw her an amused look. "Could we enjoy this bonnie day without an inquisition?"

"Maybe." She unwraps her sandwich—turkey and Havarti cheese on whole wheat, with lettuce and avocado. The sight of the food seems to stun her for a moment, then she snaps bolt upright and waves the sandwich at me. "This is my favorite. Are you sure you're not stalking me? Ferreting out all my secrets in order to seduce me into being your sex slave?"

I grin. "Caught me. I dug through your bins to find the remnants of your food and decipher what your favorites are." I lean toward her and give a low, wicked cackle like I'm the devil himself. "And I sniffed your underwear."

"A woman's underwear does not smell good, trust me."

"Bet yours would." I nuzzle her cheek. "I got my information from Gil. He said you've had a piece at their house lots of times."

"Why would Gil tell you what kind of food I like?"

"Playing matchmaker, I gather." And I might need to skelp Gil for that, the *cacan.*

I bite off a huge chunk of my sandwich.

Erica points at my jaw. "You've, uh, got something on your chin."

Vinaigrette dressing has dribbled down my skin. Bollocks. I doubt Erica will be enthralled by an eejit who doesn't notice when dressing oozes from his mouth. I snatch up a napkin and wipe my chin clean, then go back to eating and try to pretend the vinaigrette incident ever happened.

Erica makes a pained face and rips off a mouthful of her sandwich.

What's bothering her this time? I don't need to know, but my mouth disagrees.

I run a finger down her bare arm. "Care to tell me what's got you frowning again?"

"Not particularly." She reaches into the picnic basket to pluck a grape from a bunch cradled inside a napkin. "Comes under the heading of personal, comma, off-limits."

Yes, I deserved that verbal slap in the face.

With a bitter smile, I sever our eye contact. "Understood."

Peripherally, I see her chewing a grape.

Acid churns in my gut as I swivel my gaze out to the lake where gentle swells lap against the shore. A seagull swoops low overhead, its cry sharp and high. The tranquility of the setting seems out of place considering the turmoil in my life. With Erica, I feel freer and less anxious. Well, except when she chastises me for breaking the rules I set for our…whatever this is. I can't believe Erica is anything like Aisley, but taking that risk seems too dangerous.

While I'm ruminating on the lake and my life, Erica wolfs down half of her sandwich. She grabs a water bottle from the basket and gulps some of its contents, her fingers coiled around the bottle, her thumb circling over its ridged surface to smooth out droplets of condensation. "Scotland always looks beautiful in the movies."

"It is beautiful." I finish off my sandwich in two bites. "Can't believe you've never been to Scotland."

"Never been outside the contiguous United States."

"What a shame."

I pick up a grape and hold it near her lips.

She parts them to let me place the grape on her tongue and seals her mouth around the fruit. Her lips ensnare the tip of my finger.

For a long moment, we simply stare into each other's eyes.

Then she suckles my finger.

My breaths grow uneven, and a strange excitement electrifies my skin.

Erica releases my finger.

Christ, I love it too much when she teases me.

With one fingertip, I trace a path around the rim of her mouth. "You'd love Scotland. It's a land of passionate, fiercely independent men and women. A lass like you would fit right in."

She snatches up a napkin to wipe her mouth and forces a polite smile. "Maybe someday I will visit Scotland."

Casey yanks on the leash, jerking me forward. I grunt and wrestle the leash's handle out from under my erse, then give it a sharp tug. Casey trots back to us, lying down between me and Erica.

She tears off a piece of her sandwich and tosses it to Casey. The pup catches it with a snap of his jaws.

I absently rake my fingers through the sand. "Where did you grow up?"

"Isn't that off-limits?"

"Told you about my background."

"So you did. I was born in Linwood, a small town just outside of Kansas City—on the Kansas side, not Missouri. We were average, middle-class people. Me, the only child, with two loving parents. We moved to Chicago when I was fourteen." She starts to take another bite, then changes her mind and sets the sandwich down. "I'm pretty boring, really. Girl accountant, obsessed with facts and figures, friendless, loved by my parents and my dog."

"You have friends. Gil and Jayne, for certain."

"Yeah, but no one else. I'm the invisible woman."

I pause while holding a grape near my lips, and study her while I try to figure out why she feels invisible. "I'm sure someone else loves you. A beautiful woman such as yourself must have a horde of admirers."

"Nope. No adoring admirers. I'm as boring as most of my exes."

"You have had exciting lovers, then."

"Not lovers. Boyfriends."

I fling the grape into my mouth. Somehow, hearing she's had lovers before me triggers a need to batter every single one of them. Once I've chewed and swallowed the grape, I ask, "What's the difference? If you sleep with them, they're your lovers."

"The term implies an arrangement like ours—sex without commitment or attachments. I cared for my boyfriends." She grimaces. "Even the gorgeous ones."

"Why *even* them?"

She clamps her hands over her knees. "Hot guys always turn out to be hot messes. They've got cargo planes full of their baggage." She scratches the back of her neck, head bowed. "And then there are the hot guys who use women for their own ends."

I freeze while holding another sandwich near my mouth.

She freezes too, but only for a moment before she waves a dismissive hand. "I didn't mean you. Point is, hot guys are dangerous."

"Then I pray you don't think I'm hot."

"You're...good-looking and sexy."

"Thank heavens for that." I smile, but the expression fades quickly. "Who used you for his own ends? Was it the coward who assaulted you?"

"Presley didn't assault me."

I clench my jaw. "He was forcing his way into your home."

She hugs herself, rocking in place.

"What did the bastard do to you?" I ask.

"Nothing. You chased him away."

Though I try not to sound annoyed, I end up grumbling anyway. "You know full well what I was asking."

She straightens, squaring her shoulders. "Off-limits."

We stare at each other, neither of us moving even one millimeter, for so long that my eyes get dry from not blinking. She looks away first.

I pick at a stray blade of grass. "Sorry, I forgot my own rules for a spell."

Her shoulders flag. "It's okay."

We need to get back on board that fun train Erica had mentioned yesterday. So I leap to my feet and offer her my hand. "How about a walk?"

Casey launches off the ground with all four feet airborne and barks his approval of the idea.

I kneel to scratch behind his ears, and the pup licks my chin.

"Sure," Erica says. "A walk sounds nice."

She slips her hand into mine and twines our fingers.

With Casey by my side, I guide Erica away from the sheltering trees to the open beach at the edge of the lapping waves. From here, we can glimpse the skyscrapers of downtown Chicago with the Sears Tower looming over the rest—until we turn away from the skyline. Hand in hand we amble along the beach, chatting about nothing in particular, careful to avoid personal subjects like her scunner ex or my reasons for giving up on relationships. Her hand feels soft and warm in mine, and I relax even more. I feel as if I'd always been meant to hold Erica's hand in mine, but that's romantic rubbish. Even while her touch eases the tension inside me, it also excites me in every way imaginable.

She lifts our joined hands. "Isn't this against the rules?"

"No."

"That's it? No?"

What else am I meant to say? Maybe hand-holding is against the stupid rules I set, but I don't care. I will keep hold of her hand for as long as she'll let me.

I veer us off the beach, under a copse of trees that shades us from the sun. Then I spin her toward me, drag her body into me, and bend my head to kiss her. It begins softly but intensifies little by little as I brush my lips over hers again and again, wanting to keep it tender but needing to consume her mouth the way I want to consume the rest of her body. Soon, I'm plunging between her lips, desperate for even more, loving that she tastes like the snack we just enjoyed. The length of my erection is pinned between our bodies, and when Erica grinds her groin against me, I groan and clutch her hips.

She is driving me mad.

I peel my lips away from hers, my mouth kinking up into a wry smile. "It's not against the rules. It's preparation."

We stroll back to the beach, headed toward our blanket and the picnic basket.

Erica throws a hand up to shield her eyes from the glare of the sun, which has begun its gradual descent toward the horizon. Soon twilight will darken the sky. I can't believe we've spent the entire day together. Feels like minutes, not hours, since we arrived here.

"It's time to go home," I say, my lips barely touching hers. "I've got a surprise for you, and then the real seduction begins." I curl my tongue around her lobe. "If you're ready for it."

Aye, the surprise I have planned for her involves shagging. Cannae wait one more minute to strip her naked and feel that body under me.

Erica skims a hand down my belly to stroke my cock through my shorts.

When she flicks her thumb over the tip, a shock wave of lust shudders through me and robs me of breath. "I want you tonight, Lachlan."

Bod an Donais, I want her too.

A breath gusts out of me. "Thank the stars."

I have never been so relieved and excited at the same time simply because a lass tells me she wants me to fuck her. It's barmy, but I don't care.

Hand in hand, we walk down the path that skirts the house owned by Gil's mate and to the spot where we parked my hired car. I hold the car door open for her, and as I shut it, I gaze up at the ever-darkening sky. The first pinpoints of stars are just visible.

Oh aye, thank every one of those stars in heaven. Tonight, I'm shagging Erica Teague.

Chapter Eleven

*E*rica sets her fork down on her empty plate and leans back against her chair. A soft moan escapes her lips while her eyes drift half-closed. She looks almost enraptured by the steak and red wine I've fed her, as if she might climax any second. I have never seen a woman enjoy a hearty meal, especially one that includes red meat, with as much blissful satisfaction as Erica Teague displays. It makes me need to throw her down on the table and have her right here in the kitchen.

I clear my throat, shifting a little and making my chair creak.

She takes a deep breath, exhaling it slowly, her face still the picture of blissful ecstasy as she gazes across the kitchen table.

My cock is getting harder. I fidget in my chair, which makes it creak again.

Erica slides her tongue over her lips to lick away the remnants of steak sauce.

Christ, is this woman trying to give me a stroke? But I can't look away from her mouth, my gaze riveted to the movements of her tongue and lips.

She sits forward, pushing her plate away, and folds her arms on the tabletop.

And I can't stop myself from admiring her bonnie breasts, pushed up by her crossed arms. Soon, I'll see and feel and taste those tits. My mouth waters at the prospect. My *slat* likes the idea too, more than it should right now since I'm meaning to take it slow with Erica—even if that kills me.

I fidget again, cough into my fist, and swing my gaze up to hers.

"Getting sciatica?" she asks. "These wooden chairs do a number on my butt, for sure. Jayne wanted to put some cushions on the seats, but Gil thought it was too girlie."

Cheeky lass. I narrow my gaze on her. "Could we not talk about Gil and Jayne tonight."

Though my words seemed like a question, I have no doubts Erica realizes my tone means it was a statement, or maybe a command. I keep my attention nailed to her, praying I succeed at communicating to her, without words, that I intend to have her in my bed tonight. Well, in Gil's bed. But he won't be here. Only Erica and I will lie on that bed together.

Maybe she's having the same sort of problem I'm dealing with, because she wriggles in her chair as if she can't get comfortable. "Is there dessert?"

"Oh, aye." I get up, and Erica's focus swerves to my groin, which now lies at her eye level. My erection seems about to split my jeans open. Feels that way too. I saunter around the table to where she sits, holding out a hand to her. "Stand."

"Bossy much?"

I grasp her hand and tug. "Up. Now."

She pulls her hand free. "Ask nicely and maybe I'll do it."

The lass is breathing harder, and her nipples jut through the fabric of her shirt, so I know she likes what I'm doing. It makes her randy. So I lunge down, lock my arms around her waist, and hoist her off the chair. Her feet dangle several inches above the floor. Though she says nothing, she's biting her lip, and I'm sure she feels every inch of my erection pressed into her groin. My body wants me to rub myself against her until she gasps, but I promised her and myself that I'd go slow. Still, I lose ground in the battle to control my lust for her and let myself palm her erse, holding it firmly.

"Dinner was amazing," she says, sounding breathless. "Had no idea you could cook."

I knead her erse, slowly, plunging my fingers into her flesh then withdrawing, over and over.

"I love steak," she blurts out as if I give a toss about her dietary preferences right now.

Her cheeks are turning faintly pink. She's even bonnier when she's aroused, and I intend to keep her on the edge until the moment I thrust into her body. So I push a finger between her buttocks for just long enough to make her breathe harder, those tits lifting every time she inhales. But I've tortured her long enough for the moment. I let her body slide down mine inch by inch until her feet touch down on the floor. Her right hand has wound up crushed between our bodies, directly over my *slat.*

She drags one finger up my length to the head, hesitating there. Then she fumbles with the button on my jeans.

"Uh-uh." I capture her hands, restraining them behind her. "Not yet."

"Why not?" She tips her head back to look up at me.

"Patience," I grate through my clenched teeth. The way she touched me a moment ago nearly annihilated my willpower, and gritting my teeth while virtually growling at her is all I can manage.

"I suck at patience."

Releasing her hands, I back her up to the table.

She grips its edge like she might fall down at my feet if not for the table buttressing her.

I might like it if she did fall to her knees, provided she takes my cock in her mouth while she's down there.

Taking hold of her hips, I boost her up onto the table with her legs hanging off the edge. She slaps her palms on my chest, then glides them up and down like she can't get enough of feeling my body. She unhooks one button on my shirt and slips her fingers beneath the fabric to trace lines on my chest. The softness of her fingers and the warmth of her skin feel so bloody good.

With a hissed intake of breath, I haul her into me, forcing her thighs apart until I'm wedged between them. Then I grind my hard-on into her groin. "When ye lay yer wee hands on me, I cannae think."

"Stop trying to."

I nuzzle her cheek.

She wraps her arms around my shoulders.

And I shove the dishes out of the way. They clatter to the floor while silverware clinks and wine splashes out of the glasses as they topple. Donnae care about that or anything except the feel of Erica's body wrapped around mine and the scent of her desire wafting over me while I lavish her throat with wet kisses.

"You're breaking the dishes," Erica says.

"Buy 'em all new ones." I lay her across the table and hike up her blouse, revealing her breasts caged inside the cups of her lacy bra, and roughly fondle them. "Most expensive china on the market, I swear."

I thrust one hand inside her bra and tug it down. One breast springs free, landing right in my palm. I curl my tongue around her nipple, and she arches into my mouth as if she's begging for more. I need to give her what she wants, give her everything. Sealing my mouth over her nipple, I scrape my teeth over the peak and suckle so hard that a throaty moan spills out of her. Every noise she makes heightens my lust until the need is almost painful. I force myself to slow down, nipping at her skin, teasing her gently.

She cries out, bucking her hips.

I suck even harder, unable to hold back in the face of her passion.

Another cry explodes out of Erica. She clenches my shirt in her fists and yanks it up, but my arms block her from tearing it off.

I need to be naked with her *right now*. But I have to stop this before I take her in the least romantic way possible. Since I don't want romance, I shouldn't care about that.

But I do care. Bloody hell.

I jerk my head up. Gazing down at Erica, with her pink cheeks and her heaving tits, I feel like a bastard for doing this to her in the kitchen, on the table that had plates and silverware on it a moment ago.

"What's wrong?" she asks while struggling to push up onto her elbows.

"Cannae do it." I drop down onto the chair. "Not like this."

She pulls her blouse down to cover herself and levers up into a sitting position. "You can't do this to me again. Get me wound up and push me away."

"Not pushing you away." No, I'd slumped onto my chair instead of shoving her away. Is that better or worse? I scrub my face with both hands and sigh. "I don't want our first time together to be like this. A quick shag on the kitchen table."

"What makes you think it'd be quick?"

She must be joking. I give her a look meant to convey the fact that we both know I would've ravished her like a mad man if I hadn't employed every iota of my willpower to force myself to stop. The expression on her face shifts from surprised annoyance to something that suggests she recognizes the truth too.

I pull her onto my lap with her legs straddling me and rest my hands on her hips. My granite-hard *slat* pushes against her crotch, but I can't do a bloody thing about that. A few locks of hair have fallen over her face, so I sweep them away gently. "Sweet, I need more time to prepare. You deserve better than this."

"Thought this whole day was preparation."

"For you, yes." I graze the backs of my fingers over her cheek. "I want it to be an experience. One to remember."

She tilts her head to the side, studying me. "Sounds almost romantic."

"You disapprove?" Not that it matters if she does. I don't want to romance her.

"No." She spreads her palms on her thighs while I trail my fingertips down her throat. "You're confusing the hell out of me. First, you dump me for a phone call. Then, you take me on a romantic picnic and cook me a sensual dinner. Your domineering act a minute ago was wicked sexy, but now you're back to being considerate and sweet."

"Sweet?" Did my lip curl when I said that? No, that's ridiculous. I don't care what she thinks of me, so I have no reason to be annoyed when she calls me sweet. I am not a puppy, though.

Erica gives my chest a playful slap. "What is it with men and the word sweet? It's a compliment, not an affront to your manliness. Trust me, you've got no issues there."

"I don't?" Of course I don't. Why am I asking?

"Absolutely not." She leans in to press her lips to mine. Our faces a breath apart, she whispers, "You are the hottest man on the face of the earth, Mr. MacTaggart."

Now that's more like it. A compliment I can handle.

I catch her bottom lip between my teeth, releasing it with deliberate slowness, her flesh retreating millimeter by millimeter while I pull her closer. "And you, sweet Erica, are the most enticing lass on earth."

She gazes up at me with wide eyes and a slack expression, but only for a few seconds.

What was that about? She almost seemed afraid at that moment. The reasons why are none of my concern, and I shouldn't care. Maybe it's to do with that scunner Presley, or maybe I've upset her with my behavior last night when I'd run away to take a call from Rory.

I glide my hands up to her waist, spanning her back with my hands. I can't explain why, but I suddenly feel the need to apologize, again. "I know I behaved badly last night. You've no idea how much I regret it."

She fingers the collar of my shirt. "Don't worry about it."

"No chance of that. How can I make it up to you?"

Erica rolls her gaze up to meet mine. She shrugs one shoulder. "It was kind of humiliating to be abandoned on the sofa with my pants hanging open."

I wince and nod crisply, unable to come up with an excuse for my inexcusable behavior. We look into each other's eyes for a moment, neither of us seeming to know what to do now.

Erica sets her hands on her knees and turns her gaze up to the ceiling.

Is she praying for divine guidance or counting all the ways she can tell me to bugger off?

She returns her attention to me and raises one finger. "I've got it. Tell me something about you. Something embarrassing."

What in the world? Her statement is bizarre and seems completely out of context.

She taps my nose. "You wanted to make it up to me. This is how you can." She slants forward a touch. "Something really embarrassing."

I flatten my lips. Aye, I behaved like an ersehole last night. But the punishment she has meted out seems odd. Still, I suppose I deserve it.

Sighing, I relax against the chair while keeping my hands on her hips. "My mother calls me Lachie. Has done all my life. I've told her a thousand times I hate it, but she won't listen. Even called me Lachie in front of girls I dated in school."

"That's mildly humiliating." She crosses her arms over her chest. "I said *really* embarrassing."

Mhac na galla. She won't be satisfied until I've humiliated myself the way I humiliated her last night. I take a moment to consider what I should tell her, tapping my fingers on her back while I think. A memory surfaces in my mind, and I stifle a grimace. Oh yes, Erica will love this story.

I tilt my head back and let out a low groan, my eyes sliding shut. "When I was seventeen, a bonnie girl coaxed me into showing her my, ah…"

Christ, why is it hard to say the word cock? I could say *slat*, but she wouldn't understand that. Of course, I could call it my penis or even my dick. But I can't make myself speak any of those words, which leaves me squirming beneath her bonnie erse while I stare at the refrigerator.

"What'd you show her?" Erica waves a hand in front of my eyes. "Your porn collection? Your pink bunny tattoo?"

"No." Maybe I could've sounded more embarrassed if I'd wanted to, but I doubt it. I rub my eyes with the heel of one hand, contort my mouth, and drop my hands to let them hang at my sides. I still can't look at her, and when I speak, it comes out as mumbling.

"Sorry, I didn't catch that," Erica says.

Bloody hell. I squeeze my entire face into an expression that must look pathetic, then I aim my gaze at a spot somewhere near her ear. "My dick. I showed the girl my bleeding dokey." I raise a hand to my brow, as if I can hide behind it until she forgets I ever told her about the most humiliating moment in my life. "My whole family walked in on us. We were out in the barn and the family had come home early from a trip into the village. They assumed the girl was about to, ah, give me…"

"A blow job?"

I flinch, though I can't fathom why. Talking about sex does not fash me. Well, not usually. "She wasn't. The girl only wanted to see. Her friends dared her to do it. And apparently, there was a sizable wager involved. But my parents and my sisters and my brothers all saw—and they started laughing their heads off."

Erica pries my hand away from my face. "I'm sorry. I shouldn't have made you tell me that."

I swear I detect a note of empathy in her voice, which makes me wonder once again what that *cacan* Presley did to her. "Tell you anything you want to know if it'll help you forgive me."

Aye, the idea she might think of me as anything like that other bloke makes me…anxious.

She cups my face in both her hands. "Nothing to forgive."

Clasping her hands to my chest, over my heart, I give her a sheepish smile. "I have a confession. I liked telling you my embarrassing story."

"You did? Why?"

Cannae believe I said that, but I see only one way out of this conversation. So I shrug. "Now you'll wonder what I've got that lasses would make wagers about."

She glances down at my erection, visible inside my pants. "I can guess."

"No more guessing after tomorrow." Did I just decide we should wait another day? Aye, my subconscious got the better of me, or it might have been my conscience whispering to me. Erica is wounded, like me, and I feel that I should go a bit slower with her.

Not too slow. I cannae wait longer than one more day to have her.

"Good." She curls her fingers into my chest. "Cuz I don't have a barn to lure you into."

"You'll never need to lure me anywhere." I lift us both up and onto our feet. "I'm yours."

For a casual affair, that's what I meant. There is no deeper meaning in my statement, or in my need to convince Erica that I'm not a bastard.

She stuffs her hands into her pockets. "If we're not having sex tonight, how about catching a movie? *King Solomon's Mines* is on TV tonight. The good version with Deborah Kerr and Stewart Granger."

"Classic film buff?"

"Grew up watching old movies."

A woman after my own heart.

No, this has nothing to do with that bloody annoying organ in my chest.

I claim her hand and usher her toward the kitchen doorway. "To the living room, it is."

"Wait." She stops abruptly, halting us both. "Would you like to come over to my place? I mean, it's not really my place, but I've got a plasma TV. Gil's is LCD, and it has a smaller screen."

Something she just said registers in my brain at last, and though I shouldn't do it, my curiosity insists I ask. "What do you mean it's not really your place?"

"Well, you see, you're not the only one living in someone else's house." She hugs herself and veers her attention to the window above the sink. "I live in my parents' house. When my dad retired two years ago, they moved to a retirement community in Florida, but they didn't want to sell the house or leave it empty." She rotates her gaze toward me, hunching her shoulders. "I don't pay rent, just utilities and taxes and any repairs that need doing."

I close my hands around her upper arms, caressing her skin with my fingertips. "Why do you seem ashamed of your living arrangements? In Scotland, many grown children live with their parents, grandparents, siblings…"

"In America, you're a loser if you live at home. Even if your parents aren't actually present."

Hooking a finger under her chin, I push up until she raises her face to me. "I don't care where you live, as long as I'm the only man you're sleeping with for the next four weeks."

Just because this is a sexual relationship and nothing more, that doesn't mean I have to share my lover with other men.

Hand in hand, we leave the house and traipse across the adjoining lawns to reach Erica's home. I volunteer to make popcorn, though it's hardly an act of great chivalry since she only has the microwave kind. Yes, I exert a lot of energy while opening the box and taking out the bag, then tossing it into the microwave. But it's the thought that counts, isn't it?

I hate sayings like that one. How does the thought count if no real thought went into the decision?

When I amble into the living room, carrying a bowl of popcorn, Erica is already seated on the sofa with pillows artfully arranged around her. They form a cozy wee spot for us. The film has just started, and African drums are pounding out an exhilarating rhythm while the credits roll. I settle onto the sofa beside Erica, tucked into the corner, and drape an arm over her shoulders. I don't mind when she cuddles closer to me. It feels…nice.

Though I focus on the movie, peripherally I notice Erica watching me.

"How old are you?" she asks.

I swivel my head toward her. "Forty-two. Why the sudden interest in my age?"

"Just filling in your driver's license."

"I don't follow."

"Never mind."

Ah well, women are inscrutable. Every man knows it.

I return my attention to the TV, drawing Erica a little closer.

"Don't you want to know how old I am?" she asks.

"I never ask a woman's age. Was that a trick question?"

"No." She snatches up a handful of popcorn and stuffs it into her mouth. "I'm twenty-eight."

Her words were slightly muffled by the large amount of popcorn in her mouth.

The meaning of what she said finally hits me, and my entire body goes rigid. "You're just a bairn. I'm beginning to feel like a dirty old man."

"I am not a bairn. And you're not old." She nudges me with her elbow. "As for dirty… Well, that's what I signed up for, right?"

I laugh and do my damnedest to make it sound erotic. "So you did."

Erica nestles into me, tucking both legs under her, and rests her head on my chest.

My ex-wife had never liked this kind of intimacy. She hadn't liked intimacy at all, except the sexual variety—and then only if it involved things I couldn't stomach.

Sex is all I want with Erica, so the warmth of her body pressed to mine doesn't matter at all.

When she skims her hand down my chest to my waistband, my breath hitches. My pulse speeds up too.

Hell with the movie. I need to give Erica a preview of tomorrow night.

A few minutes later, I have her spread out on the sofa beneath me while I grope and caress every inch of her sexy body. I kiss her the entire time, kiss her for so long and so thoroughly that I'm amazed either of us can breathe while our lips are locked and our tongues are ravishing each other. Every time she arches her hips, I battle the almost overpowering need to take her right here, right now.

I don't do it, though. I have a plan for seducing her, and I will wait until tomorrow night. I have to wait. The surprise I've prepared isn't quite ready yet.

So instead of shagging Erica, I kiss her good night and leave.

Dreams of her torment me all night long. Fantasies of Erica Teague naked, writhing, sweat glistening on her body while I sink my cock inside her again and again.

Though I don't want to wait, delaying for one more day gives me all the time I need to finish preparing her surprise.

Chapter Twelve

Erica Teague haunted my dreams last night. All right, maybe "haunted" isn't an accurate description of what happened last night. I dreamed of Erica—naked, moaning, writhing—and my subconscious gave me vivid fantasies of what it might be like to shag her. So aye, this morning I feel less than fully rested but somehow more alive than ever before. That doesn't mean I have any sort of feelings for Erica, beyond my sexual desire for her and the fact I enjoy spending time with her.

As a mate, nothing more. A casual friendship to go along with the casual sex we'll be having tonight. Casual acquaintances, not mates. That's what we are.

I woke up with the sheets tangled around my ankles, which I assume means I was tossing and turning all night, thanks to Erica's sensual body. Aye, it's her fault I didn't sleep well. She should wear clothing that's three sizes too large, so I won't fantasize about her anymore. But I doubt that would work. Her sex appeal has little to do with what she wears. I'm too old to get this worked up over a woman, but my brain seems to have given up control of my body and put my cock in charge.

Once I've disentangled my ankles from the sheets, I get up to stretch and yawn. The sun has come up, but this room faces west, not east, so all I can see is the secondary light of sunrise glowing outside the window. I pull on jeans and a shirt that I leave unbuttoned, then I amble down the hall and into the living room, heading for the sliding glass doors. From here, I have a perfect view of the sunrise as it unfurls across the sky, growing brighter and more beautiful with every passing second. Shades of pink and gold paint the sky.

Aye, the sky is bonnie. But even sunrise can't compare to the bonnie Erica.

Bloody hell. I'm turning into a romantic fool. Not that I have tender feelings for Erica.

I groan and cover my eyes with one hand. My proclamations that I do not want Erica for more than sex, the proclamations only I hear, might seem more believable if I didn't keep thinking about how lovely and sweet she is.

Sex only. I will not think about anything except what she might look like naked.

Maybe I can't stop thinking about her because of my encounter with that *bod ceann* Presley. Aye, he's a dickhead for sure. I cannot abide any man who harasses a woman after she's told him, more than once, to bugger off. I feel protective of Erica, that's all. My feelings are chivalrous, not romantic. If I could help her with her problem, that might prevent me from accidentally developing deeper feelings for her. Aye, that makes sense.

To a ruddy eejit.

Even if that's not the case, I still want to rid her of that scunner once and for all. To do that, I need more information than just his first name. I vaguely recall the bastard mentioning his last name when he said he's the prized son of the…something-or-other dynasty. I'd been too enraged at the time to take note of his surname. If I ask Erica, she'll want to know why I care. So I won't ask her. I'll arrange it on my own, but with assistance from a trusted source.

I ring my brother Rory. Though it's morning here, back in Scotland it's lunchtime.

He answers on the third ring. "I'm working on it, Lachlan."

Rory rarely wastes time on pleasantries. Besides, he knows I'm the one calling since my name and number are programmed into his mobile.

"I know you're working on the Aisley problem," I say, and I just manage to stop myself from grinding my teeth while I speak those words. My ex-wife always has that effect on me. "I need to hire a private investigator."

"No, you don't. I already have my investigator working on this case, and he is the best in the business."

"Ah, no, I, well…" Can't speak actual words anymore. I take a deep breath and exhale it slowly. "This is a personal matter. Can you give me the name of a good investigator? Here in America?"

"What are you needing to investigate over there?"

"It's personal, Rory, which means it's none of your bloody business."

Rory falls silent for a second or two. "You really are strung tight these days, aren't you? Thought a holiday in America was meant to relax you."

"Can you give me the name of an investigator or not?"

"Only if you tell me what the problem is, Lachlan. Otherwise, no. I won't give you a name."

I want to hunt down the scunner who's harassing the woman I need to seduce so badly that I can't think straight. But I cannae tell my brother that.

"Never mind," I say. "I'll sort this on my own. Goodbye, Rory."

Without waiting for him to say goodbye, I end the call. Then I stomp over to the windows that overlook Erica's house. Why am I standing here staring at her kitchen windows? I do not need to see her. It's not a romantic impulse that spurred me to come over here. No, I'm staring into her kitchen because...

I snarl a string of Gaelic curses. I have no ruddy idea why I'm watching her house. The only thing I want from her is sex.

Well, maybe I could turn my idiotic need to see her into something erotic. Then it won't be a forty-two-year-old man's pathetic need to get a glimpse of the twenty-eight-year-old woman next door.

Erica gave me her mobile number on the day we officially met, meaning the day after our encounter at the club. I dial her mobile.

It rings several times before she answers. "Hello?"

"Good morning, sweet," I say. "You sound out of breath. Have you been exercising?"

She clears her throat. "Just had a shower."

"An exhilarating one, I gather." My mind shows me images of Erica naked, pleasuring herself in the shower. No, she wouldn't have done that. Would she?

"I—"

Silence follows that single clipped syllable. Maybe she's stunned that I've called her this early in the morning.

"Would you do me a favor?" I ask.

"Depends."

"Go to your kitchen, please."

"May I ask why?" She sounds suspicious, and I can't blame her for that.

"I want to see you."

"Um..."

I drop my voice to a whisper. "Are you in a towel? Or maybe you ran from the shower so fast you're—"

"In a towel. Yes."

"Let me see you. Please."

More silence, but only for two seconds, which I know because I count it on my watch. Then she says, "Okay."

I exhale the breath I suddenly realize I'd been holding in. "To the kitchen."

She must have the mobile in her hand, since I can hear the faint sounds of her movements while she heads for the kitchen. I grip my mobile tighter, still holding it to my ear, my gaze glued to the windows of the house next door, where Erica will appear any moment now.

She sashays into the kitchen, wearing only a white towel that she holds in place with one fisted hand, and she smiles. "Here I am."

"Yes, you are." I flatten a hand on my chest, my fingers curling into my skin. "You're a vision in the morning, wet and clean, just begging to be sullied."

"Is that your plan? To sully me?"

"And then some." I slide my hand down to the waistband of my jeans, but I keep my gaze locked on hers. The sight of her wearing almost nothing makes my mouth water, and I tap my tongue on the bottoms of my front teeth while I imagine I'm lapping at her clitoris. I cup my growing erection with one hand. "Any chance of a preview?"

"Preview of what?"

"You." I shift my hips this way and that, adjusting my cock through my jeans. I'm getting hard enough that soon she'll be able to see the crown sticking out of my waistband. "One glimpse of what you're hiding under the towel."

She scuffles backward a step, and I can tell she's breathing hard, those luscious tits rising and falling.

For a moment, I think she won't do what I asked. Not now. Tonight, aye, but this morning—

She takes hold of both sides of the towel and spreads them open.

My eyes flash wide, and I'm fair certain my jaw goes slack.

Her body is on full display, from those bonnie breasts and their dusky nipples to her slim waist and wide hips. My attention sinks lower still to the dark hairs at the juncture of her thighs. And aye, she has legs that seem well-toned and strong enough to grip me while I take her body.

"Fuck me," I say in a rasping voice I hardly recognize.

"That's the plan, isn't it?" Erica says with a grin.

She folds the towel closed, depriving me of the best view I've ever had. Not even the peak of the highest mountain in the Scottish Highlands compares to Erica Teague's body.

Something scratches my scalp, and I suddenly realize I've knotted my fingers in my hair. I shake my head slowly. "You are stunning. I cannae wait till I'm buried inside ye."

Her gaze drops to the bulge in my jeans. She tugs the towel tighter around herself and tucks one corner inside it, between her breasts, to secure the towel. Leaning back against the kitchen island, she waves at my jeans. "Your turn."

"What?" For a heartbeat, all I can do is stare at her. She can't mean it, can she? The lass is having me on. But I quickly realize she *does* mean it, and

I want to give her a preview like the one she gave me. A sly grin curves my lips. "Suppose it's only fair."

I unhook the button on my jeans.

Erica watches my every movement as I toy with the zipper pull. She crosses her ankles, and the tip of her tongue pokes out between her lips.

I ease the zipper down ever so slowly, lower and lower, my focus on her face and the way her expression changes with every second that I leisurely draw the zipper downward. The lust on her face has me breathing harder too. First, the head of my erection emerges, then millimeter by millimeter, I reveal more of my cock.

She bites her upper lip, her gaze glued to my *slat*.

I skim the tip of my index finger along the length of my shaft as I keep pulling the zipper down, and I'm imagining Erica's finger touching me instead of my own. Pressure builds in my cock, but I keep going, tracing a path down my skin, moving that finger in time with the lowering of my zipper.

Erica's mouth is open, and her cheeks and upper chest are dappled with pink. She sounds breathless when she says, "No underwear?"

"Why bother? Don't plan on wearing clothes much this month." I unveil another inch of my *slat*.

Erica lunges side to side as if she's angling to get the best view, but she keeps her focus squarely on my groin.

Aye, she's getting as excited as I am. I chuckle softly, and all my lust is infused into that sound. "Like what you see?"

I drag the zipper down to the bottom and release the pull.

She grips the kitchen island as if she needs support.

Looking at my boaby can't be so arousing that she feels light-headed and weak.

Erica glides her tongue across her bottom lip. "Can I come over for a closer look?"

As much as I'd love to do that, I won't rush it. I zip up my jeans. "This was a preview, remember? We'll both look our fill this evening."

"So, we're on for tonight?"

"Nothing could keep me away."

"What about all day? Another picnic or something?"

"Afraid I can't see you today, my plans will take time. But tonight I'll give you a fine meal and a night you won't forget."

"Until later."

"Counting the minutes."

I end the call, take one last look at the beautiful woman next door, and hurry to the bathroom. That "preview" got me so hard I need to blow off some steam before I can get everything ready for tonight. Yes, I want our first sexual encounter to be more than a quick poke. Since I've talked Erica, a sweet and clever woman, into a four-week fling with me, I feel I should make tonight something we can both remember long after our month of sex is over and we go our separate ways.

I go into the bathroom and shed my clothes, then get into the shower and turn on the water, keeping it cold. With my back to the wall, I let the water sluice over my body, though I know a shower alone won't cure my problem. I take my cock in my hand and start pumping while in my mind I relive the moment when Erica showed me her naked body. My breathing grows heavier. I tip my head back, close my eyes, and let the cold water pummel my face.

Erica naked. Erica writhing. Her slick sheath gripping me.

I pump faster, slapping my free hand on the tile wall. "*Mhac na galla.*"

Her tits. Her flat belly. Her legs locked around my hips while I thrust and she throws her head back, screaming my name.

I come so hard I can't even gasp, my breath stolen by fantasies of Erica. I keep pumping until I'm done and my ears are ringing because I've forgotten to breathe.

Tonight, that fantasy will become reality.

And I do take a shower. Then I get busy preparing for my first shag with Erica Teague.

Chapter Thirteen

I spend the better part of the day arranging everything for Erica's surprise. I shouldn't care about making her happy, but I'd come up with my plan because she seems melancholy sometimes, and I inexplicably feel the need to make her smile. Tonight, I will ensure she also comes so hard she can't speak afterward. Aye, that will take her mind off the *bod ceann* who harasses her. Presley, whatever his last name is, deserves more than a skelping. He should be in prison.

But I only thought about him twice today, too absorbed in preparing for my night with Erica to worry about anything else. Now I'm standing in the hallway of Gil's house, a few feet from the entrance to the living room where I can see Erica still sitting on the sofa. I had ordered her to wait for me. Ordered her politely. The lass is doing what I asked, not even glancing over her shoulder for a peek.

Does she trust me? She must if she's willing to follow my commands. Erica doesn't seem like the sort who does what she's told without question, not unless she feels safe with that person.

I can't decide if I like that she trusts me.

Since the living room is at a lower level than the hallway, I have a good view of most of Erica's body. She has her hands clamped over the sofa's edge and her erse balanced inches away from slipping off the cushion. Is she excited or nervous? Possibly both. I feel a bit of both too, which definitely means I'm off my head, but I don't care anymore if I am. The chance to be with Erica tonight drowns out any anxiety I might've experienced and erases the rest of the world.

After checking that she's still waiting as ordered, I hurry back to the bedroom to finish setting things up in there. Once I've done that, I move back to the doorway so I can survey what I've accomplished. Everything is perfect. I'm missing only one thing.

The woman for whom I've done all of this.

I walk carefully and quietly while I make my way back to the living room and hesitate with one foot on the top step. Below me, Erica still waits on the sofa. She looks bonnie, as always, but I love the way she's dressed tonight. Her blue jeans hug her thighs and hips, and a white satin blouse clings to her bosom, the combination of those two items of clothing making me want her even more. I think she'll like what I'm wearing, since she liked it the last time she saw me dressed this way, and I cannae wait to see the look on her face.

Erica fidgets on the sofa, then kicks off her shoes. They feature moderately high heels, and the slender straps on them draw my attention to her ankles. Or they did, at least, before she got rid of the shoes. She has the sexiest ankles I've ever seen.

She drums her fingers on the sofa cushions and shouts, "Are you done yet?"

Her words vibrate my eardrums, since I'm standing eight feet away at most and she shouted her question with more volume than I would've expected from a woman as refined and sweet as Erica. I like it, though. I like everything about her.

Tiptoeing like a burglar, I approach the back of the sofa and slide my hands through her hair from behind. She startles, but only for a second and only the slightest bit. I smooth my fingertips down her cheeks, loving the warmth and silky softness of her skin. She doesn't move, not even to glance up at me. I place a soft kiss on the crown of her head, then lean over to feather my lips over her forehead. "This is a lesson in patience."

"Already told you I suck at that."

"Shut your eyes."

"Why?"

"Please." I exhale a heated breath over her forehead.

She clenches the sofa cushions, rolling her eyes up so our gazes lock.

It's a bit odd looking at her face upside down, but the desire simmering in the depths of her golden-brown irises entrances me, and I can't think of anything except how badly I need to kiss every inch of her body. With my fingers still on her cheeks, I ease her head back to get an even better view of her eyes and her face. Aye, that also gives me a fantastic view down her blouse, where I can glimpse the slopes of her breasts. I lick my lips and skim them down the bridge of her nose, then back up again. "Trust me, sweet."

Her shoulders slacken, and her eyelids drift shut.

The lass does trust me. But why?

I push the thought aside and focus on Erica, peppering kisses on her lids and touching my lips to her temple, then I pull out the only item I hadn't left in the bedroom. I lay the scarf over her eyes and start to tie it behind her head.

"Whoa," she says, sounding uncertain. "A blindfold? I don't know about this."

"I'll take it off if you like, but I was hoping to unveil your surprise after we're in the bedroom." I brush her hair away from her shoulders. "Can you trust me?"

"Yes."

She didn't hesitate, not for even half a second. And I still cannae comprehend why she lets me do whatever I want to her.

It doesn't matter. Not tonight.

Done tying the scarf, I pull my hands away. My cock is already stiff, but I will not rush this purely to satisfy my lust. I walk around to the front of the sofa and kneel between Erica and the coffee table.

She fidgets again, rubbing her palms on her jeans, then she starts wringing her hands.

Is she nervous? Or excited? Since she's breathing harder now, it must be excitement.

Time to begin.

I lean in and seal my mouth over hers. The first touch triggers an electrical surge that enlivens my skin, and when I slant my lips over her, my teeth scraping against her lower lip, it takes every bit of self-control I have to stop myself from taking her on the sofa.

She slumps toward me, moaning softly. I pull my body away as much as I can while I've got my mouth glued to hers, but I can't have her touching me. Not yet. I crack one lid open and see she's lifting a hand toward my chest.

I move sideways just enough to evade her.

She makes a frustrated noise that's almost a whimper.

I swirl my tongue over her top lip. "Try to relax. This is meant to be fun."

"Take off the blindfold."

"Bit of a control freak, aren't you?"

"Yes." She twists her lips left and right. "So take off the damn blindfold."

"Why donnae ye remove it yerself?"

I palm her breast.

She sucks in a breath. "Don't know. I guess because letting you blindfold me is a tacit agreement I won't remove the thing until you say so."

"And ye follow orders, even tacit ones?" I curl my tongue around her earlobe. "I have trouble believing that."

"I—" She stops talking the second I blow on the shell of her ear, charting a path along its curve. "I like the blindfold."

"Let's leave it on, then, for a wee bit longer." I grasp her hips and lift her onto her feet, crushing her supple body to mine. "But when I take ye, I want yer eyes on me."

I flick my tongue out, slipping it between her parted lips.

She slaps my chest but misses the mark, grazing my arm. "Hey! Have you been eating candy and guzzling booze while I sat here waiting for you?"

Clever lass. I had sampled the offerings I prepared for her, but only to make sure everything was just right. She noticed the flavors.

"A taste test," I say, then I flip her up and into my arms. "It's all for you."

I carry her across the room, aiming for the hallway.

She walks her fingers up my cheek, pushing them into my hair. "Are you planning to get me drunk, Mr. MacTaggart?"

"The food and spirits are for after." I press my lips to the sensitive skin on the inside of her wrist. "I've no need to ply you with liquor before."

We cross the threshold and enter the bedroom.

Everything looks perfect. But will she appreciate her surprise?

I lower her onto the bed where fabric almost as silky smooth as her skin covers the mattress. I'd bought these sheets today, for Erica. The bed has plenty of cushioning, a fact I mean to take full advantage of tonight.

Her head drops onto the fluffy pillow, and she rubs her cheek against the smooth pillowcase. A sensual little smile tugs at her lips.

The scent of vanilla wafts around us, delicate and arousing.

Her head springs up, the desire vanishing from her expression. "This is someone else's bed."

"Gil won't mind." I bend over to exhale a hot breath onto the pulse point on her neck, just below her ear. "I asked him."

She stiffens. "You asked my friend if he minded you having a poke at me in his bed?"

"No, my sweet, paranoid lass." I drag my open mouth down her throat, letting my lips and tongue trace a damp trail over her skin. "I asked if he minded me entertaining female acquaintances in his home. He said as long as I wash the sheets before he gets back, it was no matter to him."

"How many females have you gotten acquainted with in this bed?"

"None—yet." I let my lips brush against her throat while I work on removing her blouse, freeing one button at a time, baring the slopes of her breasts as I move lower and lower. "You, my bonnie Erica, will be the first."

She doesn't move except to bite her lip.

"There willnae be others," I murmur against her skin. "I asked ye to be my companion for this month. You and only you."

"What makes you think I care?"

I chuckle. "Ye tensed when I said ye were the first, which means ye care."

"Maybe I'll have other men during the month."

"You won't."

She snorts. "Arrogant much?"

I free the last button, sweeping aside the halves of her blouse. Her lacy white bra barely covers her breasts, and her rigid nipples push against the flimsy fabric. I lay a hand on her belly, holding it there for a moment while I admire the delicate curve of her hips. Then I kiss my way down her chest, into the valley between those lush tits. She squirms beneath me, her breaths coming heavier and faster.

I brush my nose against her breast, relishing the scent of her skin. I touch my lips to the spot where my nose had been, teasing her with light strokes. Christ, she's beautiful. I slip a finger under her bra strap and pull it over her shoulder so it hangs halfway down her upper arm. Then I push my hand inside her bra, molding my palm to her breast, and with a quick tug, I liberate it from the fabric.

She arches into my touch.

I flick my thumb over her nipple and seal my mouth over it, suckling and nipping until she's writhing beneath me. I release her breast and let my hand travel down her belly to the button on her jeans, unhooking it.

She plows her fingers into my hair.

Relinquishing her nipple, I unzip her jeans with a sharp ripping sound.

Erica makes an irritated noise.

I laugh and peck a kiss on her nose. "Patience."

"Told you, not my strong suit."

Diving my fingers inside the waistband of her jeans, I drag them down her thighs. "I've noticed your impatience. Tonight, I'll teach ye to enjoy waiting."

Chapter Fourteen

hould I be taking notes?" the cheeky lass asks, her mouth kinking into a sexily sarcastic expression.

"Ye won't be thinking clearly enough to jot anything down."

I yank her jeans off and toss them away, then hook an arm around her, lifting her torso off the bed just enough that I can strip off her blouse with my free hand. I get somewhat distracted by the sight of one tit spilling out of her bra and the sensation of her skin on mine, so for a moment I simply cradle her in my arm, bent over so far that her back almost touches the mattress. Every labored breath she takes pushes those breasts up until they come within millimeters of grazing my chest.

When I lean sideways, reaching for the bedside table, the movement rocks her.

Erica raises her head. "Are you leaving?"

"Just grabbing a tool."

I swipe the item in question off the table and stroke it over her skin delicately so she'll feel every touch of the feather on her skin. The way her breaths quiver makes my cock ache, but I ignore my own needs and skate the feather over her body, letting it tickle her flesh in long sweeps with the vanes barely contacting her skin.

She swallows hard enough I can see the movement in her throat.

When I skim the feather over the nipple of her exposed breast, she sucks in a breath and throws her head back, crushing it into the pillow while her spine arches up toward me. Our bodies meet for a brief moment that takes my breath away, then she falls back onto the mattress. I trace the feather over her lips, then set it on the table.

Lifting her again, I reach under her body to unhook her bra, dispatching it with one flick of my wrist. I remove her knickers just as her bra flutters down to the floor. Retrieving the feather, I dance the vanes over her skin from her throat down to her breastbone, and even lower until I'm teasing her mound. I spread her legs with one knee, then drag the feather along the insides of her thighs and up again slowly, frisking it over her slick folds.

I whisk the feather away, laying it on the table.

She sinks her fingers into the pillow, almost panting. "Please."

"Please what?"

"Don't stop."

I place a kiss on the hollow of her hip.

She jolts and clutches the pillow so tightly her knuckles turn white.

Why do I love teasing her this way? I've never done this with any other woman, but with Erica, I can't get enough of watching her reactions every time I tickle her skin with that feather or my mouth.

I lick a path down her belly to her thigh, planting an open-mouth kiss so close to her mound that the hairs tickle my cheek, the sensation arousing me with such intensity that I'm having trouble breathing.

She reaches for me.

I snare her wrists with one hand, keeping my grip firm but gentle. If she lays one hand on me, I might *caith* before I even get inside her. Erica rolls her hips like she's desperate to have my mouth on her, but I restrain her wrists over her belly and seal my mouth over her clitoris, swiping back and forth. When I drag my tongue up and down in a single languid stroke, a strangled moan escapes her.

She lets her knees fall wide open, exposing all of her to me.

I lap and suckle while she bucks and writhes, fisting her hands in the sheets, but I cannae stop or slow down my relentless pace, alternating up and down, side to side, then circling my tongue around her nub only to pull my mouth away to blow a breath onto her flesh. Erica cries out with every lash of my tongue and every puff of my breath. She struggles against the constraint of my hands cuffing hers and my body pinning her to the bed, though she doesn't seem to want me to move off her. Her noises and movements are ecstatic, not angry.

She trusts me—with her body.

"Lachlan, wait. I—"

If she means to tell me to stop, I don't realize her intent. The force of her lust has shut down my brain, so I keep going, raking my tongue down her cleft and diving it into her entrance, milking all the pleasure her body can stand. Whatever she'd been about to say, she seems to have forgotten what it was.

Her entire body freezes, and her breaths shorten into sharp gasps.

"Lachlan!" she screams while her body bows inward and she squeezes her eyes shut.

And I keep going, determined to wring every last bit of pleasure from her.

She collapses, her body limp, her chest heaving.

I release her wrists.

The lass flails her hands as if she's searching for me, but she's too dazed by her climax to remember the blindfold that covers her eyes.

I settle my body on top of hers, my erection trapped between us.

Erica buries her face against my neck. "Wow, that was…"

"The beginning." I push a hand into her hair. "We've got all night."

I peel my body away from hers and sit back on my haunches.

She reaches for me but only grazes my chest. "Where are you going?"

"Nowhere." The bed creaks and rocks as I hop off it and remove her blindfold. "Nothing could keep me from you tonight."

Erica squints at the sudden brightness, blinking swiftly, but soon she seems to readjust to the lighting. The lass sits up, the beauty of her nude body complimented by the pale-green sheets, and she surveys the room—until her gaze lands on me.

I stand beside the bed, shoulders back, arms slack at my sides and wearing nothing but my kilt made from the MacTaggart clan tartan of blue and green threaded with orange. I sweep an arm wide to indicate everything I've set up inside this room. "A wee bit of Scotland brought here for you."

She lays a hand on her chest, her mouth open. "What?"

"One day you'll see my country for yourself." I step back and spread both arms. "But for now, this is what I can give you."

She studies her surroundings again, and I follow the track of her gaze with my own. Candles occupy every available surface, five on the dresser alone, and a single plump one burns on the bedside table, burnishing Erica with golden light. The windowsill has no candles since I'd drawn the curtains for privacy. But more candles adorn the wooden chest that sits beside the dresser. Fabric fashioned from the MacTaggart tartan drapes over the top of the dresser mirror and serves as a valance over the window's curtains. Eight-by-ten photographs, each framed in silver, sit propped up in strategic locations in between the candles so the flickering flames highlight each image.

Erica seems mesmerized by the display and a touch confused by it.

"Dunrobin Castle, seat of the Sutherland clan," I say as I point to a photograph of a white castle perched atop an embankment with its spires piercing the blue sky. In the next images, a row of stone arches curves over a narrow road and waves crash against craggy white cliffs. "Glenfinnan Viaduct. The coast of Caithness."

Her gaze tracks my bobbing finger while I explain each photo and the landmark it shows, giving her a true taste of Scotland, almost as if I've magically transported her to my homeland. The final framed picture rests on the bedside table beside the plump candle. It shows a hilltop view of a quaint village seated at the shore of a small loch, nestled within a valley.

Gazing at the photograph gives me a pang in my chest, and my throat tightens. "Ballachulish, my home."

I haven't been home in far too long. Maybe that's why the picture gets me slightly choked up.

"Oh, Lachlan," Erica says, leaning over to see the photo better. "It's beautiful. I wish I could visit there someday."

I sit down beside her, the bed creaking under my weight. "Why do ye say it as if it's not possible?"

She almost winces, then clears her throat and nods toward the final picture. "When were you last in Bally—Ballakol—"

"Bal-uh-koo-lish." I brush the back of my hand over her cheek. "I was there Christmas before last."

I've given her the least confusing pronunciation of Ballachulish since the Gaelic way is often hard for Americans to master. What I said is ninety-nine percent correct, which is good enough for now.

Why didn't she want to tell me why she talks as if she won't ever be able to visit Scotland? I still can't understand her reaction to my question.

"Work keeps you busy, huh?" she says.

"Aye." I tip my head to the side. "Speaking of work, do you go back tomorrow?"

"I'm sort of taking a sabbatical."

"Ah." I want to ask her more questions, to understand her behavior. Sometimes she acts like she won't be around long enough to do the things she wants to do, like visiting Scotland. But if she were dying, she wouldn't have the stamina to endure the orgasm that wrenched her whole body a few minutes ago. Whatever her reasons are for her attitude, it's none of my concern. So instead of asking, I glide a hand up her thigh and smile. "Back to the fun, eh?"

"Yes, please." Erica shimmies closer, loops her arms around my neck, and drags her lips up my throat.

I close my hand around her hip, my fingers curled against the backside, my thumb drawing circles on her skin.

She swirls her tongue up to my jaw, nibbling there while ruffling her fingers through my hair.

And I groan into her ear. Christ, this woman knows how to turn me on. I nearly *caith* when she pulls my head back to scrape her lips over my collarbone and skims her fingers over my chest like she's mapping my body. She presses her open mouth to my chest, gently biting my skin with her teeth. I groan again, kneading her hip harder and faster with my thumb.

She stretches an arm behind me to squeeze my erse.

"Och, lass, how ye drive me mad." Before she can take hold of my cock, I push away from her and jump off the bed. Scrubbing my face with one hand, I struggle to catch my breath. She'd stolen it the second she dragged her tongue up my throat. "Forgot the last stop on our virtual tour of Scotland. The botanical gardens."

"Can't it wait?"

Not if I'm going to keep hold of my sanity. How could I ever have known Erica Teague would turn out to be a siren?

I heft up a small wooden crate that had been concealed behind the dresser. Returning to the bed, I settle in opposite Erica and deposit the crate between us.

She tucks her feet under her, leaning in closer, peering down into the wooden box with an expression of excited curiosity.

No woman should ever be so adorable. It's not good for a man's health.

I shoo her away with a tsk and a wave of my hand. "Patience, *gràidh*, I'm about to show you."

"What did you call me?"

"*Gràidh*."

Why did I call her that? She's not my darling. We're shagging, that's all. But I did call her darling, without even realizing I'd said it until she pointed it out. I avoid looking at her, sifting through the crate's contents instead.

She takes hold of the box's edge with both hands. "What does it mean?"

I freeze with my hands in the box, hunching my shoulders. "*Gràidh*? It's Gaelic for darling."

When I dare to peek up at her, she looks stunned.

Bloody hell. I've derailed the fun train this time, haven't I? Time to get back to…whatever the fuck I'm doing with this woman.

Seducing her. Nothing else.

I lift a handful of purple flowers, offering them to her on my upturned palm. A thin white ribbon secures the stalks in a bundle.

Erica accepts the flowers. "They're lovely. Thistle, right?"

"Very good, *gràidh*. You're a canny lass."

Mhac na galla. I called her darling again. Whatever spirit has taken control of my voice needs to haud its wheesht. *You're the devil on your own shoulder, so shut yourself up, ye bleeding erse.*

No more calling Erica "*gràidh*." This is a fling, not a relationship.

Aye, and the fact I'm giving her flowers does not negate the casual nature of…whatever the fuck I'm doing with her.

Repeating myself doesn't stink of desperation. No, not at all.

I bring out another bundle, this one full of bell-shaped purple blossoms that hang down from the stems' tips. I skate my fingertips over the delicate flowers. "I had to give you this one. It's bell heather, but the Latin name is *Erica cinerea*." I whisk my lips over the blossoms, then clasp my hand behind the back of her head and kiss her with more passion than I probably should, but I donnae care, not tonight. Tomorrow, I might worry, but not now. "Ye are a bonnie wee flower in yer own right."

Why has my voice grown hoarse? And why did I say that?

Because I have become a bloody moron ever since I first saw Erica.

She gapes at me.

I hand her a bundle of bright-red blooms. "Lastly, Scottish flame flower for my fiery lass."

Tears roll down Erica's cheeks, and she sniffles.

I wipe her tears away with my thumbs, cradling her face in my palms. "Donnae cry, please. They're only flowers."

"I'm okay. Earth-shattering orgasms make me cry. It's a girl thing."

Though my mouth opens, I can't speak.

She sighs and stretches, the action lifting her breasts.

My gaze snaps to her chest, and I can't help licking my lips. That's clearly what she wanted—to stop me from asking any more questions by distracting me with her body. And it worked.

I gather the flower bundles, place them in the crate, and set that on the floor.

Erica crawls onto my lap.

Now I'm the one gaping.

She yanks my kilt up to expose my stiff cock, and it waves between us like my *slat* cannae wait to thrust inside her body. She dances a finger along the lines of the veins just beneath my skin, then wraps her hand around my length and pumps slowly. "No more flowers and pretty words. I want you inside me."

"Donnae have to make yer point so… ah." I crush her to my chest and flip her onto her back with me on top. Then I peel her fingers away from my cock and secure her wrists above her head with one hand. "Ahmno one to deny a lady, so I'll be fucking ye now."

"About damn time."

I let my lips curve into a self-satisfied smile.

She rolls her hips up to push my erection more firmly into her belly while she massages my erse with her fingers, locking one ankle around my leg.

I shove a hand between our bodies, straight into her folds. Her cream is hot and slick, and it smells like the most decadent food any man could crave, but I don't mean to taste her this time, so I dive my fingers inside.

Her body bows up, and her mouth falls open on a strangled cry.

"You're so wet," I almost growl, plunging two fingers into her body while rubbing her clit with my palm. "Aye, sweet Erica, go on. Show me yer passion."

"Shut up and do something." A cry bursts out of her when I lunge down to devour her nipple. "Please."

I rise onto my knees and strip off the kilt, flinging it aside.

Erica sneaks her tongue out to skate it across the bottoms of her front teeth.

Bloody hell, how could any man resist that? I snatch a condom packet from the bedside table, rip it open, and roll it on faster than I ever knew I could accomplish the task. This woman is turning me into a sex maniac.

She touches a finger to the head of my cock.

Fighting to keep from growling like the wild animal she's turned me into, I drop onto all fours above her, my face hovering over hers. "Tell me what ye want."

"Are you serious?"

"I'm at yer command." I bend down for a quick, rough kiss. "Use yer hands all ye want this time."

"Gee, thanks."

Our gazes converge as a wild grin overtakes me. I feel like a laddie again, like I'm about to shag a lass for the first time. But when I look into her eyes, I can't feel anything except hunger—for her body. How does she bring something out in me that no one else ever has?

With one knee, I spread her legs wider. "Tell me."

"Mm, I want—" She gnaws on the inside of her lower lip.

"Anything for you, *gràidh*. Ye need only say it."

"I want you to—" Her voice breaks off like she can't quite convince herself to speak the words.

Maybe I can motivate her to tell me. I pinch her clit.

She thrashes under me, shouting wordlessly. Then she looks straight into my eyes. "Fuck me."

Chapter Fifteen

I plunge inside her to the hilt, almost groaning because her body feels so bloody wonderful wrapped around my cock. Erica clings to me like she never wants to let go, her legs tight around my hips and her fingers digging into my back. I hold myself still, breathing hard, propped up on my straight arms, determined not to let this become a thirty-second shag. I want it to go on forever.

Not moving takes more effort than I'd imagined it could. I gasp for air, sweat beading on my forehead. At her rapturous sigh, I growl low in my throat like a ruddy animal.

With her hands clamped on my shoulders, Erica levers her body up to rake her tongue over my chest.

"Bloody hell, woman." I grind my hips into her, forcing my *slat* even deeper.

"More," she pleads. "Do it, Lachlan. Now."

I pull out until the only head of my erection nudges her opening. Then I rub it back and forth until she's writhing and beating her fists on the mattress. I penetrate her only an inch or two before I pull out, then I glide in further, pull out, lunge inside again, over and over. Every thrust is more powerful, more intense, as I sink in as far as I can, and even further than seems possible. She flails her head, her hair whipping around her face while sweat glues strands to her skin.

"Breathe," I command, afraid she might pass out from lack of oxygen.

She draws in one breath and then another, blinking slowly.

I sit back on my heels and grasp her hips, lifting them off the mattress while I gaze down at her body with something akin to wonder. "So beautiful. An angel couldnae be as perfect."

She still looks dazed, but it seems more like rapture than an aneurysm.

"I'll be taking you slow, my sweet Erica," I say. "Need to savor ye for as long as humanly possible."

Widening my stance, I shift side to side until my knees are spread and my cock is aligned with her entrance. I keep my hands clamped on her hips, unable to look away from her lust-darkened gaze.

She is the most beautiful creature I've ever laid eyes on.

Pushing away my barmy romantic thoughts, I sink inside her inch by inch until I can't go in any deeper, groaning from the sensation of her hot, slick flesh molding to my *slat*. She claws at my shoulders, crying out in wordless pleas for more. I grit my teeth, so focused on holding still that I can't breathe. Why am I doing this? I need to make this last forever, and torturing her with my cock feels too good to stop.

She rears up into me. "Fuck me, you bastard!"

Laughter blasts out of me. "All right, lass. No need for insults."

My arms quiver. Sweat sheaths my entire body.

She grips my arms with both hands and clenches her inner muscles around me. "Hurry up."

I splutter. "Erica, I cannae—" My eyes go wide when she tightens those muscles again. "Ah!"

The woman has driven me mad, for certain. I pound into her without a thought for how hard I'm taking her, my control shattered by what she just did to me. Erica shuts her eyes, her expression one of sheer bliss, and she shouts my name, scratches my back, bucks her hips to meet my thrusts. I plow into her, my mouth wide open, my breaths sharp and quick.

She comes so hard and so fast that she screams and thrashes while her body clenches me. I can't stop myself from tumbling over that cliff with her. A bolt of white-hot pleasure slams down my spine straight into my cock while rapid-fire spasms fire through my *slat*. I punch into her, shouting her name because no climax has ever felt this good before, then I grit my teeth, my lips peeling back, and let out a hoarse shout as I pound into her twice more until I'm spent and gasping for breath. I gaze into her eyes as a strange sensation tingles over my skin and penetrates deep inside me. This can't be...euphoria. Can it?

My heart is pounding so hard I almost feel light-headed. Must be lack of oxygen since I couldn't breathe for the last thirty seconds at least. Or is this still euphoria? No, what I felt wasn't...that.

I drop onto the bed beside Erica and pull her into my arms, cradling her to me while I wait for my pulse to slow and that strange sensation to fade away. The aroma of heather and vanilla still permeates the air beneath the scent of sweat and sex. The sheets lay crumpled and tangled around us.

She rests her chin on my damp chest. "I've never done anything like this before. Having sex with someone I just met."

"Neither have I."

"What?" Her head pops up, and she stares at me like I've spouted Gaelic phrases. "Are you serious?"

Does she have to sound dumbfounded? I twist my mouth into an irritated expression. "I understand why you'd think I'm some sort of Casanova, given the offer I made, but you've got me wrong."

She chews on the inside of her cheek for a few seconds. "So, you're not an inveterate seducer?"

Every muscle in my body relaxes, even more than a moment ago when I'd come inside her soft, willing body. I couldn't have been tensing up because I worried what she might say next. No, of course not.

To cover up whatever I experienced a second ago, I slide my lips into a lazy smile as I tug the sheet over us. "I've never been called an inveterate anything, much less a seducer."

"How many—" Erica averts her gaze to my chest, her lips clamped between her teeth. "Sorry, I was about to ask something impertinent and personal."

Every time she reminds me of our arrangement, the one I crafted, I feel pressure bearing down on my chest. Maybe I have been overly strict when it comes to the topic of personal questions. In light of her anxieties, which I don't understand, maybe I should loosen my restrictions a wee bit.

I raise a hand to caress her hair. "Ask away."

She rolls her gaze up to meet mine. "What about the no-personal-questions mandate?"

"Considering everything I've just done to you..." When I flash back to a few minutes ago, my slight smile broadens into something approaching a grin. "I think we can temporarily suspend the rules."

She drags her index finger round and round on my chest. "How many women have you slept with?"

"In my life? Six, including you."

Her finger stops moving. She arches her brows. "Only six? You're so ancient, I figured you must've had fifty or sixty, at least."

Cheeky lass. But I love it when she teases me.

I tap my fingertip on her nose. "Very funny. I was married for twelve years, and before that, I was selective. I had to care for a woman before I'd take her to bed."

"And now you're slumming it with me."

My jaw snaps shut like someone has pulled a lever inside me. I squint at her, hissing a breath out through my nostrils, and try to figure out why she believes I think of her as less than every other woman I've shagged. "Never refer to what we do together as slumming. You're not a prostitute."

"But you don't care about me. You don't even know me."

"I—" Do I want to know her? Maybe I do, but the last thing I need right now is to get emotionally entangled with anyone. I'm too damaged to be any good for Erica. I scrub a hand over my face, then press the heel of my hand to my forehead, closing my eyes. When I manage to look at her again, I force myself to maintain a neutral expression. "I like you, Erica. And I want you. Can that be enough?"

"Well, that was our agreement. Sex only." She lays her cheek on my chest. "It's your turn. Ask an impertinent question."

I skim my fingers down her spine, skimming them across each vertebra until my hand comes to rest over the dimple of her erse. "How many men have you been with?"

"Three, counting you."

"One of them would be the bawbag who bullied you."

"Presley? Yes. Unfortunately."

My hand stiffens on her backside. "I've no right to feel this way, but I hate thinking of you with him."

"So do I." She gives a fake shiver as if she honestly does dislike thinking about the *bod ceann*.

Well, at least she isn't still enamored of him. But her feelings toward Presley mean nothing to me.

Then why did I tell her I hate thinking of her sleeping with him?

"Enough personal questions," I say, sliding my hand down to squeeze her erse. "Shall we get back to the fun?"

"Absolutely." She slings her leg over mine, and her nipples scrape across my chest. A sexy smile warms her expression, probably because my *slat* is getting stiffer. "Next are you going to tie me up?"

"What?" I seize her chin, rotating her face toward me. "I would never do anything that might possibly hurt you."

"I just wondered, because you held my wrists earlier. More than once."

My lips tighten, and I close my eyes for a moment. Aisley had craved pain with her pleasure, but more than that, she'd craved depravity. I hadn't known that until after we were married, and I hadn't wanted to disappoint my new wife. So I tried some of the things she wanted. Ever since I left her more than a year ago, I haven't wanted to think about Aisley's proclivities. Some were rather tame, though nothing I wanted to try—like group sex or domination games. I might not have minded letting her be the dominant one during sex, but she also had wanted me to do things to her that I...could not stomach.

Erica isn't Aisley, or so I'd thought. But she just asked me if I want to tie her up.

She was teasing, though. I'm ninety percent certain of that.

I look at Erica and aim for a playful tone when I say, "I was trying to keep you from clawing my head."

"Did I hurt you?"

"No, but it was awfully distracting."

"Oh." She splays her fingers over my chest. "Thank you."

"For what?"

"I begged you to fuck me, and you did." She cuddles closer. "It was the best sex of my life."

"First of all, you didn't beg." I brush a stray hair away from her face. "You commanded. And I must obey the bonniest, sexiest lass I've ever met." I let my fingers roam down her arm. "It was the best sex of my life too. No thanks are necessary."

She runs her tongue along the inside of her bottom lip, then presses her lips together, rubbing them against each other. Her focus drifts to my groin.

I don't even try to quash my smirk. "Again?"

She gazes up at me through her lashes. "How did you know?"

"Because you're looking at me like you could devour me in one bite." I palm her erse, my fingers splayed over one cheek. "I could devour you for sure."

"Then please, feel free. Tonight, think of me as your all-you-can-eat buffet." She nods at my growing arousal. "Don't let that go to waste."

I feign a yawn. "Maybe I'm too exhausted. You are a handful."

She grabs a condom packet from the table.

My erection rubs against her backside as I roll over onto my side, and Erica lies down on her back. I drape my arm over her belly.

She springs upright, strips the bed sheet off our bodies, and climbs astride me.

I settle my hands on her thighs, caressing up and down, exerting more pressure with every pass until I'm massaging deep into her flesh where I can feel her strong muscles beneath all that supple flesh.

Hovering above me, she raises the condom packet to her lips.

I hold my breath, anticipating her next move. She means to put the condom on me with her delicate fingers. Doesn't she? No woman has ever wanted to do that before. I bite down on the tip of my tongue, struggling to restrain my hunger for her, but I've never had much luck with that. The thought of her hands on my cock…

Now I'm so stiff my *slat* is waving between us like it's inviting Erica to have her way with me.

"Ah, Christ," I groan. "You are going to kill me."

"No." She slides the condom packet across her lower lip. "Just torture you the way you tortured me. Make you beg. Get you so hard you can't think and the only thing you can manage to say is 'please, Erica, please.'"

I grip her thighs, right under her hips, my thumbs nudging her mound. "Please, my sweet Erica, my erotic goddess, please."

"That'll do too," she says, sounding almost breathless.

She rips the foil packet open with her teeth.

Bod an Donais. That might be the most erotic thing I've ever seen. My eyes flare wide, then drift half-closed while I drink in the vision of Erica Teague in the nude, straddling me on her knees and holding the torn edge of a condom packet between her teeth. I tug gently, urging her to bend her knees until her groin lowers to within inches of my erection. A drop of moisture from my crown rubs off on her skin. I ease a hand between her legs, my fingers grazing her mound as I brush my thumb over her clit, making her shiver the slightest bit. "Ye are for certain the bonniest, sexiest woman on earth."

"You said that already."

She rolls the condom down my length, taking her time. When her finger-tips glide over my balls, I hiss in a breath and squirm the way only Erica can make me do. I try to pull her down closer with my hand on her thigh, but she rises instead.

I'm fighting for every breath, so aroused by this woman that I can't speak. For the first time in my life, a woman has made me crave her so intensely that I've turned into a sex-obsessed bampot, but I don't care if I have lost my mind.

"Ah, *gràidh*, ahm begging ye—" I suck in a ragged breath while I scrape my thumb over her nub and down between those luscious, wet folds. When she gasps, I grit my teeth. "Yer killing me."

"Said that before." She curls her fingers around my cock, gliding her hand up and down. "Don't you have anything new to say?"

I swallow hard. "The facts bear repeating."

She sinks down onto my cock, taking all of me into her body, and moans deeply.

Bod an Donais, she's amazing. I grasp her hips, my fingers digging in, but she doesn't seem to mind. Then she lays her hands on my chest, bracing herself, and begins to ride me with languid strokes while she gazes down at our joined bodies, seeming transfixed by the sight of her flesh sliding along mine. My attention is riveted to the same spot, where I can see her cream glistening on the condom.

I squeeze words out between my teeth. "You're so wet."

"You told me that already too." She throws her head back, as lost to the bliss of our bodies merging as I am.

My hips buck at the same instant she slams down, and a choked shout bursts out of me. "Can't be original when yer driving me mad." I clutch her hips and buck into her again. "Ah! Faster, lass, faster."

She pushes up off my cock until only the head is inside her and looks at me with the most beautiful look of raw lust I've ever seen. I dart my gaze over her entire body, but I can't admire her sexiness right now, not with the painful pleasure that's mounting inside me. Swaying her hips, she cups her swollen breasts with her palms and pinches the nipples.

My breaths shorten into huffs, and sweat dribbles down my temples. When I speak, my voice is rough and strained. "Erica, have mercy on me."

"Never."

Chapter Sixteen

*E*rica impales herself on my cock, and we both cry out at the same instant. Our bodies slap together in a frantic rhythm, punctuated by my grunts and her hoarse cries. Her hair flaps around her face and fans over her cheeks while her eyes shut and her mouth falls open. She grinds her body into me, driving my *slat* deeper than ever.

I let out an explosive growl, pinning her hips to mine, and punch into her with so much force that half my body lifts off the bed. We crash back down onto the mattress while still joined, the concussion plunging her onto my cock at the instant I come. The intensity of my climax barrels down my spine, the scorching power of it wringing every last drop from my cock as my shouts echo through the house. Then I find her clit and rub it, rolling my thumb around that rigid bud while I curl my fingers over the silky hairs between her thighs.

Erica rides me faster and harder, like she's so desperate to come that she can't stand to wait one more second for that release. I keep rubbing her with my thumb while I anchor her to me with both hands. Her inner muscles clench around me in pulsating waves, and she lets out primal, unbridled cries. By the time the final wave subsides, she's panting and dazed, her cheeks and chest speckled with pink. She slumps onto my chest.

Erica has never looked bonnier than she does right now.

Still buried inside her, I glide my hands down her back and up again to comb my fingers through her hair.

The lass whispers against my chest, "Thank you for dinner—and the virtual tour of Scotland."

"You're welcome." Still combing my fingers through her hair, I lift her hand to my mouth and kiss each knuckle. "I'd be honored to take you to dinner tomorrow night."

"Mmm."

"A proper dinner." I lace her hair between my fingers. "Nothing like the club the other night."

She smiles up at me. "I would love to have dinner with you."

"I'll be honored to escort you."

"Honored? You're being sarcastic, right?"

"Of course not. You are an elegant, captivating woman." I slap her erse, making her yelp. "You're also fantastic in bed. I lucked out when I picked you for my holiday fling. And you lucked out too, since you admit I give you the best orgasms of your life." I try to restrain my grin—well, I don't try *that* hard—but it breaks through anyway, partly suppressed. "I suppose you ought to thank me after all."

She smacks my chest lightly. "Arrogant Scot."

"Cheeky American."

We both laugh.

Then I ease her off me so I can retrieve a round, black box and offer it to Erica. "Highland chocolates from Iain Burnett. These caramels are as rich and silky as you."

She peels the box open and nearly drops it when she sees the chocolate hearts nestled inside. "Uh, thanks. I love caramel."

"You don't look pleased."

Lifting her gaze to mine, she smiles, though it seems a bit forced. "I am pleased. These look yummy."

What about sweets makes her unhappy? I thought women loved heart-shaped things and all that romantic bollocks.

Bloody hell. I'm not meant to be showering her with romantic gifts. So why did I order heart-shaped chocolates?

I pull her down with me, and we lie in bed together with the sheets covering us from the hips down. After a few minutes, she leans over the bed's edge to snag her shirt from the floor and shrugs into it.

The box of chocolates lies beside me, so I flip the lid up and select a candy. I touch it to her lips. "Open up."

She complies, and I slip the sweet onto her tongue. She seals her mouth around it, not chewing, seeming to wait for the confection to dissolve on her tongue before she begins to chew. Her expression softens, her lips relaxing into a sensual smile as she relishes the treat I've given her. A barely audible moan escapes her lips.

I clear my throat and shift my hips under the blanket, as if that will disguise my growing erection. I have never thought of eating as an erotic act, but

Erica proved me wrong—starting on the day when she brought me brownies and I gave the lass her first taste of Talisker.

With a rapturous sigh, she swallows the remnants of the confection.

I lick my lips, imagining all the ways I could make her show me that expression when I'm making love to her. Sliding off the bed, I retrieve the bottle of Talisker and one glass, both of which I'd hidden in the dresser. Then I crawl under the sheets with Erica again, though she still has her eyes closed. The lass is enjoying another heart-shaped sweet with even more pleasure than the first time, while her lids slide open.

But that does nothing to alleviate my problem. The look on her face is more rapturous than before.

I pour whisky into a glass, then down it in one swig. I repeat the process twice more.

"You okay?" she asks.

"If I don't drink myself into a stupor"—I decant more whisky into my glass—"I'll take you again."

"And that's a bad thing."

I clap the glass down on the bedside table. "I've never made love to a woman more than twice in one night."

"I've never been made love to more than twice in a night, so we're even." Erica snatches the Talisker from me and gulps it straight from the bottle. She shakes her whole body in an exaggerated shudder, even flapping her lips like a cartoon character. Then she wipes her mouth with the back of her hand. "Let's break new ground together. What do you say?"

Only Erica could make guzzling whisky seem so erotic that I can't control myself when I witness her doing that. I tear the bottle from her grasp and smack it down on the table. "I must obey, milady."

"My slave?" She skims her hand down my chest to the bulge growing under the sheets. "Ooh, I could get to like this."

She takes another gulp from the bottle.

I surge toward her, lashing my tongue across her lips to lap up the traces of whisky. "Heavenly."

Setting the bottle down, she leans back against the headboard. "How about tomorrow I give you the grand tour of Chicago? I mean, you're here on vacation, so you should experience the city."

"With you as my tour guide, I'd follow anywhere." I let my gaze wander down her body. "Since tour guides walk in front, I'll get to admire your lovely erse all day long."

"Hate to burst your bubble, but we'll be walking side by side."

"Even better." I shove a hand under her bottom. "I get to hold your lovely erse all day."

She slaps my arm playfully.

With an enormous effort, I convince myself to pull my hand away from her.

Erica threads her fingers through mine, and I curl my fingers around her hand.

"Tomorrow," she says, "I'll show you all my favorite places in the Windy City."

"Can't think of a better way to spend the day." I brush a kiss across her lips. "Thank you."

"Wait till you see where I take you before you thank me."

"I appreciate the offer." Lifting her hand to my lips, I feather kisses over her knuckles one by one. "But the taking bit can happen right now."

"Well, get to it, mister."

I sweep her up in my arms and lay her down on her back, flat on the mattress with the pillow tucked under her head. Then I slither up her body until my erection is trapped between us. My mouth hovers a hair's breadth from her ear. "Time to break new ground."

"Three times in one night?" She rakes her tongue up my throat to that tender spot just under my jaw. "Are you sure you're up for this, an old man like you?"

"Ye won't be asking me that again." I rock my hips, grinding my cock into her. She gasps, and I murmur into her ear, "I'm up for it, lass."

For the next hour, I prove that.

Once we're done, I have no energy left to do anything except go to sleep with Erica curled up against me, her sweet body snuggled under my arm. Memories of everything we'd done earlier whisper through my mind as I drift down toward the oblivion of slumber.

"Gotta pee."

Erica's half-whispered statement barely registers in my mind since I'm on the edge of sleep, and all I can manage to do is mumble wordlessly. A few seconds later—or maybe it's been hours, I don't know—a mobile rings, loud enough to rouse me. I yawn and roll over, throwing a hand out to the bedside table and feeling around for the device that woke me with its incessant ringing. I push up into a sitting position, braced with one arm, and blindly fumble around for the mobile, but it's not on the table. I blink several times, trying to make sense of my surroundings.

The ringing sounds farther away than this room.

Still groggy from sleep, I stumble down the hallway and into the living room, where the sound seems to originate. Did I leave my mobile out here? Damned if I can remember. Rubbing my eyes, I finally spot the offending device on the table by the sofa and grab it. Yawning again, I swipe the screen.

"Hello?" I say to the caller.

"Do I have the wrong number?" a woman asks. "I'm trying to call Erica Teague."

Mhac na galla. I've answered Erica's mobile by mistake, and I doubt she'll be happy with me for this. But since I have answered, I might as well find out who's ringing her.

"Aye, you've got the right number," I say. "But Erica is in the bog at the moment."

"What did you say, dear? The bog? Why is my daughter in a swamp?"

"Ah, sorry, no. I meant the bathroom."

"Oh, I see. You're Scottish, aren't you?"

"Yes, and we sometimes call the bathroom the bog." I start down the hallway, aiming for the bedroom. "Didn't mean to confuse you."

"That's all right, dear. You must know Erica very well, since you answered her phone."

"Ah…" Though she seems quite nice, I don't know who this woman is, so I probably shouldn't reveal too much. Aye, and I shouldn't have answered Erica's mobile either, should I? "Erica and I met recently. I'm staying in the house next door to hers while Gil Friedman is away."

"Funny she hasn't mentioned you." The woman pauses, then clears her throat. "I'm Deb Teague, by the way, Erica's mother. Who are you?"

I veer into the bedroom, now fully awake. "Lachlan MacTaggart. I'm, ah, Erica's friend."

"Casual acquaintance who only wants to fuck her" is more appropriate, but I can't say that to Erica's mother. What can I tell her? Nothing personal, that's for dead certain.

"So, you really are Scottish, right?"

Does she think I'm faking my accent? "Aye. My family lives in the Highlands, but I've been living mainly in Edinburgh."

"Are you married, Lachlan?"

Leave it to a mother to ask that question thirty seconds after I introduced myself. "Divorced. Erica and I are not dating."

What sort of bleeding moron have I become? Telling a mother I'm "not dating" her daughter will lead to more questions I can't answer. Well, it's more that I *shouldn't* answer.

I drop my erse onto the bed and rest my elbows on my knees.

"Are you spending a lot of time with Erica?" Deb asks.

"I suppose so."

"How is she? The last time we talked on the phone, Erica sounded tired or depressed, but she swore she's fine. We haven't heard from her in a while, though."

Though I've thought the same thing about Erica, the answer to that question is none of my concern. But her mother is worried, and I can't ignore what she asked me. Bowing my head, I say, "Aye, she's well. We had a picnic at the beach yesterday—with Casey, of course. Couldn't leave the furry little fellow at home."

"Oh, that's wonderful. I'm so glad she's having fun." Deb sighs. "I wish Erica would tell me what's bothering her, but she can be as stubborn as a mule sometimes. Maybe you can sweet talk the truth out of her. Since you're friends."

She makes friendship sound like we're filming a pornographic movie together. And I suppose we did do that, without the filming part. Tonight, we enjoyed each other's bodies in ways I will not describe to Erica's mother. "You are right, Mrs. Teague. She can be stubborn when—"

Two shapely legs move in front of me half a second before a delicate hand yanks the mobile out of my grasp. A breath explodes out of Erica as she holds the mobile to her ear.

"Mom?" she says, then listens to whatever Mrs. Teague is telling her. "I— well—" She drops her lovely erse onto the bed, turning her back on me. "I didn't think about it? It's a recent development."

I watch in silence as the woman I shagged earlier reverts to the demeanor of a teenage lass caught with a boy in her room after midnight. It's so endearing that I want to kiss her.

"Mom!" Erica cries out, jerking as if she means to get up, but then she clamps her fingers over the bed's edge instead. She angles away from me more and mutters something she must think I won't hear. "One hundred percent grade-A certified."

I did hear that, though. What or who is "grade-A certified"? I can't imagine why they would be talking about poultry, but that's the only thing I can think of that has letter grades assigned to it.

"Bye, Mom." Erica disconnects the call and turns to me, her lips puckered. "Why did you answer my phone? It was in my purse."

"I..." Rubbing the back of my neck, I shrug one shoulder. "I was groggy, and when I heard a mobile ringing, I tracked it down." I flash her a frown. "You left it on the table by the sofa, not in your purse. Didn't realize it was yours until I answered."

She tilts her head back and grumbles. "Fine, it's not your fault."

I stretch out on the bed behind her. "Your mother says you haven't called in some time. Why is that?"

Erica throws a hand up. "Off-limits."

Bollocks. My rules just slapped me in the face, again. But my talk with Mrs. Teague made me wonder even more about Erica's state of mind. I should ignore it, but I suddenly find I can't.

I place my lips on her back and pepper kisses on her skin until I reach her nape. "I'll make no judgments, you have my word. You can tell me anything."

"Forget it."

I nibble on her shoulder and flick my tongue out to taste her skin. "Please tell me."

"It's against the rules."

With my mouth on her shoulder, I sit here without moving for a long moment. She's right, and I'm a *bod ceann*. A sigh gusts out of me. "Understood."

She glances around as if she's unsure of something. "Do I stay? It's fine if you want me to go. I'm not up on the etiquette of flings."

"Course I want you to stay."

She focuses on fiddling with her mobile, which results in her lips tightening and trembling faintly, but the quivering passes in a few seconds. She sets the device on the bedside table.

I coil an arm around her waist. "Come back to bed."

Erica lies down on her side, facing away from me, and nestles her body against mine.

Soon, I will fall asleep. But I know I need to keep to the rules I set for these four weeks with Erica. I long to know all about her and to help her in whatever way I can, but it's too dangerous. Aisley ruined me, and I won't risk another disaster.

No, never.

Chapter Seventeen

Today, Erica is showing me her favorite places in Chicago. I've been to America before, but never this city, and I've never had such a sweet, sexy tour guide. Right now, we're standing beside the gigantic skeleton of a dinosaur that died millions of years ago, and Erica is gazing up at the skull of the *Tyrannosaurus rex* with a look of sheer wonder on her face.

I never would have guessed she loves dinosaurs. But then, I don't know much about her.

Because I told her we shouldn't talk about anything personal. *Mhac na galla.*

Erica cranes her neck back for a better view of the underside of the huge *T. rex* skull. Sunlight streams down from the skylight onto the bones, but I'm not admiring the prehistoric skeleton in front of us. No, I'm watching Erica's face and the way her expression turns from wonder into excitement, her lips curving up at the corners right before she breaks into a big smile.

I come up behind her, slipping my arms around her waist to link my hands over her belly. Resting my chin on her shoulder, I sigh with contentment, though I have no reason to feel satisfied this morning. Last night, aye. But today? I haven't even shagged her yet.

She leans into me, her head falling back against my chest.

"Tell me," I say, nuzzling her cheek, "why do they call this monstrosity Sue?"

"I don't know."

"But you're my tour guide, the one who knows all."

"Are you calling me a know-it-all?" she says in a teasing tone, turning her head to peek at me over her shoulder.

"I wouldn't dare." I straighten, and my chin brushes the top of her head. "Are you a dinosaur aficionado?"

"Suppose you could say that." Her head falls back again, nestled against my neck. "When I was a kid, I wanted to be a paleontologist."

"Why didn't you do it?"

"Eventually, I realized I needed to be practical. Jobs at universities are hard to come by."

"Do you love accounting?"

She hesitates before answering, but I can't see her expression. "It was more of a safe choice than a passion."

"What is your passion?"

She settles her hands over mine on her belly. "Well, I've always loved animals. Maybe someday I'll buy a farm, grow my own food and lots of flowers. Raise chickens, cows, horses, whatever."

"On your own?"

"Maybe." She twists her head around to look up at me. "Why do you ask?"

Good question.

"No reason," I say, pretending to survey the *T. rex* in front of us though I'm really wondering why I asked about her job and her secret passion. I nod toward the skeleton. "Tell me more about this charming lass."

Aye, that's called deflection.

Erica rattles off a litany of information about the skeleton and dinosaurs in general while I nod occasionally and make "hmm" noises where appropriate so she'll think I'm fascinated by the facts she has given me. Maybe I would find it interesting if I weren't distracted by wondering why I keep dragging us into discussions of sensitive issues. I told her "nothing personal," but I keep asking for details about her life.

"Sue is the most complete *T. rex* ever found," Erica says, and it seems like she's wrapping up her mini-lecture. "Replicas of her have toured the world."

I make an appropriate noise, as if I've absorbed every word she said when I've heard only half of what she told me, at most. Stepping up beside Erica, I clasp her hand. Why? I have no bloody idea. But holding her hand feels natural and comfortable. The other visitors in the museum must think we're a couple enjoying a tour. No one would guess I'm a dirty old man who seduced a sweet lass into spending four weeks in my bed.

Erica shifts her weight from one foot to the other, glancing up at me before returning her attention to the *T. rex* skeleton. "Turnabout time. Is finance your passion?"

I lean sideways, our shoulders bumping. "No, it's not."

"What is your passion?"

"Haven't found it yet." Since I met Erica, my passion is to have a poke with her as often as possible. Other than that, I have no ruddy idea what I want out of life—except to be rid of Aisley.

A family of four wanders past us, the mother and father holding hands while the children scurry this way and that, their round little faces excited.

Erica watches the family with her face pinched, her lips crushed between her teeth. Her eyes glisten faintly.

Is she about to cry? No, I'm imagining things.

But I feel an inexplicable need to reassure her, so I smile and lean in to peck a kiss on her cheek.

Her expression becomes more pained, and I swear her lips tremble, though only for a moment.

I tilt my head to the side, studying her for clues as to why she's unhappy. Her mother has noticed Erica's melancholia too, so I'm not imagining that. "Sometimes I think you're not here, you've gone somewhere else in your head. Those lovely eyes are seeing things far away that I can't see. Unhappy things." I grip her hand more firmly, surprising myself with the fervency in my voice. "I don't like it."

She shuffles closer, her hand floating up to rest on my shirt, her thumb grazing my skin where I've left a button undone. Her gaze connects with mine. "Why do you care what I think about?"

I look away, my throat suddenly tight. Why do I care? Not a sodding clue. I shouldn't care, and I don't want to, but the more time I spend with Erica...

"Don't know, it just bothers me," I say, glancing at her sideways, then I stare straight ahead at nothing while I search for a way to avoid answering more questions. "Is there a gift shop here?"

"Museum store, yeah."

"I'd like to buy souvenirs for my sisters." I lead her away from the dinosaur display and down the gallery. "Which way?"

"All the way down to the other end."

I capture her hand as we stroll away from the *T. rex* display and straight into the museum gift shop. Just as we cross the threshold, entering the store, I realize I'm holding Erica's hand again and release it. Then I browse the store's offerings and let choosing gifts for my three sisters distract me from everything else. Fiona, Catriona, and Jamie always love it when I bring home trinkets for them after I've been away.

Erica trails behind me but doesn't speak.

I grab a stuffed *T. rex* that has mottled green skin and red eyes but that still manages to be friendly and sweet thanks to its broad grin. I hold the stuffed animal up for Erica to see, waggling its puffy wee arms. With a smile and a wink, I say in a silly voice, "Wouldn't you like to hug me? I love to cuddle."

Her lips twitch, almost forming a smile.

She snatches the toy from me—and then seizes the back of my head to kiss me.

A child shrieks in delight somewhere behind us.

Erica pulls away, hopping backward, and fusses with her blouse as if it needs fixing, though it looks fine to me. She must be embarrassed by her sudden impulse to kiss me.

I cup her cheek with one hand. "No need to be embarrassed. I love your impulsive side."

"Not appropriate here." She straightens, rolling her shoulders back. "You said you wanted souvenirs for your sisters. Brothers don't rate gifts?"

"Their tastes aren't this refined." I glance down at the grinning dinosaur toy, feeling like a fool for telling her I love something about her. Christ, it's not like I said I love *her*, but I can't shake this unease. "I'll find gifts for them somewhere else."

For the next twenty minutes, we roam through the store selecting items for my sisters. With Erica's advice, I buy an embroidered purse for Catriona, a scarf with bicycles on it for Jamie because she loves biking, and souvenir spoons for Fiona because she collects those. We even find a spoon that features Sue's image. On the way out of the museum, I insist on buying Erica lunch at the museum's bistro. It seems like the least I can do considering…everything.

The least isn't good enough. I need to buy a gift for her. She deserves much more than a trinket, but right now, this is what I can give her.

A few yards from the museum's exit, I halt us both.

"Hold this." I thrust my shopping bag at Erica. "I need to run a quick errand."

"I'll go with you."

"No." I try to soften my tone since that word sounded too sharp. "Won't be long, I swear."

Taking my bag, she shrugs. "Fine, I'll just…stand here."

I jog off down the gallery, skirting around the imposing skeleton of Sue, and head straight for the gift shop. Maybe I shouldn't have left Erica alone. It seems rude, but I can't choose a surprise gift for her if she's standing right here next to me. I'd seen an item in this shop that I want to buy for her, one I hope she will appreciate. I think she will. It seems like an appropriate thing to give to the woman who is letting me ravish her at will. Once I've purchased the item, I rush back to Erica.

She is not alone. Erica is chatting to a young couple while their two children huddle around their father's legs. I assume they're a family, at least. The wee ones resemble the man and woman, so they must be related.

Erica wears that pained expression again, though she tries to hide it with forced smiles. The pair she's chatting to doesn't seem to notice her discomfort.

I walk up behind Erica. "Ah, there you are."

She sways ever so slightly, not enough anyone else would see it, and flutters her lashes like she has something in her eyes.

I sling an arm around her waist to support her.

Erica loops an arm around me, her embrace tighter than a simple hug would be.

I can't help wincing, just a touch. Blimey, she's strong.

She lifts her face to gaze up at me, her smile tinged with gratitude.

I kiss the top of her head. "Sorry I took so long, sweet."

My attention shifts to the man she'd been talking to, then back to her. Will she introduce me? Not sure she'll want to since we're not dating. But the couple in front of us seems to be waiting for her to tell them who I am. Erica opens her mouth, then shuts it, and repeats the action three times.

Should I introduce myself?

"Lachlan MacTaggart," I say, offering my hand to the chap whose wife is whispering to their children. "I'm Erica's friend."

"Danny Liao," the chap says. "I used to work with Erica. And this is my wife, Mia."

"Pleasure to meet you both." I shake hands with the couple, then I give Erica a quick squeeze and a quick smile. "We should be going, don't you think? Plenty to do before our dinner reservation at Everest."

Maybe I shouldn't have mentioned that in front of Erica's mates, but the words flew out of my mouth before I realized what I was saying. I'd once again experienced a strange urge to make Erica feel better. She seems anxious about meeting up with Danny and Mia, though I can't imagine why since Danny works with her.

No, Danny said he *worked* with her. Past tense. That must mean something.

Aye, it means she changed jobs, or maybe he did. There's no deeper meaning.

"Wow," Danny drawls, his eyes widening. He slaps my arm and grins. "Pulling out all the stops, eh?"

"Nothing's too good for my Erica." My Erica? Why the bloody hell did I say that? Despite knowing I've bollocksed things up again, I can't resist nuzzling her hair and lowering my voice to a murmur when I say, "That's for certain."

Erica throws me a panicked sideways glance, but then reasserts her pleasantly bland expression as she faces her mates.

A few minutes later, we've said goodbye to the Liaos and are heading across the parking lot to the Mercedes convertible I'd hired for the duration of my holiday in America. I open the passenger door for Erica, and once she's climbed in, I shut it and get in on the driver's side.

She scowls at me. "You could've warned me."

"About what?"

"Dinner." She enunciated each syllable carefully, hitting the consonants hard. "Five-star dining? I have nothing—absolutely nothing—I can wear to a place like Everest. I don't own a skirt, much less an evening gown."

I shrug. "I'll buy you one."

She crosses her arms and frowns again. "I won't be your kept woman."

"Kept?" I open my mouth but can't speak, so instead, I shake my head. What have I done now? Dinner at a posh restaurant was meant to be a good surprise, not cause for annoyance. I raise my hands, spreading them palms out. "The dress will be a gift, nothing more."

She eyes me sideways. "Accepting gifts from rich men in exchange for sex is the definition of a kept woman."

I jerk my head back as if she slapped me, which it almost feels like she has done. "It's not in exchange for anything. You're worried about not fitting in at the restaurant, so I offered to buy you a new dress." Don't women love it when men buy them things? Apparently, I've had it wrong all my life, or else this is more of her unexplained anxieties. I stretch out an arm to drape it over the back of her seat, leaning in close. "Stop acting like you're a prostitute. We have nothing to be ashamed of. Do we?"

For a moment, she says nothing, her expression slack. Then she rests her head against the seat and swivels her face toward me. "No, we're not doing anything wrong."

I slant closer, our lips now within kissing distance, and lay my free hand on her thigh with my fingers splayed over it. "Let me buy you a dress. Please."

"Are you trying to impress me? With haute cuisine and haute couture to match?"

How can I change her mood? Only one thing comes to mind, so I do it. I plunge my fingers between her thighs, molding them to her groin.

Her erse lifts off the seat, and her lips form an O. "Honestly, Lachlan, I'm not impressed by money."

"Not trying to impress you." I reposition my other hand above her head and lazily caress her hair with my fingertips. "I want to earn you."

Earn? What on earth am I saying? But I mean it, don't I? Yes, I suddenly realize I do mean that. I want Erica to trust me, and I need to earn that from her.

How? My only way in is through sex.

I mold my hand to her body, feeling the heat of her desire even through her clothes.

She exhales a shaky breath. "I give."

"What?"

"Please buy me a dress." She rests her hand on mine, pushing it more firmly into her groin. "If you insist."

A groan resonates deep in my throat while I stroke her with my fingertips. "Thank you."

"Don't thank me yet. You haven't seen the bill."

"Anything for you."

She grips the edges of her seat.

I caress her with my fingers, though her jeans keep me from massaging the parts of her I most need to touch.

"Why are you so determined to have me spend your money?" she asks.

I stop stroking her and watch her expression for a long moment, then I raise my hand to her cheek, leaning in until our lips nearly touch. "Because it matters to you, having the right clothing for the restaurant. I want you comfortable, not embarrassed." I rove my gaze down her body, from her breasts to her hips, where I pause while I remember the heat of her body against my palm, then I let my gaze wander down to her sexy ankles and back up again to her face.

The corner of my mouth curves up. "Though I say you'd stun every man in the place wearing exactly what you've got on now."

She rolls her eyes. "You are so full of it."

"You don't credit yourself enough."

"Nerdy girls don't stun—"

I crush my mouth to hers, silencing her protest. The feel of her lips on mine makes me crave more of her, and I dive my fingers into her hair to tilt her head back. I thrust my tongue between her lips, and deeper still, devouring her with all the hunger she inspires in me, loving the way she responds with equal ardor.

Though I'd love to kiss her for hours, I give up her lips. But I keep our mouths a breath apart. "Never call yourself a nerd again. Never." I brush my lips over hers. "You are perfect, *mo leannan*."

"What are you calling me now?"

I jerk my head up, and a cold wave crashes through me. "*Mo leannan*."

"And what does that mean?"

For several seconds, I can't move or speak. Why had I called her my sweetheart in Gaelic? She is nothing more to me than a casual lover. Why, then, do I keep trying to make her feel better? Doesn't matter. I will not get entangled in a relationship with anyone. Maybe Erica will forget about *mo leannan* if I erase it from her memory using the only method I know will work.

I knot my fingers in her hair, catch her lower lip between my teeth, and let it slide out little by little, lapping at her lip until it pops free of my teeth. Then I kiss my way up her cheek and murmur into her ear, "Doesn't matter."

"You're not going to tell me?"

What *mo leannan* means? No, I will never tell her that.

I nibble on her earlobe, then suckle it until her body relaxes and she exhales a soft sigh.

Pulling away, I face the steering wheel and crank the key in the ignition. "Tell me where to go for this new dress you need."

Peripherally, I see her glance down at my groin and my cock that's already thickening.

She almost smirks as she relaxes into her seat and lets her knees fall open. "You're paying. The choice is yours."

I give her a wolfish smile. "The most expensive shop in town, then."

Chapter Eighteen

Dinner at Everest with Erica... How can I describe it? The best date ever can't apply since we are not romantically involved. Why, then, did I insist on taking her to a posh restaurant? I've given up worrying about that—for the moment. For one night, I'm letting myself enjoy spending time with her and sharing a gourmet meal with the only woman who has ever made me feel lust and tenderness in equal measure.

Now, we're standing on her front porch having just returned from our date that wasn't a date. Erica wears a designer dress fashioned from emerald silk that clings to her body but leaves just enough room for the fabric to move with her instead of plastering to her skin. Her already beautiful body looks even more enticing in that frock. The neckline plunges between her breasts, giving me a tantalizing view of those bonnie tits. But it's the slit in the dress's skirt that makes my mouth water, the way it extends halfway up her thigh.

The lass belongs in expensive clothes. Though she'd been uncomfortable with the idea of me buying a designer dress for her, once she'd recovered from the shock, she seemed to enjoy trying on different frocks and stepping out of the fitting room to show me every single dress.

Erica leans back against the door to her house, inhaling deeply, her lips curving into a relaxed smile. The word beautiful can't adequately describe her when she smiles that way, like she hasn't a care in the world.

I know she does have cares—and worries, and fears. I've witnessed the sudden shifts in her mood, but as much as I want to know everything about her, I can't do it. Giving her the wrong idea about us will only lead to heartache.

She sweeps her gaze up and down my body, and her smile warms with desire.

Aye, she likes the suit I'm wearing. I know this because she told me so when I'd picked her up for our date that's not a date. Erica had told me, "You look soooo hot in a spiffy grey suit. Makes me want to fondle and lick you everywhere." Oh aye, her statement had made me as randy as a teenage virgin, but I marshaled all my willpower to keep myself from taking her right there in her living room, or on the porch, or in the car, or on the table where we shared a meal.

We didn't have a private table, but I still would've loved to shag her right there in full view of everyone and with a stunning view of Chicago through the picture window beside us. Getting arrested would've been worth it. Besides, my brother Rory is a lawyer.

My focus returns to the present when Erica speaks.

"Dinner was amazing," she says.

Aye, it had been. We shared a bottle of champagne, but Erica daintily sipped it instead of letting herself fully enjoy it. I'd told her to "indulge yourself, *mo leannan*," but she still held back. I held back too, but only from thinking about why I kept calling her my sweetheart. It was a pet name, nothing more.

I slant toward Erica to brace one hand on the door frame beside her, then duck my head near hers. "You are so bloody beautiful."

"The dress makes the woman," she says, glancing down at her feet.

"You've got it the wrong way round," I tell her while coiling a lock of her hair around my finger. I brush the lock's tip across her lips. "You make the dress, *gràidh*."

Releasing that lock of hair, I slip a finger under the slender strap of her frock, whisking it up and down. My breaths come faster and shallower, as if the slightest touch of her skin on mine excites me more than anything ever has before. It's true. She does excite me like no other woman could. Not even drinking an entire bottle of Talisker could intoxicate me the way Erica does.

I glide my finger up and down her skin. "I'm positive you'd make a paper sack look seductive."

She shivers the slightest bit, and her breath hitches.

I move my finger down to the neckline of her dress, skimming it along the slope of one breast. She follows the movements of my finger with her eyes while I dip it into the valley between her breasts. With a long, sighing groan, I lift my hand to catch her chin with it, encouraging her to meet my gaze. Rubbing my lips over hers, I dart my tongue out to taste her skin. Another, deeper groan rumbles out of me.

Bod an Donais, every inch of her body tastes as good as sweet cream and honey.

Erica yawns, then grimaces and clutches her hands over her belly. "Sorry."

"Don't be." I cradle her cheek in my palm, resting my forehead on hers. "We've had a long day—wonderful, but long—and you're jeeked." I step back and prop my shoulder against the door frame, then sweep a hand over my eyes. "I am too."

She smiles. "Jeeked means exhausted, I'm guessing."

"Aye." I reach out to caress her cheek, and without thinking about it, I smile too. Every day I do more and more things that suggest I have tender feelings for her, but that will never happen. Even if I wanted a relationship with Erica, I'm far too damaged for it to work out. I'd cock it up, and she would wind up hating me.

Erica deserves someone who appreciates her, a man who can give her everything she deserves. That man is not me.

She digs her keys out of the emerald clutch I'd insisted on buying for her since it matches her dress. The little purse is studded with real emeralds. Shoving the key in the lock, she hesitates and peers over her shoulder at me. "Wanna come in?"

She can't want sex, not when she's jeeked. Why else would she ask me to come in? I stare at her, unable to move a muscle except to speak."Are you sure?"

"Uh-huh." She unlocks the door and pushes it inward. "I'm not that tired."

She yawns, her mouth gaping open so far I can see her back molars.

Not that tired? Rubbish.

I settle a hand on her back, between her shoulder blades. "I would love to come in, but no sex tonight. You're far too tired."

"Losing interest already?"

"Never." I skate my hand up to her neck and gently knead her nape, gratified by the way she relaxes into my touch, giving up the pretense of not being exhausted. I kiss her cheek. "I plan on debauching you plenty tomorrow. But for tonight, I'd be honored just to sleep beside you."

She gazes at me, not blinking, her lips parted. But it isn't desire triggering that expression. It's surprise.

I suppose the lass can't believe I'd want to sleep with her, actually sleep, with no sex involved. It does contradict my claim that all I want is a four-week fling, but I don't give a toss. For one night, I need to lie in bed with her and fall asleep with her body nestled against mine.

Erica shuffles into the house.

I follow and shut the door.

A furry body sails through the air at us.

Casey lunges right past Erica to tackle me. I stumble but stay upright and ruffle the pup's hair with vigorous strokes while havering to Casey the way dogs love.

"Do you have a dog at home?" Erica asks.

"No, but I always had them growing up." I straighten, and Casey switches his attention to his mistress, greeting her with a slap of his tongue on her hand. I scratch the back of my neck, eyes averted. "My wife did not like animals."

Casey nuzzles Erica's hand, whimpering and wagging his tail.

"He wants a snack," she tells me, then heads for the kitchen with the pup following close behind.

I trail after them and can't help smiling when Erica retrieves a plastic bag from the refrigerator and tosses small pieces of some sort of meat to Casey. "What is that you're feeding him?"

"Raw chicken gizzards. Casey loves them." With a playful smile, she holds out her palm, and I see one gizzard seated in it. "Wanna try some?"

"No, thank you. I had raw sheep intestines for breakfast."

Her nose crinkles. "Please tell me that's a joke. It's hard to tell. I mean, you Scots love haggis which looks like something a dinosaur barfed up."

"Maybe I'll cook haggis for you sometime. You might like it."

"Doubtful."

She goes back to tossing chicken gizzards to the dog, who clearly loves his snack.

When she's finished, I raise my brows and smirk. "Planning to touch me with those hands?"

She wiggles them in the air. "Yep. Still want to sleep with me?"

"That's why God made antiseptic soap. Besides, I've been all over that body several times, in the most intimate ways."

She turns away from me to wash her hands in the sink.

I come up behind Erica to grasp her shoulders, resting my chin on the crown of her head, and coast my hands down her arms with deliberate slowness, relishing the feel of her skin, the warmth and softness of it against my rougher palms. I barely hear it when she sucks in a shallow breath. When I reach her wrists, I pause there for a moment with my thumbs over the pulse points, then I move my hands to envelop hers.

With our fingers interlaced, I nuzzle her hair. "We'll risk the germs together. Eh, lass?"

"That's a strange thing to say to a woman you're trying to seduce."

A chuckle vibrates in my chest. "Told you, I only want to sleep together tonight." I rotate our joined hands so the warm tap water sluices over them, rinsing away the soap. "Besides, I've already seduced you."

She gazes at the water splashing over her hands with an almost lustful look on her face, making me wonder what she's imagining right now.

My attention falls to her breasts, and the familiar hunger flares to life again. "In the morning, I promise to ravish you with multiple orgasms. Tonight..."

I sweep her up into my arms and saunter out of the kitchen, through the living room, straight down the hallway to Erica's bedroom.

She raises her head, scrutinizing me. "How did you know where my bedroom is?"

"You mean because this is the first time you've invited me into your bedroom?" I set her down on her feet, and she wobbles on her high heels, though only for a second. I tuck a wild lock of hair behind her ear. "It was common logic, sweet. Your house has one hallway with two doors down it. One of those doors had to be your bedroom."

"Oh." She hunches her shoulders.

"Bit suspicious, aren't you?" I study her for a moment, wondering what in her past makes her paranoid now. I don't need to know. So I give up thinking about it and start undoing my tie. "Imagine you have your reasons."

I shed my tie and jacket, then begin to unbutton my shirt. After freeing the second button, I hesitate with my fingers on the third button and eye her clothing. "Are you planning to sleep in that dress?"

She blinks several times in quick succession but stays rooted in place with her arms hanging slack at her sides. Her jaw is slack too.

Is she staring at me because I'm undressing? It shouldn't be a shock.

"But, uh, y-y—" she stammers. "Are you going to, uh, keep your boxer shorts on or something?"

I tip my head to the side, my lips ticking up at the corners. "Last night I stripped us both naked and did wicked things to you for hours. Now you're shy about seeing the full monty?"

Still paralyzed, she chews on her lip. "Well, see, nudity feels kind of different tonight. We're not doing anything, and besides, last night you undressed me while I was blindfolded which is kind of different and—"

I surge forward to seal my mouth over hers and silence her havering. When she opens her mouth to me, I want to kiss her deeply—but that would lead to sex. Instead, I pull away, giving up her lips. "If you like, I'll handle the task of removing your dress from your supple little body myself." I bend to graze my lips down her throat while I trail my fingers down her arms. "Would ye like me to?"

"Yes."

I settle my hands on her hips and slide them around to the small of her back, then skate them up her spine until I can reach the zipper on her dress. She sucks in a breath when I tickle her bare skin with my fingertips. While I pull the zipper down in slow motion, I let my fingers flit over her flesh. Once I've exposed her entire back, I flatten my palms on her skin and tug her closer.

The warmth of her penetrates my shirt, and her natural scent teases my senses.

"Soft as silk," I purr into her ear, then I push my hands under the fabric to spread the dress wide.

I angle toward her slightly as I flick the straps off her shoulders. The dress tumbles down to pool around her feet. I take half a step back, raking my gaze over Erica's body and her bra and knickers, all that remains of her clothing. "Take off the rest."

My voice sounds rough even to my ears.

Erica shimmies out of her bra and knickers. When she kicks her shoes off, I find myself licking my lips like a beast about to pounce on his prey.

I get rid of my shirt, trousers, socks, and shoes faster than I ever have in my life, paying no mind to the clunks that ensue as everything I discard sails down to the floor or lands on a chair or the dresser. Now naked, I pause to catch my breath. Stripping at lightning speed takes a lot out of a bloke.

Erica's hand rises to her throat, and her fingers stroke her skin.

I want to be the one stroking her that way, everywhere on her body.

"To bed," I all but snarl.

She tosses the blanket and top sheet out of the way and drops onto her back on the bed, one arm bent above her head.

That pose, combined with the hungry look on her face, makes me need to shag her like mad. But I will not do that tonight. I might be a bastard for the way I've treated Erica so far, but I never renege on my word.

I crawl over her body on hands and knees, settling in beside her on my back. Then I tug the covers over us both. "Good night, Erica."

She swivels her head toward me, pushing up on one elbow while giving me a peevish look. "How do you expect me to sleep?"

Despite my *slat* twitching, I assume the appearance of relaxation. "Now you've got something to look forward to in the morning."

She slugs my arm, but I barely feel it. "Jackass."

Only then do I turn to gaze at her with feigned innocence. "There's no need for insults, *gràidh*."

"You got me all wound up on purpose." She flops back onto the mattress amid a flutter of sheets and a faint puffing sound from her pillow. "You're a tease."

"No, I'm an inveterate seducer. Remember?"

"Hmph."

I lift one arm, making room for her. "Come here."

She gives me a fake scowl, then cuddles up against my side. The lass glances at the covers, which are now tented by my erection, and squirms a little.

"Shh," I murmur, lowering my arm to cradle her close. "I'll help you relax."

Before she can complain again, I begin to hum softly. It's an old Scottish lullaby my mother used to sing to me when I was a wee laddie, but I won't try to sing it. Not sure I remember all the words, and I have no singing talent. As for humming, I can manage that passably.

Erica stretches an arm across my chest, snuggling closer, her cheek pasted to my skin. Her lids gradually slide shut, and her body slackens.

While she drifts down into the peace of slumber, I whisper to her, "Sleep well, *mo leannan.*"

Chapter Nineteen

I wake in the morning to find Erica is crawling up my body while lick-ing and kissing my skin, her mouth traveling up my belly. She slurps at my flesh and pants softly, her hot breaths blustering over my chest and saliva dripping onto my skin. Then she chuffs once and wags her leg.

That doesn't feel like her leg, though. It's too small and moves too quickly. Besides, I haven't known Erica to drool on me.

I crack my lids open.

Casey lies sprawled between my thighs, on top of the covers, with his front paws and chin resting on my belly. When he sees my eyes are open, he wags his tail again.

Scratching behind his ears, I whisper, "Good morning, Casey. Let's try not to disturb Erica, all right?"

His ears prick up.

I decide to assume that means he agrees with me about not waking Erica. "Good boy."

The dog turns his head so he can lick my arm.

And I start muttering nonsense to him the way I always do because he seems to enjoy it. Casey pants and chuffs, and I swear he's smiling at me.

A throat-clearing makes us both glance at Erica.

"Am I interrupting?" she asks.

"You're awake." I aim a playful smile at her. "Thought you'd sleep all day."

"What time is it?"

"After ten."

She looks at the bedside clock. Her face goes blank for a moment.

Casey leaps up and lunges toward Erica to slop a kiss on her cheek. Splutter-ing, she pushes him away. The pup bounds off the bed, rocking it wildly.

Once the aftershocks settle down, I roll onto my side to face Erica and steal a quick, soft kiss. "Good morning, lass."

"Morning."

"Have a good sleep?" I run a fingertip along the sheet's edge, where it just covers her breasts.

"Mm." She flips onto her stomach. The sheet slips off her breasts but still covers her erse. When she props her torso up with both elbows, those mouth-watering tits dangle beneath her. "Haven't slept that soundly in years."

I skate my fingertips up her spine. "And all without sex."

She peeks at me over her shoulder. "You made me a promise last night."

"And I intend to keep it." I place an open-mouth kiss on her nape. "But first, I have another gift for you, if it won't offend my *gràidh*."

"No, of course not." She spreads her fingers over her pillow and stares down at them. "I'm sorry about last night. I love the dress."

My fingers freeze halfway up her back. She loves the dress, and I love that she told me so. But I called her darling again in Gaelic. Didn't mean to. The word came out of my mouth before I realized what I was about to say.

Erica throws me a sideways glance. "I'm just not used to men buying me expensive presents."

"Ah, but you deserve it." I sit up, twisting around to reach down to the floor and retrieve the plastic sack I'd hidden just under the bed. Last night after she fell asleep, I'd sneaked out of Erica's house and over to Gil's place to get the gift I'd bought for her at the museum. I pull the item out of the sack, which makes the plastic rustle. Still leaning over, I tell her, "Shut your eyes, please."

She shuts them, resting her chin on her linked hands.

I sit up again, this time with the dinosaur toy in my hand. It's the same one I'd shown her in the museum store when I had used it as a prop to make her smile. Now, I touch the plush dinosaur to her back and move its wee feet in a waddling motion the way Godzilla does in those old Japanese films. Erica wriggles just enough that I know she likes the feeling of fuzzy dinosaur feet tickling her spine, though she can't see that's what I'm doing. The creature's tail drags behind it while I continue walking its wee feet up to her shoulders.

Then I duck my head near her ear, just close enough that my lips graze her skin. "You can look now."

She opens her eyes, and they fly wide for a heartbeat when she notices the fuzzy dinosaur perched on her shoulder.

I keep holding the toy there until she takes it, holding the creature in one hand.

Erica stares into the amber eyes of the plush *Tyrannosaurus rex* while its pudgy wee arms reach out to her. The words "Field Museum Chicago" are embroidered on the dinosaur's erse. That seems like an odd place to put the museum's logo, but maybe someone thought it would be a good joke.

Erica bumps her nose into the dinosaur's snout. "I love this too. Thank you, Lachlan."

I lie down on my side again and rest one hand on her back. "It seemed the perfect gift for a dinosaur enthusiast like yourself."

Her lips pucker slightly, and I swear they tremble too, though it's so faint that I can't be sure.

I trace the backs of my fingers up her cheek. "What troubles you on this bonnie morning?"

"Nothing."

She falls silent for a moment, her attention on the dinosaur toy while she fiddles with its stubby arms. Then she turns her face toward me, inadvertently pushing one of my fingers between her lips. I withdraw my finger and suck it into my mouth, humming with pleasure. Aye, her skin always tastes good, but the flavor of her mouth is even better.

She tries to smile, but the expression falters. "Don't you ever wonder about me?"

"Wonder?" I feel my brows tighten.

"Aren't you curious about me? About my life? My past?"

"Of course." I give her a half-hearted shrug. "But it's against the rules. You reminded me of that when your mother called the other evening."

Her lips twist into an expression that seems like half annoyance, half disappointment.

She kicks her feet out from under the sheet, so it covers only her buttocks, and bends her knees to swing her feet in the air. Fingering the stubby arms of the stuffed *T. rex*, she affects an air of indifference that fails to convince me. "You could, you know, ask me a few questions. If you want."

"Ah…" Didn't we say no personal questions? Aye, but then I bought her a dress and a toy dinosaur, and I keep calling her *gràidh*. Our simple arrangement has turned into a right fankle. What Erica would call a hot mess. And it's entirely my fault. How many times have I broken the rules I set for our fling? Time to reassert the parameters. So I roll onto my back, linking my hands under my head. "That would be violating our agreement."

Erica springs up into a sitting position, swinging her legs off the bed to perch on the edge of the mattress with her hands clamped over it. Shoulders slumped, she stares down at the floor.

Bloody hell. How am I meant to stick to my own rules when she keeps looking so…dejected? Hurting her gives me a strange sensation in my gut, like icy worms slithering around in there.

I can't stop myself from settling a hand on her back and gliding it up in slow circles.

She leans into my touch.

And those worms stop slithering. An odd warmth sprouts in my chest—until she speaks again.

"Don't you want to know anything about me?" she asks. "I don't know that much about you. You have brothers and sisters and once showed a girl your penis in a barn, that's about it." She yanks the sheet around her waist, covering her erse and groin. "I don't know your favorite color, your favorite song, anything."

I groan and let my hand fall away from her back. She wants answers, and I can't blame her for that. Maybe she'll be satisfied with a piece of the truth.

While I pluck at the sheet, I grumble, "My favorite color is blue. I don't have a favorite song. What else would you like to know?"

She covers her eyes with her hands.

Mhac na galla. My grumpy tone has made her miserable again, and those worms come back to life in my gut. Why her unhappiness makes me feel miserable too, I have no ruddy idea. It does. That's all I know.

I exhale a long, resigned sigh, then slip an arm around her waist, urging her to lie down on the bed. She lands on her back, her head on the pillow. I straddle her body with my face hovering above hers, those hazel eyes shimmering with an emotion I refuse to consider, though the look she's giving me triggers that odd warmth in my chest again, and my throat goes thick. I brace myself on my elbows with my hands on either side of her face and comb my fingers through her hair. "I want to know everything about you, but I'll be leaving soon. Can we not just enjoy this time together?"

"Yeah. Sure."

"Good."

The sadness has vacated her expression, so I believe she means it.

And I feel better, happier, knowing she isn't upset anymore. Not for the moment, at least.

I nibble on her lower lip, thrusting my tongue out to sneak it between her lips for a quick taste of her. She moans, shoving her hand into my hair as if she's desperate to tug me closer. I resist at first, scraping my mouth over hers until she opens for me. Then I seize the chance to plaster my lips to her mouth while I forge my tongue deep, lashing it against hers, starved for the flavor of her mouth. She sucks on my tongue, making me groan.

As much as I'd love to kiss her for hours, I have a promise to keep. So I peel my mouth away and shift off her, my leg pressed to hers and my erection jutting over her belly.

She runs the tip of her tongue over her bottom lip, then drags her teeth across it.

I push my hand between her thighs and urge her to spread them wide, granting me full access to her rosy, glistening flesh. Parting her folds with my thumb and forefinger, I slide my middle finger down to stroke her.

She chokes back a throaty cry and fists her hands in the sheets, planting her heels on the mattress, knees bent.

Erica is the most sensual woman on earth. I need to make her come for me, several times, before I take her body and give us both what we need. I pet her folds with my thumb and forefinger while I sweep my middle finger up and down her slick flesh. Her soft, panting breaths spur me to swirl the tip of my finger around her nub, over and over, harder and harder, until I finally thrust my fingertip into the stiff head of her clit.

Erica bucks into my fingers, thrashing her hips in a desperate plea for more.

"You like this," I rumble, pressing my cheek to hers. "What else do you like?"

"Oh," she breathes while I toy with her nub. She clutches at my shoulders, clawing and whimpering. "I like e-everything you do to me."

I plunge my finger into her sheath.

Her back arches, and her mouth falls open, though no sound emerges.

My breaths come heavier and faster, just like hers.

"Erica." I almost growl her name, my voice roughened by the need pulsating through me. "Do ye want mah hand or mah mouth?"

She writhes and sinks her nails into my shoulders while I twirl my finger around her clit. "Mouth, please."

I gaze down at her wet flesh, my senses filled with the intoxicating scent of her desire, and drag my tongue across my lips in one long sweep. "I need to feast on ye. Now."

"Yes, please, yes."

She squeezes her eyes shut as I lunge my head down to lave her rigid nub with gentle strokes of my tongue. Her desperate noises and sharp breaths compel me to lash her flesh with ravenous swipes, the flavor of her cream permeating my mouth. When she plows her hands into my hair, clawing at my scalp, I know I need to make her come right now so I can shag her mindless before I *caith* all over her.

Somewhere in the distance, a doorbell chimes.

The sound barely registers in my mind. I plunge one finger inside Erica, then two, curving them into the sweet spot just inside her opening.

Erica thrashes, flinging her hands up to clench them in the pillow.

The doorbell chimes again. Casey begins barking, and something in the tone of his barks snaps us both out of the spell our shared lust has woven around us. She jolts upright, pushing me away. On my knees, off-kilter with one hand on the bed, I gape at her.

"I have to see who's at the door," she says, then she jumps off the bed to snag a robe from the back of the door and yank it on.

"Ye've gotta be kidding me." My jaw drops open, and I follow her movements without blinking or moving a muscle. My shoulders sag.

As she rushes out the bedroom door, Erica flashes me an apologetic smile. "Sorry."

Should I go with her? Can't remember where I left my clothes, so I lie back on the bed with my hands linked behind my neck. I hear voices, though not loud enough that I can tell who the other person is or if that person is male or female. Gradually, the voices grow louder. Not because they're moving toward the hallway. No, the voices get louder because Erica is almost shouting at the visitor. The anger and distress in her tone tell me everything I need to know to make my decision.

I am going out there.

When I'd sneaked over to Gil's house to retrieve Erica's gift, I'd also grabbed some daytime clothes. Now, I spot the jeans I'd brought and snatch them off the dresser, pulling them on so quickly that I almost trip over my own feet. Though I jerk the zipper up, I don't fasten the button. The argument going on out there has gotten more heated, and I forget all about my clothing, sprinting down the hallway and halting at its end.

Presley the *bod ceann* has just shoved his foot over the threshold, though Erica is blocking him with her body and one hand on the door. The *cacan's* body is inches from hers. She kicks at his posh running shoes.

The *cacan* chortles. But then his attention swerves to me, and his eyebrows lift. "So, you are banging Scotch Tape."

Erica looks over her shoulder at me, but I only glance at her for a split second before I sharpen my gaze on Presley.

The *bod ceann* glowers at me. "What's your game, Scottie?"

I raise one brow. Is that the best his puny brain can come up with? If I wanted to insult and harass him, I'd do much better. But not in front of Erica.

"Go away," she hisses at Presley, shoving against his chest. "No way in hell you're ever getting inside my house."

The *cacan* bores his gaze into her for a moment, then spins on his heels and stomps away from the house to his Alfa Romeo. I can see it through the windows.

Just as Erica shuts the door, tires squeal out on the street.

I watch the canary-yellow car roar away.

She rests her forehead on the door but doesn't seem to notice when I approach her until I grip her shoulder. Then she jumps.

"Easy," I say. "He's gone."

She raises her head, shuffling around to face me. "You didn't throttle Presley this time."

Did she want me to do that? Women can be very confusing.

I back her up to the door, planting my hands on either side of her shoulders. "You seemed to have things in hand, and I didn't want to barge in where I'm not wanted, like last time."

"You were wanted then." She places a palm on my bare chest, her soft skin slightly cool. "And you're wanted now."

"Am I?" Pinning her to the door, I sweep aside the halves of her robe and rub myself against her so she can feel my erection, where it strains to escape my jeans.

"Oh, yes." She rolls her hips into me.

"Well then." I pick her up and race down the hallway into the bedroom, dropping her onto the mattress, and strip off my jeans. "Best take advantage of the moment, eh?"

She grins. "Take advantage of me anytime, for as long as you want."

That's all the invitation I need. I pounce on the lass and finish what I started a few minutes earlier, before that bastard interrupted us. Here in this room, I will set aside all my questions and worries. Nothing else matters right now except giving Erica pleasure.

Everything else can wait.

Chapter Twenty

"Please," I murmur against Erica's neck, then I drag my lips down her throat to place a damp kiss on the spot right at the base that I've learned makes her shiver. With my tongue, I tease and stimulate her skin until she shivers again and arches her back. I flick my tongue over the slope of one breast while imagining all the things I want to do with her in this bed. I can't see all of her breasts. Her low-cut shirt hides them.

"Why do you want it?" she asks, her words emerging on a soft moan.

I sneak my hand under her shirt, gliding it up her side. "I want unfettered access to you, my sweet rose."

"You mean you want me to be your twenty-four-hour love slave."

My hand bumps into the band of her bra, but that doesn't slow me down for long as I track the band behind her until I find the clasp. I unfasten each tiny hook slowly, loving the way she squirms impatiently until I've freed all the hooks and her bra hangs loose. I slide one hand around to the bra's front, pushing it inside the cup so I can pinch her nipple with my thumb and forefinger. "Lass, I like surprising you, and I have proof you like it too. Give me a key, and I'll surprise you more often. In many and varied ways."

Erica and I have spent three weeks enjoying each other's company, aka shagging each other relentlessly. We don't sleep together anymore, though, because that would only confuse an already confusing arrangement. Still, every morning when I walk over to Erica's house or she comes over to mine so we can have breakfast together, I feel strangely excited by the prospect. Once, I even found myself skipping across the lawn like a dafty. Every time I pass by Erica's rose bushes, I want to pick a handful to give them to her as a surprise.

But casual lovers don't do things like that.

One day, we were sharing a picnic lunch in a park Erica chose. I don't know where anything is in Chicago, except for Gil's house, Erica's house, and the restaurant Everest. I could probably find my way back to the airport too.

Casey had come with us to the park, and I held the pup's retractable leash.

Erica sat beside me on our blanket. Suddenly, she set down her sandwich and announced, "No more fancy-shmancy dinners at places where I couldn't even afford a glass of water."

I jerked my head up. "You didn't like Everest?"

"No, it was great." She took a sip from her can of root beer, eying me sideways. "You told me once you don't care about the trappings of wealth and your needs are simple. I let you know mine are simple too." She tapped a fingernail on the can. *Tick, tick, tick.* "Which is why I don't get the Everest thing. It was sweet and all, but you know you don't have to try so hard to impress me."

"Don't I?"

"No."

Of course I didn't. She was right about that. I scratched my cheek, staring down at the sandwich perched on my thigh. But I *did* want to impress her.

She hooked a finger under my chin, urging me to look at her. "Trust me, money does not impress this girl."

"What does?" I fussed with the collar of my shirt and cleared my throat. Though she tickled me with her finger that was still hooked under my chin, I couldn't pull off a smile. "I'd like to know."

Casey chose that moment to hop up from where he'd been lounging on the grass and nuzzle my hand. Maybe the pup sympathized with me.

"You impress me, Lachlan," Erica said. "You're a good man. The best."

I captured her hand, but her finger was sticking up between my thumb and forefinger. "Good, bad, I don't know. But you make me feel like a man, Erica."

Why the bloody hell did I say that? It might've been true, but telling Erica that was a barmy thing to do.

She stared at me, clearly dumbfounded.

I needed to change the subject immediately. So I drew her finger into my mouth, sucking lightly until she forgot everything we'd just said to each other.

Now, back in the present, I chase the memory away by ducking my head under her shirt to latch onto her nipple with my mouth. I swirl my tongue around the taut tip, earning a breathless moan from her.

Since our discussion in the park, we've preferred eating at home to having dinner at a posh restaurant. Why I had felt the need to impress Erica with a five-star meal still confuses me. But I avoid thinking about it by cooking for Erica, though sometimes she cooks for me too. This morning, I had fed the lass a good Scottish breakfast consisting of sausage links, bacon, scrambled eggs, tattie scones, and black pudding. I needed to explain to her that tattie scones were made from potatoes, but it was the black pudding that caused a problem.

Maybe I shouldn't have waited until after she'd eaten the pudding to explain the ingredients in that dish. But being a bloody stupid erse, I did wait.

Done with her meal, she sighed and smiled with satisfaction. "That was yummy. You are one awesome cook. I've never had that pudding stuff before. What's in it?"

Since she had asked, that meant what happened next was not my fault. Right?

"It's traditional black pudding," I told her, "made with pig's blood."

Erica froze for several seconds. Then she gagged and smacked my arm—rather hard. "How could you let me eat that?"

I shrugged. "I eat it all the time."

"Yuck." She rushed to the kitchen faucet to cleanse her tongue with the sprayer. "It's disgusting, Lachlan."

"Sorry." I did feel bad about unintentionally tricking her, but I couldn't stop my mouth from tightening with a repressed smirk. "You were wolfing it down until I mentioned the key ingredient."

"Not the point, Lachlan." She picked up a bottle of dish soap like she was considering scrubbing her tongue with that, but then she set it down again. "Warn a girl before you let her eat something like that."

"Next time, I will. Maybe you'll want to try haggis, then."

"Uh-uh, no way. Told you already, I don't eat sheep stomach."

"These days, it's made with synthetic casing."

"My answer is still no." She gave me a sarcastically chastising look. "Can't trust you to inform me of all the ingredients, can I?"

"Let me apologize properly."

My apology involved pulling Erica down onto the sofa for a round of "who comes first," as she decided to call it. Naturally, I make sure Erica always comes before I do. A gentleman doesn't get his end away before giving his partner pleasure. This time, our sofa interlude had no interruptions because I'd switched off my phone.

Back in the present, I shove her shirt and bra up over her breasts in one swift motion. Then I pull her nipple into my mouth and suck hard until she cries out and scrapes her nails down my back. Without detaching my mouth from her flesh, I mutter, "Key."

"Okayfineyes." Those four syllables emerge as one breathless word.

I catch her nipple between my teeth and tug gently, elongating it while I lave the swollen peak with my tongue. She digs her nails into my scalp, her breaths quickening, and I release her nipple. "I'll give you mine too."

A slow, sexy grin stretches her lips. "Then *I* can surprise *you*."

"Hmm." I feign concern, my lips compressed. "Should I worry? You might steal into my bedroom to massage my…account ledgers."

She slaps my shoulder. "Better be nicer to the woman who gives you the best sex of your life. Especially after you tricked me into eating pig's blood."

"Point taken. Though I really didn't think the black pudding would be a problem." I tear off her sweatpants and knickers, hurling them to the floor. When I lower my mouth to her groin, she writhes beneath me. Aye, she's close to the edge. I keep tormenting her with my mouth until she stops breathing, a sure sign she's about to come. Then I pull away. "Is this nice enough?"

"Bastard."

"Give me the key, and I'll be even nicer to you. So nice you'll forgive me for the black pudding debacle."

"There was no debacle."

"You shrieked and punched me."

"I smacked you on the arm. And I did not shriek."

Maybe I exaggerated the sound she'd made at breakfast, but I'm not giving up until I get what I want. I coil my tongue around her stiff clit. "Key."

"It's in my house." She gestures at her body. "I can't go get the key. You've taken away my clothes."

"You've got a key in your sweatpants pocket." I hold up a warning finger when she opens her mouth to protest. "And there's a spare under the potted plant beside your back door."

"How do you know about that?"

"Gil told me."

Bending over the bed's edge, she fishes a key out of her sweatpants pocket. Her tits dangle, swaying slightly.

I pat her erse. "I rather like this view."

She rolls her eyes at me.

I snare her around the waist and haul her back up to sit facing me.

Erica wags the key in my face, but when I reach for it, she closes her fist around it. "Uh-uh-uh. Yours first, you sneaky Scot."

I yank open a drawer in the bedside table, nab the key, and offer it to her. When she plucks the key from my open palm, I close my hand around her wrist.

She spreads her fingers.

I take her key but keep my hand fastened around her wrist.

She tugs. "Let go."

"A kiss first."

"Sure."

Though I keep hold of her wrist, she manages to scramble around until she's on her knees, braced with one hand on the mattress. Then she dips her head to plant a kiss on cock.

I grumble under my breath.

"What was that?" she asks, cupping her hand over her ear. "Couldn't quite make it out."

"A *real* kiss."

"Coming right up." She lavishes the head of my cock with a ravenous, full-tongue kiss.

A strangled noise gets caught in my throat while she licks and sucks on me until my cock is throbbing and I know I'll *caith* any second. Though I would love to come inside her mouth, I won't be able to shag her right now if I do that. A man of my age needs time to get up for it again.

So I surrender, releasing her hand and relinquishing the key.

Erica drops onto her elbows, hoisting that bonnie erse high in the air, and swallows my *slat*. I groan, but it mutates into a gasp when she withdraws and circles her tongue around my crown. I grasp her erse with both hands while she thrusts in and out, over and over, while I groan and growl and sink my fingers into her backside. I should stop this, but I cannae move. When her breasts graze my thighs, a hot surge of pleasure barrels down my spine and straight into my cock.

"Erica!" I shout as my body goes rigid, and I cannae breathe anymore, not unless she makes me—

She releases my cock and sits back on her heels.

My hands fall away from her erse. I'm still breathing too hard to speak.

Erica stretches her lithe body, making sure to hoist those breasts. "I could go for some brownies."

The only thing I want to consume right now is her.

I lean in, boring my gaze into hers. "You stopped."

Struggling not to smile, she shrugs one shoulder. "So?"

"You're in for it now...Erica."

"Bring it on...Lachlan."

The way she spoke my name, her voice rife with hunger and sensuality... I cannae wait another second. I seize her hips and flip her erse out from under her. She drops onto the bed flat on her back.

I brush my nose against hers. "Thank you for the key."

"Ditto."

"I'm already planning my surprise for you." I grab a condom from the table. "What have you got in mind for me?"

"Something wicked your way comes."

"A Shakespearean girl, eh?"

Erica wraps her arms around me. I push inside her with deliberate slowness, relishing every sensation and the look on her face. This woman is more than bonnie. When she's aroused and reveling in the pleasure of our lovemaking, she looks more exquisite and erotic than any work of art. No one has ever made me feel this way, like I could leap off the tallest building in the world and land on my feet, unscathed—all because she wants me.

Aye, Erica Teague means more to me than a fling. I need her to care for me. Why else would I do everything I can think of to make her smile and to show her I'm not a bastard? I need her to feel the way I do whenever I'm with her.

I need her to love me. But I can't risk that again. I won't do it. After what Aisley did to me, I know I can never again give all my trust to anyone.

One more week, and then I'm gone.

Chapter Twenty-One

For the next three days, I avoid Erica as much as possible. My revelation that I have deeper feelings for her than I'd realized has left me raw and edgy. I do not love her. I can't. My wounds go far too deep to ever be healed, not even by the love of a good woman like Erica.

Does she love me? I pray she doesn't, because I will break her heart.

Every evening, I stop by to say good night to Erica. She always invites me to stay, with or without sex, but I decline. Distance from her is what I need, but keeping away makes me even edgier. When she asks me what I'm "up to" all day, alone in my house, I inform her I have important video calls to take care of, via something called Skype, and I don't have the time to entertain her.

She winces when I use the word entertain.

I've hurt her feelings, but I can't help that.

Twice, my mobile rings with the caller ID announcing it's Aisley ringing me. I don't answer. Instead, I block her number and delete it from my contacts list.

My video calls are real. I've been consulting with Rory that way, which was his idea. He claims he needs to see me and make sure I haven't become "a recluse who doesn't bathe or bother with clothes anymore." I dress the way I always have, and I shower every morning.

"But you sound grumpier than everyone says I do," Rory tells me on the second day since I started hiding from Erica. "Are you competing for the title of Ogre of Loch Fairbairn?"

"I don't live in Loch Fairbairn, but even if I did, I could never take that title away from you."

"But you are fashed about something, Lachlan."

"Donnae be telling anyone else that. I'm fine."

We say goodbye, though Rory refuses to accept my claim that nothing is fashing me. I can't tell him I've done the one thing I swore never to do again. I've gotten entangled with a woman.

On the third morning, Rory and I have another video call. During every call, I have paced the width of the living room while behaving like the ogre Rory thinks I've become. Maybe I have been acting like a selfish *bod ceann*, at least where Erica is concerned.

Rory's investigator has been having trouble rooting out the reason for the "clerical error" that's cocked up the divorce proceedings. Rory has repeatedly assured me he will sort the mess. But today, on the third morning of my voluntary incarceration in Gil's house, Rory has news.

But it's not what I want to hear.

"Aisley is taking advantage of the clerical error," Rory says, "to renegotiate the divorce settlement."

"What? She cannae do that."

"Relax, Lachlan. We will sort this, but it might take time."

"Time? I gave her twelve years of my life. That's all she gets."

Rory sighs. "I don't suppose I can convince you to tell me what happened between you and Aisley."

My silence gives him my answer.

"All right," he says. "But if you want this to be over soon, you might need to sweeten the pot."

"The bitch gets nothing," I shout. "Nothing. Ye hear me, Rory?"

"Aye. We'll keep at it."

I say goodbye to Rory and glance out the window.

Erica has just hopped off the porch and is scurrying back to her house.

Had she been at the front door while I was talking to Rory? She couldn't have overheard most of our conversation, but I had roared those last words about the bitch getting nothing.

I can't worry about Erica right now. My call with Rory has not eased my anxieties. I head into the kitchen to grab a piece because stress always makes me hungry.

But no food tastes as good as Erica.

I do not love her. I'm incapable of feeling that way. But I do like her and want her. *Bod an Donais*, do I want her, even more after spending three days away from the lass, three days without touching, kissing, and shagging her. My good-nights have been brief and chaste, but tonight, I need to drown my tangled emotions in the body of the sweet, sensual woman next door.

I did promise to surprise her. She gave me a key to her house, so she must want me to sneak in and fuck her.

The more I try not to think about Erica's body and the look on her face when she comes, the more I need to go over there. My *slat* is firming up already, which means I'll either need to wank off or…

Sneak into Erica's house.

I grab something from the kitchen, then leap off the sofa and race out the door, heading straight for Erica's house. As I approach her porch, I slow to a walk. It's after sunset, so I have the cover of night to help me. At the door, I press my ear to the surface and listen, but I can't tell if she's in the living room. Unlocking the door, I slip inside and shut it quietly. The living room and kitchen are dark, but I see a light on in the bedroom. Hurrying down the hall, I stop just past the threshold.

Casey lies at the foot of the bed, sleeping. He opens his eyes to look at me, thumping his tail twice.

I scratch behind his ears, which makes him thump his tail again. When I pull my hand away, the pup closes his eyes and goes back to sleep.

Erica's clothes lie in a lump on the floor, and I hear the shower running. I take a moment to prepare the rest of her surprise.

"Lachlan, yes!"

That cry came from the bathroom, but it didn't sound distressed. No, Erica shouted those words with a hunger that makes my cock go hard. I crouch to dig out the condom packet I'd stashed in my jeans pocket, then I get rid of my clothes and roll the condom on.

I walk into the bathroom and push the shower door open.

Erica yelps, dropping the showerhead she'd been holding to her groin. It clatters on the tile floor.

My gaze flicks to her hand positioned inches from her groin, and lower to the discarded showerhead, then gravitates back to her face. The flush of arousal dapples her cheeks and chest, and her nipples are rigid.

Aye, she was wanking off while thinking of me. I'm certain of that.

I tip my head to the side, gazing straight into her eyes. "Screaming my name, and I haven't even touched you yet."

Erica fumbles to hook the showerhead back in its clip but misses. "W-what are you doing here?"

"Surprising you."

I saunter into the shower, backing her up to the wall, and raise her hand to hold the showerhead at my shoulder level. Hot water drizzles down our bodies, between our bodies, beading on her breasts and spraying up to soak my body and my hair.

The showerhead slips from her fingers.

I catch it. "I see ye started without me."

"What happened to your all-important Skype stuff?"

"Hell with it." I grasp her hip with one palm, the showerhead clasped in my other hand. "I'd ask what ye were thinking of just now, but ye gave me a good clue when ye shouted my name."

She ducks her head, and her chin almost touches her chest.

I brush my cheek against hers. "Don't be embarrassed. I've climaxed while daydreaming of you too."

She peeks up at me. "Really?"

"Aye."

"I like that." When I run my thumb over the sweet spot just next to her hip bone, she tilts her head up. "I'm glad you're here."

"Cannae stay away." I should be able to do that, but I can't, not with her. "I donnae know why, it's never happened to me before. I…missed you."

She rakes her fingers through my hair. "I missed you too."

I make a rough sound deep in my throat, part lust, part raw emotion. She missed me. I love hearing her say that, and for tonight, I won't worry about what that means.

I snap the showerhead into its clip on the wall. "Ye won't be needing this anymore."

Flipping her around, I crush her to the wall with my body and nudge her feet apart. Her mouth has fallen open, and her breaths come faster. I'm breathing harder too, so desperate to feel her around me that I can't think about anything except fucking her. I push one hand in front of her to work her clit, already swollen and slick for me. She rocks into my caress, slapping her palms on the tile wall while I pinch her nub.

She cries out.

I rub harder. "I need you, Erica."

Cannae hold back anymore. I pull my hips back and drive into her.

She throws her head back.

I growl into her ear, "Ye've got to be mine, only mine."

No time to examine what I just said. Lust has me in its scorching grip, and I slam into her again, pumping with relentless force and speed. She gouges her nails into the tile walls while our sharp breaths reverberate around us and wet skin slaps against wet skin. The scent of her arousal fills my senses even through the steamy haze of the water sluicing over us. My heels lift off the floor with every thrust, flattening her against the wall.

"Erica," I growl, dropping my chin to her shoulder. Words burst out of me, punctuated by grunts. "Ah, God, *mo leannan*, yer so soft and sweet and—och!"

"Don't stop, please."

"I willnae." With our bodies glued together, I pound into her harder, faster, teetering on the edge of climax. "Come fer me now, *gràidh*."

"Lachlan, yes!" Her inner muscles clench me over and over.

Bod an Donais, her orgasm hurtles me over the edge too. My *bagais* slap on her erse as I unleash everything inside her body, my feral cries resonating off the walls. I sag against her back, my lips on her shoulder. "Now that's how you scream my name."

"A shower was supposed to relax me."

I lift her hand to kiss the palm. "Are you saying I haven't relaxed you?"

"Oh, you sure did. Just not in the way I'd planned." She wriggles around to face me. "We probably scared Casey half to death with our caterwauling."

"Men don't caterwaul. We give masculine shouts of appreciation."

She holds my face in her hands and kisses me. It's a raw, primal kiss that leaves us both breathless. We ravage each other's mouth while I grope every inch of her body and she does the same to me. I never want the kiss to end, but we'll both pass out from lack of oxygen if we don't stop.

We peel our lips apart.

Moments ago, I said I wanted her to be mine and only mine. Should I tell her I didn't mean it? But I did mean those words, and I don't want to lie to her. I can't assure her I was speaking the truth either, though, because she'll think I want more than four weeks with her.

Aye, I do want more. Much more.

Barking erupts in the bedroom.

That's not a playful bark. Casey is upset.

I shut off the water and hustle to the bathroom door. "Casey, what's the bother?"

The pup stands at the window with his front paws on the sill.

Erica hurries out of the bathroom wearing a towel.

Casey's barking becomes growling. His lips, flapping from the ferocity of his snarls, draw back from his sharp canine teeth.

I race to the window and jerk the curtains aside.

"What is it?" Erica asks, hurrying to my side.

A shocked face gawps back at us from the other side of the glass. Presley the *bod ceann* spins around and takes off running.

I yank my jeans on and sprint out of the house.

"Wait!" Erica yells, running after me.

Hurling the door open, I gallop into the night.

Casey rockets past me and latches onto Presley's trouser leg, snarling and preventing the *cacan* from fleeing. Presley tries to kick at the dog but loses his balance and stumbles.

I seize Presley's shirt and hoist him off the ground.

"Casey!" Erica shouts, clapping her hands until the dog detaches his teeth from Presley's trouser leg.

The dog scampers over to her.

I shake Presley hard.

He sputters and flails his fists at me but can't land a punch on anything more sensitive than my biceps. The bloody ersehole is a weakling too. I'm hardly surprised by that fact. I doubt a spoiled bastard like him has ever lifted anything heavier than a wine glass.

Erica herds Casey into the house, shutting the door after him.

"What the hell do ye think yer doing?" I roar while rattling the *cacan* again. "Spying on a wee lass? I'm gonnae skite mah fist on yer face till yer spitting teeth."

"I was looking for Erica, that's all," Presley whines.

"Haud yer wheesht, ye bloody bawbag!" My spittle spatters Presley's face. "Ye've been rummeled this time, and ye willnae get away with it."

"With what?" The ereshole's voice squeaks faintly. "I haven't done anything. You're the one going ape shit and hollering nonsense. I came to see Erica, heard a weird noise, and checked it out."

"And then yer erse fell off." My breaths huff out my nostrils, and I can't stop my lips from curling with disgust. "Means yer a liar, ye eejit."

Erica sprints up to me and slaps her hands on my left arm. "Put him down, Lachlan. Please."

I rotate my gaze to her but maintain my grip on Presley.

She squeezes my arm. "Do it for me."

Grudgingly, I unlatch my fingers from the *bod ceann*'s shirt.

Presley crumples to the ground in a jumble of legs and arms.

I swipe my palms together like I'm ridding myself of his filth and tip my chin up, aiming a flinty glare at the man lying in a heap on the grass.

Presley scrambles to his feet and flounders to straighten out his disheveled clothes.

I hold my ground, shoulders back, my fingers twitching from the urge to throttle the bastard.

Erica steps sideways between me and the *cacan*.

Presley glowers at her. "Still screwing Scotch Tape, huh? Shouldn't he get back to the zoo? Bet the girl gorillas miss him real bad."

"Shut up," Erica snaps. She lodges her hands on her hips and scowls at him. "What on earth is wrong with you? I know you're the lowest level of scum in the pond, but I never pegged you for a peeping tom. What, you haven't ruined my life enough?"

"I did nothing." Presley sets his lips in a defiant line. "You did it all to yourself."

"You know what? You're right. I did do this to myself." She jabs a finger at him. "I trusted you."

He rolls his eyes.

What the bloody hell did this man do to her? How could he ruin her life? I can't believe she means that in an offhanded way. He must have hurt her badly, which might mean she still has feelings for him.

No, Erica is too clever for that. And she clearly despises him.

So do I.

Baring my teeth, I crack my knuckles and slant forward, ready to launch myself at the bastard.

Erica edges closer to me, splaying her hands on my chest. "Let me handle this, okay? Trust me."

I do trust her, so I take one step back. "If he makes a move toward ye, I willnae be responsible fer what I do."

"If he makes a move, you have my permission to skelp him till he's roadkill."

"Hey!" Presley waves his arms. "I'm still here, ya know."

Erica whirls on him. "I'm aware of that. Maybe I should call the cops to report a prowler."

"Who do you think they'll believe?"

She stares at Presley for several seconds, her determined expression melting into something akin to shame. Her eyes swivel to me.

I squint at Presley, drilling my gaze into him.

Turning to Presley, she points at the Alfa Romeo parked along the curb. "Get out of here."

He sneers at me.

I clench my fists and squint at him again.

Presley's face pales, and his smirk falters. He scurries to the Alfa Romeo.

Neither Erica nor I speak or move until the sports car zooms out of sight, the purring of its engine fading into the night.

Erica's knees buckle.

I swoop in to gather her into my arms before she hits the ground. The rush of adrenaline must have flooded out of her, weakening her body.

"Easy." I press a kiss on her forehead. "Slow, deep breaths."

I carry her to the door and open it without letting go of her. Casey follows us into the bedroom where I lay Erica down on the bed. The sheets are already pulled back, and her body crushes the soft, slippery rose petals I had scattered across the bed before I joined her in the shower.

She pushes up on one elbow, blinking slowly as she takes in the sight of the pale-pink petals strewn across the bed and on the pillows.

I can't blame her for not noticing the rose petals when we came out of the bathroom. A peeping ersehole had distracted us both. Now, she surveys the room and everything I have set up for her, including candles on the dresser and the bedside table as well as a silver tray on the table that holds a plate of strawberries and a fondue bowl brimming with liquid chocolate, alongside a bottle of Cristal champagne.

When I sit down beside her, the bed jostles, the mattress sinking under my weight. I sweep my fingers down her cheek and let my thumb fall onto her lips. "This was the other part of your surprise."

"It's amazing." Erica picks up a rose petal and buries her nose in it, inhaling deeply. She skates the petal over her lips, then uses it to tickle my mouth, making my lips twitch. She twirls the petal in the air. "Thank you. I love all of my surprise."

"You're exhausted." I blow out the candles on the table. With only the ones on the dresser for illumination, shadows engulf us. "I can recreate this for you tomorrow night."

"I'm okay."

I nod at the arm propping her up. "Your arm's shaking."

"I'm still okay to—"

"No." I pat the mattress behind her. "Lie down. We're going to sleep."

"We?"

I tap a finger on her forehead. "Lie back."

She sprawls on her back amid the roses.

And I crawl over her body to stretch out alongside her, curling an arm around her shoulders to draw her close.

She turns onto her side, her head tucked against my shoulder, one hand on my chest. Her palm rises and falls with my every breath. "Tell me, why do you get so angry at Presley?"

I snort. "He harasses you, spies on you, upsets you so much you shake. And you wonder why I'm angry?"

"Good point." She sighs. "Truthfully, I kind of like it when you throttle him. Does that make me a bad person?"

"Truthfully…" I slide my fingers into her hair, combing them through the silken locks. "I rather enjoy throttling him. Am I bad, then, too?"

"No." She wriggles to snuggle even closer to me, her warm body cradled to mine. "You're not bad. You're very, very good."

I exhale a groaning sigh. "Never been a violent man, but that—that—"

"Scunner?"

"I was going to say 'ersehole,' but scunner works too." I wrap my arm tighter around her. "He's a bully, and I hate bullies. No one should try to bend another to their will just for the sake of control."

"Mm." She seems to have grown sleepy, her body slack and her eyes half-closed.

"Sleep now, sweet."

I thread my fingers through her hair again, hoping to soothe her with the gentle rhythm of the movements. Her eyelids flutter shut, and her breathing grows shallower.

Why do I assault her ex whenever I see him? He's a bastard, but I've met my share of scunners like Presley. I don't lash out at them. Yet I can't restrain myself when that *cacan* harasses Erica.

I am not in love with her.

She murmurs in her sleep, nestling closer to me.

My chest aches, but that means nothing. I can't love her.

Erica will be better off when I leave.

Chapter Twenty-Two

In the morning, Erica and I relax on the living-room sofa while we share a breakfast that isn't quite healthy—chocolate-chip pancakes slathered in maple syrup with whipped cream on top and crispy bacon on the side. When I woke up this morning, I decided Erica needs comfort food, not bran muffins and prunes. I don't eat either of those things, anyway. I had never tasted chocolate-chip pancakes until today. Erica suggested them, and I will give her anything she wants.

Almost anything. If she wants love… No, I can't give her that.

Erica slides a forkful of pancake into her mouth. Whipped cream sticks to her lips, and maple syrup dribbles down her chin, but her lips curve into a sweet smile of appreciation. Her eyes are half-closed too as if the taste of pancakes is pure ecstasy.

To me, they just taste like pancakes. Good, but not ecstasy-inducing.

Her smile evaporates. She picks up a strip of bacon and pulverizes it between her fingers. Her eyes shimmer, like she's about to cry, but she doesn't. She squeezes her eyes shut.

"All right?" I ask, caressing her cheek with one finger.

"Fine." She affects a smile, but it's not convincing. "Dust in my eye."

Like hell it's dust. She's sad, and I'm certain the blame lies squarely with me. Aye, that scunner Presley has upset her, but she wouldn't cry this morning because of his ridiculous antics.

In seven days, I will fly home—and never see Erica again.

She knows that. Would she cry because I'm leaving? I haven't given her a reason to care that much about me, though I care for her more than I should.

We have seven more days together. That's it.

She skims her palm down my cheek, her expression full of emotions I don't dare examine too closely.

I sigh, staking a slab of pancake from our joint plate, balanced on my knee. Erica sits right beside me, her body leaning against mine. I love being this close to her. I love being with her, full stop. As I shove the pancake bite into my mouth, I wonder if I should stay longer to have more time with Erica. Why? I'll need to go home eventually, and extending my holiday would only make it more difficult to leave her.

Erica scoops up a bloody great chunk of pancake and stuffs it into her mouth.

Something is fashing her, but I doubt she would tell me what it is if I asked. Or that might be an excuse for me not to ask, so I won't find out I'm the problem. *Act like a man, ye damn eejit.*

I wipe syrup from her chin with my thumb. "You've gone serious all of a sudden."

"Have I?"

"Don't pretend you've no idea what I'm talking about." I lean in and try not to notice how good she smells or how much I want to hold her. "I can see the cloud over your head. It's grey and heavy with rain about to pour onto you." I twist my mouth into a crooked smirk. "I like you wet, not drowned."

"There's no cloud. I was thinking, that's all."

"About what?"

She slouches into the sofa, avoiding my gaze. "You'll be gone in a week. There must be things you'd like to do before you go."

"Besides you?"

She nudges me with her elbow. "Yes, besides me."

"Yes." I set our plate on the coffee table. "I would like to experience this country a bit more. And I've got an idea of how to do that."

"What kind of idea?"

I glance at her sideways. "You probably won't like it."

She folds her arms over her breasts. "Tell me."

My plan occurred to me only a few seconds ago, right after she said there must be things I'd like to do before I go home. Maybe I'm experiencing a slight need to spend as much time with her as I can over the next seven days. All right, it's more than slight. I need more time with her like I need to breathe, and a week won't be enough. A lifetime wouldn't be enough.

I scrub a hand over my face, then fix my gaze on her. "I want you to take a trip with me, to drive around as much of the country as we can in the time I've got left."

"You make it sound like you're dying."

"I'm not dying." I settle a hand on her thigh. "Will you come with me, Erica?"

She gets that look on her face again, the one that tells me she's upset but doesn't want to tell me why.

How can I help her if she won't let me? Not that I ought to be helping her. Erica's life is her business, not mine. I can't blame her for not sharing her problems with me since I've refused to share mine with her.

I prop one ankle on the other knee, then drop it again and drum my foot on the floor while running a hand up and down my thigh. "Say something, please."

"Um…I can't."

"But you're on sabbatical from your work."

"Yeah, but I can't just pick up and go. I have…obligations."

"Such as?"

She grips her knees. "Off-limits."

Every time she throws my rules back in my face, I get a feeling like I've swallowed a cold steel ball and it's about to rip through my guts. My shoulders sag. "If you don't want to go, it's fine."

A car horn beeps outside. Erica jumps.

I stare at her, my foot drumming faster.

She wrings her hands. "I want to go with you, Lachlan. But I just can't. My life is way more complicated than you realize, and I know you have zero interest in hearing about it. Which leaves me with no way to explain." Her shoulders cave in, and her lips tremble ever so slightly. "I can't—I can't leave the area. My reasons are personal."

"Ah." I angle away from her, though only by a few inches. I've slammed into the wall I built between us, and I don't like it at all. My eyes want to look at her, but I can't do it.

Erica lays a hand on my arm. "Why is this so important to you?"

Aye, that's the question I've been asking myself since I suggested we take a trip together. My gaze shifts to the window that overlooks the backyard and the park beyond it. Children climb around on monkey bars while their mothers watch from a bench nearby.

I used to want children, but two months after I married Aisley, she had announced she never wanted bairns. Maybe I should've left her then and there, but I was raised to believe a man shouldn't abandon his wife without serious cause. So instead, I'd accepted my wife's decision and let her whittle away at me for twelve fucking years.

Erica deserves better than what I can give her.

I turn toward her, but for a moment, I can't speak. She's so bonnie, so sweet, and clever too. Maybe I can't offer her a lifetime of happiness, but I can give her something close to happiness for the next seven days.

Enjoy whatever time you have with her.

I take my own advice and smile at Erica, infusing the expression with all the good things she makes me feel. Then I squeeze her hand. "I enjoy your company. Nothing more."

Her spine snaps straight, and she puckers her lips a touch. "Right, no personal involvement. I needed the reminder, thanks."

Maybe I could've phrased that better, but we need to work within the parameters of our arrangement before we both start to feel things we shouldn't.

Unless it's too late.

I rub my forehead with my thumb and forefinger. "I'm sorry. It came out all wrong." I drop my head back against the sofa and groan. "Och, you make me lose my mind. I can't drum up the right words when I'm with you." With a rueful smile, I tilt my head toward her until our gazes meet. "My bum's oot the windae now."

She laughs and leans her head on my shoulder. "I can't leave the state, but I could go for a little road trip. Get away from the city for a few days." She props her chin on my shoulder. "How's that sound?"

"Perfect. We've had the main course—these weeks together here. It's time for dessert."

"A road trip sundae with sex and a cherry on top?"

I feel my brows tighten. "There are times when I think Americans speak an alien language."

"Right back atcha, Mr. Highland Sex God."

"Sex god?"

"Don't let it go to your head. If your ego swells any bigger, you'll never fit on an airliner."

I haul her onto my lap, and she straddles my hips. I love the weight and warmth of her body, but more than anything, I love her sweet smile.

I rove my hands up and down her back. "Tell me one thing?"

"Okay."

Settling my hands on her hips, I clear my throat. "Am I a substitute for Cliff? The eejit you were meant to meet at the club."

"I don't understand what you're asking me. Cliff was a jerk who stood me up."

"But you wanted to meet him. He...excited you." She must wonder why I care if another man excites her, though she will probably assume I'm jealous. The truth is much harder to explain. Aisley had cared about excitement above everything else, and when I wouldn't give her the sort of thrills she craved, she made my life hell as punishment.

Erica splays her hands on my chest. "It wasn't Cliff that excited me. It was the idea of a fling, of chucking all my inhibitions and letting my inner wild child come out to play. I needed to feel alive."

"You chose me because I was the first man to approach you."

She slides her hands up my chest to my shoulders. "Actually, a rather enticing specimen bumped into me before you showed up. He smelled like beer and vomit, and he said I was hot but my breasts are too small for his taste. He staggered out of my life forever. I was devastated."

I almost smile at her joke, but I can't shake my memories of Aisley. "I'd no right to ask you about that."

"The topic is borderline off-limits." She glides her hands up behind my ears to bracket my head and sweeps her mouth over mine, back and forth, while our breaths mingle. "From the second you spoke my name that night, I wanted you. Cliff could take a flying leap. Every other man in the club disappeared. I saw only you. I wanted only you."

"The same for me, lass." My throat has gone dry and tight, making my voice hoarse. "You excite me like no other."

She brushes her tongue over my bottom lip. "You're no substitute, Lachlan."

I cradle her nape in one hand and pull her in for a kiss so passionate that it takes my breath away. Erica always does that to me, but even more so when we kiss. Our tongues dance, and I savor the taste of her—maple syrup, pancakes, and bacon—while she wraps her arms around my neck and moans into my mouth. I could devour her forever and still not get enough.

Erica pulls away first, breathing hard, her lips swollen and her cheeks pink. "Lachlan, do me one favor."

"Anything you want."

She rests her forehead on mine. "Never stop surprising me."

"Wouldn't dream of it."

I fold my arms around her, never wanting to let go.

She rubs her cheek against mine, seeming oblivious to the roughness of my morning stubble. "I'm sorry I keep calling you a bastard while we're having sex."

"I am a bastard. Just ask my wife."

Her head springs up, and she studies me intently. "You're divorced, right?"

I shrug one shoulder. Since I can't tell her about Aisley, I also can't explain that my ex-wife is not legally my ex yet because she managed to bollocks up the paperwork, probably on purpose. But I can tell her the truth in another way.

I smile with all the tenderness I shouldn't feel for her. "My wife is out of my life, permanently."

"Oh. Good." She studies me again, but only for a heartbeat. "Did you have any children?"

Should I answer? Does it even matter whether I do? We'll part ways much sooner than my heart wants. But the thought of having bairns with her triggers a sort of excitement I've never felt before.

Erica slides her hands down to my chest. Chewing the inside of her cheek, she stares at her own hands. "Sorry, that was too personal a question, wasn't it?"

I blow out a long sigh. "I've no bairns, though I want them very much."

"So do I."

That excitement rushes through me again. I told her the truth, but I left out the bit where I will never have children because I will never marry again.

"I didn't have any siblings," she tells me, "and I guess that made me want a family of my own. Lots of kids scampering around the house. And of course, a husband who loves me as much as I love him."

"A lovely dream." I sink my fingers into her hair, my palm on her cheek, and wish like hell I could be the one to give her what she wants. When she leans into my touch, that old pang throbs in my chest. "I hope you get it someday."

"I hope you get yours too."

A silence settles between us, not quite awkward but echoing with all the questions I long to ask her and all the things I wish I could tell her. She nestles her head on my shoulder, her face buried against my neck. I hold her and inhale the sweet scent that always surrounds her, and for a moment, I allow myself to fantasize about a life with her—a life with children and happiness that will never fade away. Seven days. That's as much as I can give her. I never want to let her go, but I know I must do it.

The words I can't speak whisper through my mind. *I love you, Erica.*

Chapter Twenty-Three

When I wake up the next morning, all that sentimental rubbish I wallowed in yesterday has evaporated. I like Erica and love shagging her, but that's all it is. I'd wanted a holiday from my life, and she has given me that. My ex-wife wants to cause me trouble in every way possible, and I let the stress of all that divorce bollocks get to me.

No more. It's time for a road trip with the sexy lass who's lying in bed with me. And I know just how to start our morning.

I roll onto my side and gaze at the woman sleeping beside me. Erica lies on her side too, facing me, her eyes closed and a soft smile on her lips. What is she dreaming of? The two of us naked, I hope, with our bodies entangled. A lock of hair has fallen over her eyes, so I tuck it behind her ear.

Then I grab my mobile off the bedside table and head into the bathroom, shutting the door as quietly as possible to avoid waking her. I mean to wake her in a special way.

I lean my erse against the sink counter and dial Erica's mobile number.

Out in the bedroom, her mobile starts ringing. After four rings, she answers drowsily. "Hello?"

"Ah, sweet Erica, it's time to wake up, so I can do wicked things to that body of yours." I imagine I'm doing exactly what I describe to her. "I want to massage your entire body, starting with your feet, and work my way up to your legs, where I'll spread your thighs and feast on all that luscious cream. Your body is the canvas, and I mean to paint it with my lips, tongue, and hands until you're thrashing under me and begging to come."

"Mm, Lachlan, yes," she mumbles. "Get your ass over here and make me come with your mouth."

"Ahm meaning to do that, *gràidh*. Over and over."

She moans softly, still sounding drowsy.

"After I massage your body," I tell her, "I'm going to flip you over and fuck you from behind."

"Mm, I'd love—" Her words cut off, and silence follows for a few seconds. When she speaks again, she doesn't sound sleepy anymore. "Lachlan, where are you?"

"Right here." I swing the bathroom door open and amble out, tossing my mobile onto the bedside table. "I'd never leave you, especially when you're naked and wet."

"I'm not wet. Haven't taken a shower yet."

I crawl onto the bed and inch my way up her body, licking her skin as I move. "Not that kind of wet."

For the next half hour, I show Erica exactly what kind of wet I meant.

We make breakfast together and eat it in the kitchen, at the table where we had shared brownies three weeks ago. I'd never known a chocolate dessert could be erotic until that day. I remember the soft, sensual look on her face while I had told her about Talisker whisky. She is incredible, and I couldn't have found a better partner for my month-long fling in America.

Erica's mobile rings, shattering my reminiscences.

She looks straight at me, a question on her face.

"You don't need my permission to take a call," I say. "But I'll give you some privacy and wait in the living room."

The devil on my shoulder whispers that I should linger just outside the kitchen doorway and listen in on her conversation, but I ignore the impulse. Instead, I drop onto the sofa and wait for Erica.

I can hear her voice, but I can't make out the words.

A moment later, Erica shuffles into the living room and perches on the coffee table's edge. "I have to go somewhere this morning. It's personal, and I can't tell you any more than that."

"Is everything all right? You seem anxious." Aye, I noticed that the second she walked into the room. Hard to miss the signs. She'd been wringing her hands and chewing on her lip.

"My emotions are private." She stands, giving me a cool look that doesn't fool me for one minute. "I don't know how long this will take, so don't wait for me."

But I want to wait for her. I want to go with her, actually, but I can't do that.

"I'll be here," I say. "Come find me when you're done."

She nods and walks out the front door.

What can I do until she comes back? Everything I've done on my holiday so far has involved Erica. I don't have a bloody clue what to do with myself when she's not here.

It's been too long since I took a real holiday. That's the only reason I'm sitting in the living room, staring across the way at Erica's kitchen window, and it's the only reason I keep jogging to the front door so I can peek outside. After an hour of that nonsense, I get on my computer to look for destinations Erica might like to visit during our road trip. I'm not obsessing over her. I'm being a good, ah, traveling companion.

Making all the arrangements for our trip doesn't take as long as I'd hoped, but I get everything set up. I even find a dog sitter for Casey since the places we'll be going to don't allow pets. The older woman who lives across the street, Mrs. Abernathy, is more than happy to help. Once I've got the pup's accommodations settled, I pack a suitcase and take it out to the car so I'll be ready to go whenever Erica comes home.

When she returns, she goes straight into her house instead of coming over here. I don't care. She is not my girlfriend.

Mhac na galla. Is this what I've become? A whingeing ersehole? I'm too old to act like such a numpty.

To distract myself, I ring my brother Aidan. Even his jokes can't take my mind off the woman in the house next door. I ring several of my cousins too and have pleasant conversations with them, but I still keep thinking about…her.

Someone knocks on the front door.

I leap off the sofa and bolt for the door, my heart racing, anticipation tingling over my skin. I'm off my head for sure, but right now, I don't give a toss because my mind insists the visitor must be Erica. But I'd given her a key, so she doesn't need to knock.

At the door, I pause. The ridiculous joy that had overcome me seconds ago has faded just enough to make me wonder—worry, actually—about what awaits me on the other side of the door. I take a breath, iron the excitement out of my expression, and roll my shoulders back.

Then I swing the door open.

Erica smiles at me. "Sorry to keep you waiting for so long."

"Donnae mind. You're worth waiting for. But why didn't you use the key I gave you?"

"This is more dramatic. Don't you think?"

"Aye, but you don't need to impress me with grand gestures."

"I know, but I liked surprising you this way. And I have some news." She spreads her arms wide. "Let's go on our road trip right now."

"What?"

"I said let's do it right away. Why waste more time? I'm ready for a road trip sundae with lots and lots of hot, caramel-y Lachlan on top."

When did I become an ice-cream sundae? Not that I mind if Erica wants to lick me. I plan on tasting her body from head to toe too.

"Are you comatose?" she says teasingly. "I said let's get on the road immediately. Unless you have something better to do…"

I swoop her up in my arms and whirl us both round and round. Her feet sail through the air, though not as high as my spirits have soared in the last few minutes. I step backward and kick the door shut behind us. Why am I so excited? The answer doesn't matter. She wants to go with me, and that's all I need to hear.

I deposit her on the wood floor of the entryway, though I keep my arms around her, unwilling to let go yet.

"It's true?" I ask, as my grin gets bigger.

"Yes." She pecks a kiss on my mouth. "I want our road trip to start today. I thought about it all night and this morning and then in the car I realized—"

I silence her ramblings with my lips. When I finally make myself stop kissing her, I ask, "How soon can you be ready?"

"Already packed. Got ready last night."

I feel almost light-headed, and I can't stop grinning, not even when I crush her to me. "You're a miracle, *gràidh*."

Before she can say anything in response, I seal my lips over hers again and kiss the lass so thoroughly that we're both breathing hard by the time I pull away.

She breathes one word. "Casey."

"I asked Mrs. Abernathy. She'll take him while we're gone." I duck my head. "Where we're going, they don't allow pets. I'm sorry, I tried to find a pet-friendly place."

"It's okay. Casey loves Mrs. Abernathy."

"Gave her my key to your house. Was that all right?"

"Yes." Her lips find mine, and she thrusts her tongue into my mouth, rasping it over mine like she's starved for more. "Thank you for taking care of all the arrangements."

"Welcome. Shall we go?"

She grins. "Absolutely. Let's get on the road."

I brush kisses on her temple, her cheek, the corner of her mouth. "Got my bags in the car. Let's go grab yours, my sweet lass, and get on the road."

Her joy fizzles like a candle that's been snuffed out.

I graze a hand over her cheek. "Feeling unwell?"

"Uh-uh."

Slipping my hand around her nape, I draw her in for another kiss, determined to erase her worries with my lips and my tongue—and whatever other parts of me she wants. When I pull away, I'm not convinced I've done my job. "You still seem unhappy. Where did you go this morning?"

The words spilled out before I had time to think about them.

She opens her mouth as if to speak, but then her shoulders wilt and she shuts her eyes, exhaling a long breath. She stares at my chest. "I went to see Presley."

"The erse who's been harassing you? Why?"

Erica wraps her arms around me, burying her face against my chest.

I caress her hair, threading my fingers through it. "What happened?"

"Sure you wanna know?"

"Positive." I curl one arm around her, holding her close.

She turns her head to rest her cheek on my chest. "I thought I needed to confront him, to get some kind of closure. But he just made fun of me. Can't believe I was ever involved with him. Can't believe I actually thought he might—" She squeezes her eyes shut. "Guess I needed to believe he wasn't a total slimeball. But he is."

I enfold her in my arms and kiss the top of her head. "What did he do to you?"

"Today? Not much. He was sarcastic and dismissive."

"I meant in the past."

"Don't think you really want to hear about it."

Well, I haven't given her much reason to think I care enough to want to hear her story. I rest my chin on the top of her head, and when I speak, I'm surprised by my melancholy tone. "Whatever he did—and I won't push you to tell me, since I have no right to—but whatever he did, I hope it's over now. I hate seeing you like this."

"It is over. Way over." She wriggles out of my embrace, rubbing her arms. "Couldn't even get him to tell me why he keeps coming to my house." She slips her hands into mine, holding on tight. "Let's forget the serious talk. I want to go away with you and have fun."

"That I can give you."

Keeping hold of one of her hands, I lead her out of the house and across the lawns to her front door. We collect Erica's bags, piling into my hired Mercedes convertible. I'd put the top down so we could enjoy the fresh air and scenery.

Erica settles her bonnie erse onto the plush seat, wriggling like she's very comfortable.

The car rocks when I climb in and yank my door shut. The engine rumbles to life, but so softly that it's almost drowned out by the classical music emanating from the stereo. Vivaldi's *The Four Seasons*. I'd left the radio on a classical station, but maybe I should tune it to something livelier.

Erica looks a touch melancholy again.

I lay my hand over hers on the center console. "I won't ask what's been eating at you these weeks, but I want you to know you can tell me if you like. Maybe I can help."

She twines our fingers and gives me a half-hearted smile. "Let's get on the road and have fun. That's all I want to think about right now."

I nod, though I'm not convinced by her attempt to brush off her anxiety. Despite my command that we don't talk about anything personal, I get an ache in the pit of my stomach when I think about the look on Erica's face every time she mentions Presley the scunner. I want to pull her into my arms and kiss her mindless, then vow to do whatever it takes to solve her problems, whatever they might be.

But I can't do that.

Vivaldi concedes to Mozart by the time we've merged onto the freeway, headed for a destination I chose. I hope she'll like it, but if she doesn't, I will find something else to make her smile.

A police car passes us on the left.

Peripherally, I see Erica tensing up and biting her lip while she glances sideways at the police car. Once it's passed by, she relaxes again.

Why did that fash her?

She crosses her legs and massages my thigh. "Where are we going, Sex God?"

I wince and shift position while she slides her hand higher, dangerously close to my cock. "Our destination is a surprise."

"Oh?" She edges her fingers closer to my burgeoning erection.

I grasp her hand, settling it on the center console beneath mine. "You'll like it, I promise."

"Will it be sexy?"

I flash her a secretive smile. "Patience, *mo leannan*. Patience."

On our drive south from Chicago, I show Erica every silly tourist destination along the way to make sure she smiles and laughs instead of slipping into sadness again. We stop at the Paul Bunyan statue in University Park, where the giant lumberman slumps as if he's too knackered to hold himself up and lets his ax drag on the ground. The second I notice Erica's good mood waning the slightest bit, I take action.

I rush at Paul Bunyan's giant ax, pretending to strain to lift it and contorting my face strictly to make my performance more believable. I don't care if the other tourists think I'm a dafty. I will suffer any indignity to make Erica smile. So I fall on the huge blade and act out a death scene that involves enough overblown silliness to make even a confirmed cynic smile.

And Erica laughs so hard she clutches her belly while happy tears gather in her eyes.

Mission accomplished, I give up my bloody awful one-man show and march back to Erica's side. I lay a hand on her cheek, running my thumb over the upturned corner of her mouth. "That's better. I'll humiliate myself anytime to see that beautiful smile."

She gazes up at me with an expression that almost seems like…adoration.

Christ, the last thing I want is for her to develop feelings for me. I'm leaving in less than a week, and anyway, I can't give her the sort of relationship a woman like her needs. I probably misinterpreted her expression. She doesn't adore me.

After paying our respects to Paul Bunyan, we get back on the road and visit several other tourist destinations, all featuring bizarre statues or some other barmy monument, like a water tower emblazoned with a smiley face, and a Nazi buzz bomb. When we reach the statue of Abraham Lincoln holding a "Go Bears" sign, I don't understand the reference.

"Was Lincoln afraid of bears?" I ask, and I'm not being cheeky.

"No," Erica says with a half-suppressed laugh. "The Bears are a professional football team."

"I assume you mean that daft game Americans play with an oval ball. But that's not football."

"Yes, it is. Not that I'm into sports, but football is super popular in this country."

"But you lot don't know what the word means." I sling an arm around her waist to pull her close, then I speak in a low, husky voice. "Everywhere else in the world, football means the game where blokes kick a ball around with their feet, not the bloody stupid game Americans play."

"I don't care what you call it," she says in an equally soft voice, rubbing her body against me. "Sports are dumb and boring, unless they take place in bed."

"You have a point." I dip my head to whisper in her ear, "Shinty is a real man's game, and we Scots are very serious about it."

A family walks by, the parents giving us odd looks, probably because Erica and I look like we're about to shag right here in front of them.

We continue our tour of roadside attractions, and I find I enjoy seeing the barmy sights with Erica. Her mood improves even more as we go along. The prospect of taking a detour off the interstate to see the first Dairy Queen franchise makes her clap and shout, "Yay!"

She honestly is the most adorable woman in the world.

And I learn that Dairy Queen is a fast-food restaurant that also sells ice cream. I still don't understand why she loves seeing the first example of that restaurant, but I love anything that makes her happy.

On we go, traveling south down Interstate 45, with the scenery whizzing past our windows in a blur. At the town of Loda, I exit the freeway to head for another attraction. When Erica asks me what it is, I simply tell her, "You'll see."

When we pull up to the village park, and the attraction comes into view, Erica goes stone-still and stops blinking.

I can't see what has upset her. On the grassy lawn of the park stands a large metal cage marked with a sign identifying it as the Loda Jail. According to my research, this is a popular tourist attraction and just the sort of thing Erica ought to enjoy. Maybe I need to explain it. She's probably confused.

I point at the cage. "A hundred years ago, they kept prisoners in that contraption. Must've been a pleasant experience, eh?"

She fidgets in her seat, and when she speaks, her voice almost cracks. "Yeah, I'm sure it was a pajama party."

I swerve my gaze to her, noticing the way her eyes glisten. "What's wrong?"

"Nothing." She starts to lean back as if to get comfortable, but instead, her posture seems awkward and tense. "Jails aren't fun, that's all."

I cup her face in both hands, leaning in until my breaths reflect off her skin, and search her gaze for a clue to her distress. "Erica, please don't cry."

She blinks rapidly, as if to chase away the tears forming in her eyes.

I brush my lips over hers. "I never meant to upset you, but clearly I have. I'm sorry."

"You didn't do anything." She clears her throat, avoiding my gaze. "Can we just go somewhere else, please?"

Nodding, I release her so I can steer the car back toward the freeway. I decide Erica has had enough of the roadside attractions and head for the bed-and-breakfast where I've arranged for us to stay. Her reaction to the Loda Jail baffles me, but I can't ask why it fashes her. If she wants to tell me, I will listen. But I won't press her for answers. After all, I'm leaving soon.

This trip is my way of saying goodbye.

Chapter Twenty-Four

Just outside of Champaign, we pull into the semicircular, brick-lined drive of a historic mansion. Sky blue trims the white house, and slender Corinthian columns buttress the wraparound porch while lacy railing lines the porch and the second-floor balcony. I chose this bed-and-breakfast because I thought Erica would appreciate its historic and aesthetic appeal. Once I've parked the car, I hurry to Erica's side to open the door for her and offer my hand to help her get out. I keep hold of her hand as we mount the brick steps toward the mansion's front door.

Her mood has been melancholy ever since we visited the Loda Jail.

A sparrow lands on the brick steps to Erica's left, flutters its wings, and flies away. Her mouth turns down at the corners, and she hunches her shoulders.

Now a wee bird upsets her? I can't ask why. *Bloody hell.*

We enter the bed-and-breakfast hand in hand, like any normal couple might. The interior is stunning and historically accurate, with hardwood floors and wall paneling along with a crystal chandelier suspended over the entryway. Erica's frown softens into a slight smile as she surveys our surroundings.

A bonnie grey-haired woman called Mrs. Wilkins signs us in while regaling us with tales of the mansion's early days. Erica doesn't seem to pay attention to anything Mrs. Wilkins says, and her unfocused gaze tells me she isn't here with me. She has retreated into herself again.

Mrs. Wilkins hands me our room key, then looks at Erica. "Have a wonderful stay, Mrs. MacTaggart."

Erica startles at our host's statement. "I'm not—"

"Thank you, Mrs. Wilkins," I say, tossing an arm around Erica's shoulders. "I'm sure we'll both love it here."

And aye, I'm also sure Erica had been about to inform Mrs. Wilkins that she is not my wife. I don't see the point in declaring our marital status, and for reasons I can't fathom, I don't want to hear Erica say those words.

I haul her away from the desk toward a sprawling staircase upholstered in crimson carpeting.

Erica twists around, bound by my arm, and waves at Mrs. Wilkins. Then she elbows me in the side, muttering out the corner of her mouth, "Why'd you let her think we're married?"

"It made her happy. She adores newlyweds." I experienced another of my too-frequent needs to make Erica smile and spoke the last two words in a silly imitation of Mrs. Wilkins's voice. Erica would have known the woman loves newlyweds if she hadn't been lost in her own anxieties while our host was talking to us. "Where's the harm in letting her believe it?"

Erica's mouth twists down at one corner, and she averts her gaze to the floor.

A moment later, I usher her to our room on the second floor, which has balcony access and picture windows that grant us views of both the tree-shrouded drive in front and the lush gardens behind the mansion. We stand outside the closed door to our room, but I'd seen pictures of this place on the establishment's website. I had requested this room specifically, because it has the best view.

I unlock the door and crack it open a few inches.

Then a strange impulse overtakes me. I pick Erica up and kick the door inward to carry her over the threshold. I kick the door shut behind us.

Erica seems mildly startled, but she looks bonnie that way.

I set her down on her feet beside the bed. Our bags already await us, tucked in between the dresser and the wall, across from the four-poster bed. Mr. Wilkins, the husband of Mrs. Wilkins, had brought our luggage up here while I got us signed in at the desk.

Erica shuffles toward her wheeled suitcase, glancing out the windows.

Ivy surrounds the panes while flowering trees and bushes add color to the landscape. The bed-and-breakfast boasts a magnificent garden with tables for outdoor dining. Maybe I shouldn't have chosen such a romantic place for us to spend a few nights, but I'd hoped the beauty of this mansion and its garden would lift her spirits.

Hooking an arm around her waist, I turn her toward me and pull her body snug against mine. "Like the surprise?"

"I love it." Linking her hands behind my neck, she rests her cheek on my chest. "I wish we could stay here forever, on a never-ending honeymoon."

Her statement makes me flinch, and my entire body goes rigid. Honeymoon? She'd been annoyed when I let Mrs. Wilkins believe we're married. Now she wants a honeymoon with me? I've made a mistake bringing her here. It's too romantic. I've given her the wrong idea about my intentions.

Erica jerks her head up and clamps her lips between her teeth. She also seems to stop blinking. Then she clears her throat and laughs nervously. "I meant a fake honeymoon. You know, like Mrs. Wilkins thinks we're doing now."

Like hell that's what she meant.

I let my arms fall to my sides, suddenly ill at ease with this conversation. Are my hands trembling? No, that would be daft. But I do feel cold inside, as if I've swallowed a bucketful of ice cubes. My gaze converges with hers, and for a few seconds, I wonder if she can read my mind and hear all my idiotic thoughts. Does she know how conflicted I am? I didn't until right now.

The green flecks in her hazel irises seem to shimmer as if they're lit from within, and I can't rip my focus away from her. A hint of tears glimmers in her eyes.

I veer my gaze away and scrub my hands over my face. "You know I'm leaving in a matter of days."

A sigh deflates her shoulders, and the movement seems to drag her spirit down too. "What's your point?"

"You said…" I start pacing the width of the room, between the door and the opposite wall, afflicted with a sudden need to stay in motion. "Have I given you reason to think I won't go?"

"No." Her voice turns sharper, almost acidic. "Don't worry, I won't chase you to the airport and throw myself at your feet, begging you to stay. I can find another sex partner at Dance Ardor."

The place where she'd wanted a one-night stand with a random stranger?

I reel around, seizing her arms. "Donnae ever go back to that club again!"

She punches my chest. "Let go of me, you—you—*Homo heidelbergensis*."

I gape at her, dumbfounded. "What did you call me?"

"*Homo heidelbergensis*." She wrests free of my grasp. "It's an ancient species of prehuman hominid. I was going to call you a Neanderthal, but then I remembered they didn't live in the UK, but *heidelbergensis* did."

I can't help it. My closed lips stretch taut, one corner curving up. "A timekeeper, an accountant, and an anthropologist. My, you are a Renaissance woman."

She scowls and stuffs her hands into her jeans pockets. "I read a lot."

"Sorry." I reach out to touch her cheek, but pull my hand away. "I shouldn't have shouted at you. But I can't stand the thought of you going back to that…den of iniquity. Men would take advantage of you."

"Oh, you mean like you've done?"

Bod an Donais, is that what she really thinks of me? I grimace, shoving a hand through my hair. "Is that what you think I'm doing? I told you honestly what I could give you and left the decision in your hands."

I feel a touch nauseous when I speak those words, but I need her to understand this is still a temporary arrangement. I won't be here for much longer.

But I get even more nauseous thinking those words.

Erica squeezes her eyes shut, her lips quivering.

"I've upset you again," I say, disheartened by the way my voice has thickened with emotions I shouldn't be feeling. "Forgive me, *gràidh*?"

She grunts, opening her eyes.

I kneel before her and raise my clasped hands, like I'm about to beg for her forgiveness. Which I am. Upsetting Erica makes me feel like the worst sort of *bod ceann*.

She waves for me to get up. "Fine, I forgive you."

I bow my head, a breath rushing out of me. "Thank heaven for that."

Rising, I stumble backward a step, off-balance in too many ways. Then I regain my equilibrium, in body if not in mind, and stride over to an antique chair that sits near the bedside table, dropping onto it.

Erica sinks onto the bed with her feet dangling six inches off the wood floor.

The gulf between us feels much larger than the width of the table.

I brace an elbow on the chair's arm and let my forehead fall onto my palm, pushing my fingers into my hair and spreading them wide. My fingers tighten over my scalp. I can't squeeze sense into my brain, though. Can't control my body either, since my eyes insist on glancing sideways at Erica.

She shifts position to sit cross-legged on the floral bedspread. With her hands on her knees, she taps her fingers in a staccato rhythm and stares at the floorboards. "Are you okay?"

I make a noise that's somewhere between a grunt and a sigh.

Erica rocks on her erse. After a moment, she snatches a brochure from the table and reads it, then slaps it down again.

"You're fashed," I say, "but I don't know why."

"Really."

She unzips her boot and kicks it off. The boot ricochets off my shin, and though I wince, it's not because of the brief pain. Erica is angry, because of me. She kicks off the other boot, sending it sailing.

I bolt upright with my hands latched onto the chair's arms, anticipating another blow, but her boot flies wide to whack down near the bathroom door.

Erica scowls at me. "All I said was I wished we could stay here forever—which is, by the way, a common thing Americans say when we're happy—and you freaked out."

I cross my ankles, uncross them, link my hands, and finally fasten them on my thighs. "I did not freak out."

"Right. I imagine there's a masculine Scottish word for it."

"Erica—"

"Chill out." She tears her socks off, lobbing them toward the dresser. One catches on a drawer handle while the other plops onto the floor. "I am fully aware of the rules, Lachlan."

I heave my body off the chair and scuffle over to her. Kneeling before her yet again, I settle my hands on her thighs. Aye, that bloody stupid need to appease her has gripped me again, and I can't fight it. I slide my hands up and down twice, then curl them over her knees. "I am sorry, for whatever I've done to upset you this time. I seem to have a knack for it. *Gràidh*, what can I do to make it up to you?"

"Stop calling me that. I'm not your *gràidh*. I'm your American fling."

Hearing her speak those words, I experience a strong need to batter something. Instead, I brace my hands on the bed at either side of her hips, straightening them to raise myself so my eyes are now level with hers. Another need grows stronger, erasing my anger.

The need to comfort her.

"I know what you are, *mo leannan*," I say as I drag my mouth up her jawline, from her chin to her ear. I forge a trail down her throat, punctuating my words with feather-light kisses. "Sweet. Kind. Strong. Stubborn. Clever."

Moving my mouth even lower, I graze my lips across the slope of one breast and follow it down.

Her head falls back, and her spine arches.

I slip my tongue under the edge of her bra, drawing a gasp from her.

"Beautiful," I whisper, nuzzling the valley between her breasts. "Sensual. Soft. Irresistible."

"I—" She stops abruptly after speaking that single word, her breasts heaving.

"The bonniest of all," I murmur, diving one hand inside her jeans to palm her erse.

She sucks in a breath and opens her thighs.

I tilt my head back to gaze into her golden eyes. "Are ye ready for me?"

Erica says nothing, but desire burns in her eyes.

With lazy strokes, I caress her erse inside her jeans, loving the warmth of her skin and the way her flesh yields to my fingers. I rub my chin over the mound of her breast. "Find out for myself."

I hold her close as I ease her down onto the bedspread, then get rid of her clothing before I shed mine. Her naked body is spread out beneath me, and I can't resist taking a moment to admire every curve and swell—and the scent of her desire for me. Aye, she wants me as much as I want her, and here in this room, I need to show her exactly how much she means to me.

Kneeling at her feet, I close my fingers around her ankles in a light hold, barely grazing her skin. When I skim my hands up her calves, she shivers faintly—and my cock starts to harden. Her breathing has become more labored, her breasts bouncing with every rise and fall of her chest. Those taut, rosy-red nipples bob in front of me. I should be ravishing her, but instead, I gaze at her body with reverence while I take slow, deep breaths to savor the scent of her.

My tongue sneaks out to moisten my lips.

She lifts her head, her body held up by her elbows. "Wha—"

That word cuts off when I glide my hands over her knees and higher still. She lets out a long, shaky breath. I ease her legs apart with both hands and touch my damp lips to her inner thigh, kiss my way up to the apex, and hesitate there. Fuck, she's perfect. Her body, her smile, her voice, everything about her is wonderful.

With my fingertips, I caress the curly hairs on her mound, amazed anew by how soft those hairs feel. I plant a wet kiss on her hip, earning a ragged moan from her.

She stretches a hand out to comb her fingers through my hair.

I turn my face into her palm, darting my tongue out to taste her skin, then I move my head down between her thighs where the scent of her envelops me, sweet and musky and rich. Our gazes connect, and I swear I feel a genuine connection between us, though I know that's bollocks. She believes I want only sex from her. That's what I told her, and it's the reason she doesn't feel comfortable telling me about her problems. As much as I long to comfort and help her, all I can offer her is this—sex, but imbued with all the confusing, conflicting emotions she inspires in me.

I seal my mouth over her clit, suckling and licking it, stimulating her nerves little by little while she watches me, her face tightening from the pleasure ratcheting tighter every second.

Erica aroused is the most beautiful thing I've ever seen.

Lifting my head, I crawl up her body, skating my hands over her skin, caressing every inch of her while licking and nibbling my way over her belly and breasts until my face hovers above hers. I wrap my hands around her breasts, my thumbs drawing circles around the nipples.

She blows out several short, uneven breaths. "What are you doing?"

I flick my thumbs over her nipples. "Worshiping you."

"Lachlan—"

"Shh." I slant my mouth over hers with firm pressure, then soften the kiss, rubbing my lips back and forth, running my tongue along the seam of her mouth. Her lips part for me, and I murmur into her mouth, "Let me show you."

"Show me?" she whispers.

No explanations. I'm going to show her and hope she understands.

At the instant I thrust my tongue between her lips, I plunge my cock inside her and lower my body to cover hers. My breaths fan her hair across her cheek while she writhes and moans into my mouth and I push my tongue deep, in time with every stroke of my cock. I stop fighting what she makes me feel, stop trying to hide it for as long as I'm inside her, using my body to show her what she means to me. I rove my hands over her body, exploring it with all the tenderness I'm incapable of expressing any other way. I take her slowly and sweetly, and when I come with one long, powerful thrust, I feel Erica's climax break through her too. Wave after wave of contractions grip my body as every muscle inside her fastens around me in the most incredible embrace.

Tears roll down her cheeks.

I sweep hair away from her face and touch my lips to hers. When more tears trickle down her skin, I kiss away the drops and drag my fingers down her cheeks. "Why are you crying, love?"

She rubs away the tears, hauls in a deep breath, and clears her throat. "It's nothing."

My jaw clenches. Nothing? That's bollocks, and we both know it. But since I refuse to share my feelings with her, I can't push her to confess.

She feigns a laugh. "Guess you're such a great lover, I cry from the pure ecstasy of it."

My frown tenses my whole face. "You aren't going to tell me, are you?"

"No."

I roll off her, flopping onto my back. "You can't keep crying and not tell me why."

"You don't want to know."

"Stop saying that." I jump off the bed and scoop her up in my arms, then I shove the covers aside with my foot and drop her back onto the mattress. She squeaks, bouncing a little. I leap over her body to lie down alongside her, tugging the covers over us both, and pull her against me with our chests crushed together. "I'll be holding you until you tell me the truth."

"Oh, darn."

My lips twitch but don't quite form a smile. "If we're not talking, then go to sleep, woman."

"Woman?" She tries to kick me but can't get leverage. "I'm not your chattel."

"I know. I have no claim on you."

"Do you want to? Have a claim, I mean."

Aye, I want it so much I can't breathe when I think about leaving her. But I'm incapable of giving her what she really needs. "Go to sleep."

She flattens her lips, but then rolls over, turning her back to me.

I pull her close again, my front to her back.

Erica holds still for a moment before she relaxes into me. We snuggle under the sheets, my hand over her belly while the heat of her permeates my entire body. I listen to her breathing as it slows and becomes shallower, a sign she's falling asleep. My breaths come slower too as I let my muscles slacken, allowing myself a few moments to revel in the feel of her body tucked against mine. The world sifts away, and I relax even more deeply.

"Stay with you forever."

Did I mumble those words or only think them? Doesn't matter.

I can't stay, but for tonight, I will pretend I can.

Chapter Twenty-Five

The sun has sunk below the horizon by the time we turn onto the street where we both live—or rather, where she lives and where I'm temporarily in residence. The mood on the drive back from the bed-and-breakfast had been tense and melancholy, on both our parts. We'd spent two more nights at the quaint mansion and visited more tourist attractions in the vicinity during the day, but always I sensed tension beneath the surface. We're both pretending I didn't make love to her like she means more to me than a fling. If Erica heard what I think I mumbled on that first night while I was falling asleep, she hasn't given any indication that she did. Maybe she wishes she hadn't heard me say that. Either way, the distance between us has grown to more than the width of the center console in the Mercedes.

I want to touch her, kiss her, convince her to share her troubles with me. But it's a bloody awful idea. If I know everything about Erica, I won't want to leave her. It's possible I already feel that way, but that changes nothing.

Maybe I shouldn't have worshiped her body on that first night, but I couldn't stop myself. Knowing I will leave soon infected me with a growing sense of dread, and I needed to show her how much I cherish her. But I can't stay. I would only hurt her more if I tried to make this work between us.

Until the day I go home, I will spend every moment I can with her.

Earlier today, I received a text from Rory informing me of Aisley's new demand. She wants everything I have including my Edinburgh apartment and my house in the Highlands. When I'd read that message, I wanted to pound my fists on…anything. But I'd been in the bathroom of our room at the bed-and-breakfast, so instead, I had raged on the inside while I took a shower. Even pummeling my body with steaming-hot water hadn't helped, and neither had cold water.

That's why I hadn't said much during our drive home. I still don't understand Erica's reticence, though.

I pull the car into the driveway of Gil's house and get out to open Erica's door for her. "You must be jeeked. I'll bring your bags over to your house after I drop mine off. Then I'll make you a good meal. All right?"

She nods weakly, and I swear her lips tremble a touch.

Erica and I walk across the lawn to the concrete path that connects her driveway to her front steps. I lace my fingers with hers as we approach the porch where her automatic light has already switched on, flooding the vicinity with its warm glow.

We both stop. I grip her hand harder as the meaning of what I'm seeing penetrates my mind.

The front door hangs ajar, though the interior is dark and silent.

For a few seconds, all I can do is stare at the door while my jaw clenches and my muscles go rigid, tensed in preparation for whatever awaits us inside Erica's house. Someone has broken in. They must've done.

I let go of her hand. In a crouch, I creep toward the doorway.

Erica tugs my sleeve. When I glance back, she mouths, "Nine-one-one."

I nod and mouth, "You call."

Then I push the door open further and sidle through the opening.

My eyes haven't had time to adjust to the gloom inside the house, so I tiptoe into the living room, hoping to avoid crashing into furniture if I move more slowly. I also don't want to surprise the intruder and get myself shot or stabbed. I will make my presence known as soon as I find out who has breached the house.

Halfway across the living room, I freeze. Is that breathing I hear? Or the central air kicking on?

Something scrapes across the carpeting nearby.

I clench my fists harder, my jaw too. I've found the intruder, but I can't see the bloody ersehole.

A shadow moves across the kitchen doorway, heading this way, but I can't distinguish the intruder from the walls.

"Show your face," I snarl. "The police are on the way, so you might as well give up."

More scratching of shoes on carpeting. More breathing noises.

The intruder moves into a wedge of wan light that's spilling through a window.

I lunge for the bastard.

He punches me in the gut.

"Och!" The shout bursts out of me along with all the air in my lungs.

The intruder hits me in the jaw, but when he tries to punch me again, I throw my fist out to catch his in my palm, closing my fingers around his fist and twisting his arm behind him.

He kicks me in the shin.

I lose my grip and stumble sideways, then knock into the wall when my opponent pulls his arm back for another swing. This time, I slug the *bod ceann*, making him cry out like a mewling bairn, then I lock my arm around his neck in a choke hold.

The overhead light comes on, blinding us both for a moment.

My captive thrashes and paws at my arm but can't break free.

Finally, my vision adjusts enough that I can see the face of the ersehole who has broken into Erica's home. It's the whingeing wee scunner, Presley.

Erica stands just inside the living-room threshold, not far from where I'm restraining Presley beside the sofa.

I fist my hand in his hair and yank it back so hard his eyes bulge. "What the hell are ye doing in mah woman's house?"

Erica's hand flies to her chest, positioned over her heart, and her eyes widen as she glances back and forth between me and Presley.

"Tell me!" I roar.

Presley gags and splutters.

Erica points at my arm that's locked around Presley's neck. "I don't think he can speak."

I stare at her for a couple of seconds before I realize I'm behaving like a rabid beast. Aye, Presley deserves to be throttled, but it's not worth going to jail over a scunner like him. I release my choke hold, but before Presley can run away, I grasp his wrists and use my hands to cuff his behind his back.

Presley spits blood. The skin along his jaw and around his left eye has begun to turn faintly purple.

My jaw aches, though not only from clenching my teeth. Presley had gotten in one good punch before I caught him.

The twat glowers at Erica, probably because he can't turn around enough to aim his fury at me. "Scotch Tape attacked me for no reason. Your pit bull's out of control, babe."

Erica anchors her hands on her hips, seeming remarkably calm, though I know her well enough to realize she's putting on a brave face. "Answer Lachlan's question, or I'll cut the leash and let my pit bull tear your throat out."

She wants me to batter the slimy *cacan*? My lips tick up at the corners as I gaze straight at Erica. Her lips tick up a little too.

I jerk Presley's hands, making the *cacan* bellow. "Once more, ye filthy bawbag. What are ye doing in mah woman's house?"

"Door was open when I got here," Presley says. He struggles against my hold, then sags his shoulders. A deep scowl tugs his brows down. "I came in to check on Erica."

"Gimme a break," she says. "First, you try to force me to let you inside. Then, we catch you spying through my bedroom window. And to cap things off, you've broken into my house."

"Did not."

"Stop lying. I don't swallow your crap anymore." She stalks up to him. "I know you broke in."

He juts his chin up, lifting his nose too. "Prove it."

Erica clasps a hand around her left arm, and everything about her wilts, from her posture to her expression.

"Did ye call the police?" I ask her.

She rubs her arms, shoulders hunched. "No."

Presley sniggers. "She knows."

What hold does this bastard have on her? I wrench Presley's hands so roughly that he whimpers and his face contorts in pain. "What do ye mean she knows?"

Erica sidles closer to me and lays a hand on my upper arm. "Let him go."

"What?" I shake my head and huff out several short breaths. "Ye cannae mean it. This bastard is tormenting ye."

"Yeah, I know, but you have to let him go." She squeezes my arm. "Please, Lachlan. I'll explain everything later."

I stare at her for a long moment while anger hardens me into concrete. The scunner should not be allowed to get away with committing a crime and harassing an innocent woman.

Erica keeps her hand on my arm and her gaze nailed to mine, but something in her eyes convinces me she wants me to release the bastard. Why, I have no idea. But I will do what she wants because I'll do anything for her. Anything except stay forever.

I shove Presley away.

He sprints out of the house.

And I pull Erica into my arms, noticing that tears glisten in her eyes. I hold her face with both hands, tracing circles on her cheekbones with my thumbs. "Why, lass? What hold does he have on you?"

"There's a lot to explain." Erica glances at the sofa beside us where blood stains dot the fabric. Wincing, she scratches her arm. "Would you mind if we continued this conversation in the bedroom?"

I usher her down the hallway, shutting the front door along the way.

Erica is about to confide in me, but I should tell her not to do it. I need to know, though not for any reason that makes sense. I will let her share her pain with me.

For tonight, I will be what she needs.

Chapter Twenty-Six

I slouch on the bed with my back to the headboard and my legs outstretched while Erica huddles beside me, inches away though it feels like the entirety of the universe separates us. She tucks her feet under her, angling toward me, and moves her fingers restlessly for a moment. Then she shoves them under her legs.

She leans one shoulder against the headboard.

I settle a hand on her knee. "You owe me no explanations."

"Yes, I do. Lachlan—" Whatever she'd meant to say is cut off by a sharp intake of breath. Her eyes are glistening again, and I can tell she's fighting the tears. Though I want to drag her into my arms and kiss away her pain, I know that's the last thing I should do. So I squeeze her knee instead.

"I'm in trouble," she says. "It's bad, and I don't see any way out of it."

Erica shifts her weight side to side, edging closer to me though I don't think she realizes she's done that.

I glide my palm up to her thigh.

She stares at my hand, not speaking for several seconds, then she lifts her gaze to mine. "I trusted the wrong man. He was one of those hot guys who turn into hot messes. He charmed me, and I fell for it hook, line, and sinker—except this hook ripped me apart from the inside out."

Anything I might say would sound trite, so I don't speak. I will let her tell the story in her own way and in her own time. But I do clasp her hands and keep my focus on her.

"I was involved with Presley Cichon. He seduced me, and I believed every honeyed word he fed me." She shakes her head, her lips curling slightly in a rueful expression. "I should've known he was using me. Chicago's most eligible bachelor wouldn't date an accounting nerd."

"Nerd?" I spit, then touch my lips to the back of her hand. "I told you never to call yourself that again. You are a stunning, sensual woman. The kind any man would be fortunate to take as a wife."

Her eyes flare wide, and she doesn't blink or move, her mouth partway open.

What did I say that stunned her? The truth smacks me in the face. I said any man would be fortunate to have her as a wife. I didn't mean I want to marry her, though she must have assumed I did mean that.

Erica shakes off her shock and continues. "Anyway, Presley comes from a rich family. Old money, the kind that buys anything and anyone, and I guess I let myself be seduced by the luxury of wealth too. I slept with him, gave him all my trust, let myself be happy with this amazing guy. Only he wasn't amazing." Her shoulders crumple, and she slants forward, catching her forehead in her palm. When she speaks again, her voice quivers and her tone is rife with pain. "He was a goddamn fucking liar."

My entire body tenses, and I compress my lips. That bastard Presley should be the one who's anguished, not Erica. He used and discarded her like rubbish.

"What did he do to you?" I ask carefully.

"I worked for his family's accounting firm, one of many businesses they own. His mother put him in charge of the firm after he got his MBA because she thought the job would force him to grow up. That's where I met him." She lifts her other hand to cover her forehead with both palms. "I should've known better than to date my boss."

"You did nothing wrong."

"That's not what everyone else thinks." She grasps her upper arms. "Presley embezzled a quarter of a million dollars from a dozen of the firm's clients, all of them senior citizens. He framed me for the crime. The day after I was arrested, when I got out on bond, Presley tracked me down and bragged about how he set me up. It was my word against his, and the Cichon family is connected everywhere. I'm screwed." She hugs herself tight and rocks a wee bit. "And it's my own fault."

I grind my teeth, my hand on her thigh curling into a fist.

"Presley kept asking to use my computer, said his was glitching, and I... I am such an idiot. I gave him the password for my work computer." Tears escape her lids to trickle down her face. She sniffles and swipes at her eyes with the back of her hand. "About a month ago, someone gave the police an anonymous tip that I was embezzling funds from the firm. Since Presley used my computer, it looked like I was guilty. I told the DA my suspicions about Presley, but there was no evidence. All of it pointed to me. When the shit hit the fan, Presley came out smelling like fresh linen and I stank of guilt." She sniffles again, her whole body trembling while the tears flow faster. "I was fired. They're pursuing criminal charges. I found a lawyer to take me on pro bono, but she doesn't have the resources to investigate Presley. Odds are, I'll go to prison—unless I take a plea deal, which I will not do because it means admitting I'm guilty. So, it's off to the big house for me."

I drag her onto my lap, enfolding her in my arms and cradling her to my chest. The tears pour out. She buries her face against my neck and clings to me like she never wants to let go. I stroke her hair, murmuring words that might not actually be words. I have no idea what I'm saying, only that I need to comfort her. Christ, she's been betrayed and used so badly that it's no wonder our arrangement distresses her.

"You're staying with me tonight, not here," I say. "Then I'm hiring you the best bloody solicitor in the world."

Her head pops up, and she gazes at me through a haze of tears. "Solicitor?"

"A lawyer. To defend you."

Sniffling, she shakes her head. "I like Doretta. I'm not firing her. And besides, I can't let you do that. I didn't tell you about this so you'd give me money. Considering you attacked Presley to protect me—three times—I needed to tell you the truth. But this is my mess, not yours."

"Wrong." I cradle her in my arms, slanting my head down until our noses touch. "This is Presley Cichon's mess. And he will pay for what he's done. I'll make damn sure of it."

She rubs her eyes and pushes off my lap. "You're leaving in four days."

"No." I swing my legs off the bed, turning my back to Erica, and snatch my mobile off the table. "I won't leave until you're settled."

Glancing over my shoulder, I see her retreating into the bathroom.

That pang I've been getting often lately throbs in my chest even harder than before. Can I leave her once we've sorted her legal mess?

I have no fucking idea anymore.

Seconds after Erica hurries out of the room, I realize I can't ring Rory to ask for his help with Erica's problems. It's the middle of the night in Scotland. I'll have to wait until morning, Chicago time. Since I can't do anything else at the moment, I head for the kitchen, intending to make something for us to eat. Something light. A wee piece will do.

When I walk into the kitchen, I notice her laptop computer sitting on the counter. That wouldn't seem strange, except that the laptop has its lid flipped up, and it looks like someone has been working on the computer. Erica just came home and hasn't had time to sneak away to surf the web.

I perch on a stool at the counter where the laptop awaits me. On the screen, I see web pages that someone has opened. It must have been Presley Cichon, though I can't imagine why he would want to rifle through Erica's computer.

My jaw starts to ache, but when I rub it, that makes it hurt even more. I gently palpate the area. I've got a swollen sore spot where that *cacan* hit me.

Erica walks into the kitchen and stops when she sees me. After a few seconds of just standing there, she goes to the refrigerator and nabs a bag of frozen peas from the freezer. My gaze now fixated on the computer screen, I barely glance at Erica when she presses the bag of peas to my jaw.

I place a hand over the bag, though my gaze returns to the computer screen. "Thank you."

She climbs onto the stool across the island from me. "What are you doing with my computer?"

"Not framing you for a crime, that's for certain."

Erica sits up straighter and folds her arms on the island. She's smiling at me.

I arch an eyebrow. "What are you smiling for?"

Her expression broadens into a grin. "I was remembering all the times you beat on Presley."

"And that makes you happy?"

"Mm-hm." She swivels her stool back and forth. "Nobody's ever tackled anyone for me before. A chivalrous, attack-ready man like you must be very popular with the lasses in Scotland. No matter what we might say, women all fantasize about men who'll skelp scunners for us."

I rub my neck, averting my eyes. "I don't make a habit of it."

"Still, you must have to beat the ladies off with a caber."

I grimace, then spin the laptop so the screen faces her. "I know what the bawbag was doing here."

She squints at the screen which displays a travel booking website. "I don't get it."

"Look." I point at the middle of the screen. "Either you were planning a trip to Switzerland and paused in the midst of making the reservations to go on a road trip with me, or that filthy snake was making your travel arrangements for you."

She leans forward to study the computer screen, her brows rising.

Aye, the scunner had not only opened an account on the travel website in her name, but he'd also started the process of booking a flight to Switzerland for tomorrow afternoon.

"What's the point of this?" Erica asks. "I doubt he was surprising me with a free trip to Geneva."

"I found something else too." I hold up a flash drive no bigger than my thumbnail. "I interrupted him before he could get this back. It was still plugged into your computer. The files on here would've made it look like you had a Swiss bank account with a quarter-million dollars in it. I checked, but he didn't get a chance to transfer the files to your computer."

"That sneaky, conniving little scumbag." She stomps her foot on the stool rung. "Gah! No wonder he was so intent on getting into my house. He's not done framing me." She grips the edge of the island. "I bet he was planning another anonymous tip to the police. Hey guys, she's about to bolt for a neutral country." Erica kicks the island, wincing briefly. "My bail would be revoked. I'd have no chance of finding any evidence to implicate him."

"That will not happen." I stretch my arms across the island to cover her hands with mine. "You have my word."

"Lachlan, I can't let you—"

"Aye, you can and you will." I roll my shoulders back and look directly into her eyes. "This is not charity. I help my friends when they're in need."

"Thought I was your fling."

I cradle her hands between mine. "You are my *gràidh*, Erica. And I will help you whether you like it or not."

She hesitates, but only for a second. "Okay. I accept your money and your investigators and whatever you give me. I do want to keep Doretta as my lawyer, though."

"Fine."

"Thank you, Lachlan."

Why do I feel relieved that she's agreed to accept my help?

I march around the island to pull her into my arms. With her body nestled against mine, I comb my fingers through her hair and feel all the tension inside me melting away. "Anything for you, *mo leannan*."

She hugs me like she never wants to let go. "Don't leave me, Lachlan. I love you."

Chapter Twenty-Seven

I freeze and stop breathing too, so stunned by her words that I can't think of what to say even if I could speak. My heart is pounding. All because she said the L-word? Christ, I wish she hadn't said that, but I also wish she'd say it again. She shouldn't repeat it. Even if I want to be with her permanently—and I have no ruddy idea how I feel about that—I can't drag her into the disaster my life has become.

Erica lifts her head just enough that she can shake it, her hair flapping around her face. "I-I didn't mean to say that. Forget it. I'm still in shock from all the Presley stuff and I—"

"Hush, Erica," I say in the calmest tone I can marshal, since everything inside me has gone cold, from my skin down to my bones. "I won't hold you to anything you say tonight."

She grabs fistfuls of my shirt and shakes me, anger twisting her bonnie face. "You know what? Forget what I said about forgetting what I said."

"Your bum's oot the windae again."

"No." She raises onto her tiptoes to level our gazes. "I love you, Lachlan. I don't want you to go home unless I can go with you. Stay with me, or take me with you."

The coldness inside me has plunged into the subzero range, and I feel stiff, like icicles have formed all over my body. I struggle to breathe, but I swear there's a massive iron weight crushing my chest. I stare at Erica, though I can't even blink, and my eyes start to burn. My throat has constricted, and my mouth has gone dry.

Finally, my lids slide closed. At least now I don't have to see the look on her face—anger and pain mixed with a deeper, more intense emotion than I've ever witnessed from anyone.

She cannae love me.

My shoulders collapse. My jaw goes slack, and I stumble backward with my arms raised partway, as if I can steady myself that way, but I can't. I retreat so abruptly that Erica loses her balance and careens into the island.

I hoist my head up, though it seems to weigh ten times more than it should, and I look at Erica. Her anguish shows on her face, which stabs a pang into my heart. I take a tentative step toward her, reaching out, but then let my hand fall before I've even grazed her skin. My arms hang limp at my sides. "I'm sorry, Erica. I can't stay with you."

Speaking those words breaks something deep inside me, but for her sake, I have to do this.

Erica shoves away from the island and rolls her shoulders back, chin lifted, though her eyes shimmer with burgeoning tears. "Yes, you can. If you want to."

I swallow, trying to get rid of this lump in my throat, but it won't budge.

She rubs her palms on her jeans as if she's got something on them, then she crosses her arms only to uncross them half a second later. "Do you want to stay with me?"

I shift my weight from one foot to the other and back again, almost rocking in place, and rub the back of my neck. *Tell her yes*, a part of me commands. That voice is too small and weak to hold any sway. All I can hear in my mind is Aisley's voice telling me what a bloody awful husband I was to her.

You're a worthless coward, Lachlan, and sex with you was like shagging a sloth. Go on, run back to your precious Ballachulish. You won't find another woman who will put up with you.

Aye, Aisley had spoken those words two days before I left her. What if I stay with Erica and after a few weeks or months she realizes she can't stand me either?

"Well?" Erica demands. "Do you want to be with me? Do you love me?"

What I feel doesn't matter. I've ceased my restless movements, and I swivel my gaze toward her. I hardly recognize my voice when I speak. It's rough and unsteady. "I cannae stay."

"Yes. You. Can."

"Aye." I drop my chin to my chest, locking both hands behind my head. "I owe you no explanations, just as you owed me none."

"Very clever," she says in a hard tone, though her voice quivers the tiniest bit. "By telling me I owed you no explanations, you freed yourself from any similar obligations to me. Presley Cichon would approve."

I jerk my head up, my jaw clenched. "I am nothing like him."

"Really." She rests a hand on the island's rim, tapping one finger on the surface. "Why did you call me your woman? Why tell me I'm more than a fling, I'm your *gràidh*? What the hell was all that about?"

"You are more."

"I'm beginning to understand why your ex-wife thinks you're a bastard."

I flinch. "Donnae talk about things ye cannae understand."

"Then explain it. I just poured my heart out to you and got skelped with a caber for it."

"Forget the bleeding caber and skelping." I rush toward Erica and pen her between my body and the island with my hands rooted on the countertop at either side of her. "Listen, because I'll tell you this only once. Aisley, my wife, was a posh lass from the day I met her. Not wealthy, but elegant. Her hair had to be perfect and if the wind touched it, she had to fix it. She pursued me, a flattering event for any man. But after we were married, she stopped flattering me."

Erica cranes her neck to meet my gaze.

I bend my head near her ear. "On our first anniversary, she told me I was a bore, and I wasn't delivering the excitement she needed. I'd suspected she was unhappy for some time, but whenever I tried to talk to her about it, she laughed it off as nothing." I brace my forehead on her shoulder for the space of two slow breaths, then raise my head and level my gaze on hers. "That's when it started. The little jibes, the constant complaints, the endless demands for more, no matter how much I gave her. A man can only take so much. I…" Swallowing hard, I turn my head away. "Before Aisley, I was what Americans might call a macho man. I won the caber toss often. I'm not saying this to impress you, but to help you understand. Aisley turned me into a weakling. I began to believe her complaints about me, and I tried to be what she wanted, but I never could please her. The last strong act I managed was moving us to Inverness. She hated the Highlands, so things only got worse after that."

The entire world seems to have frozen, and the only sound I hear is the faint ticking of the clock on the wall above the sink.

I lean into the island, head down, my lips achingly close to hers. "One day, Aisley announced she'd had enough and was leaving. I asked why. She told me I was a right bastard because I'd failed to give her the excitement she needed, in bed and in life in general. She wanted to travel to exotic places, make love in public, drink and smoke and experiment with shamans' drugs." I give a harsh laugh. "I'd no clue she craved such things. For pity's sake, I thought we had a good life together. And now she tells me she wants a hedonistic life of traipsing around the world. We didn't have the money for that, not yet, and besides—" I shut my eyes and shake my head, then tip my head forward. "I like my simple life in the Highlands."

Aye, all I want is the simple life I've craved for twelve years. Longer, actually. But I let Aisley ruin me, and I don't know if I can recover from that. There will be no more picnics on the beach or road trips to see silly statues. There will be no more nights of making love to Erica or days spent making her smile. Never again will I cradle her in my arms. Never again.

I can't look at Erica while I tell her the rest. "Aisley changed her mind about leaving when she realized my financial consulting business was becoming successful. She seduced me into taking her back for another three years." I start to turn my head but stop, bumping my nose into hers. "It was hell. I will never go down that road again."

"Oh, Lachlan." Erica loops her arms around my neck, caressing my skin with her fingertips. "I'm so sorry for what you went through."

My breathing has grown labored, blowing over her face and fluttering her hair. I feel like I can't pull in a full breath, like that weight has gotten even heavier. Awareness of Erica shivers over my skin, awareness of her attention on me and her body so close to mine with the scent of her surrounding me. I long to bury my face in her hair and hold her close forever.

Of its own volition, my left hand sneaks onto her back to draw her closer to me. "Erica, don't ye see." I face her at last, my lips grazing hers. "I cannae be with ye in the way ye want. I told ye no relationships."

"I don't—"

I crush my mouth to hers in a bruising kiss, lashing my tongue against hers, demanding a response that she gives without reservation. I feel lightheaded and weighed down simultaneously, but I can't stop myself from deepening the kiss with a fervor that transforms into desperation so intense it tears at my soul. *Speak the words*, that voice in my mind urges. *Tell her now before it's too late.*

I wrench my mouth away from hers. "Ye know the rules, Erica."

No, those aren't the words I'd longed to say. But it's what I have to tell her.

She shoves me away. "The rules? Are you kidding me? Screw your rules, just tell me what you feel."

"I told you."

"You think I'm like her. Your bitch ex-wife."

"She's not my ex-wife. We're still married."

Erica stares at me, slack-jawed. "You said you were divorced."

"You assumed I was. I never said it."

"But…you let me go on believing it. That's the same as lying."

"No, Erica. It was the rules. Nothing personal, remember? You agreed to it."

She flinches as if I've struck her. "I'm surprised you didn't make me sign a contract. A formal tryst agreement. Then again, you would've included all your loopholes in that too. You're a liar."

"I didn't lie." Maybe I had misled her, but I can't change that now. I take a shuffling step toward her. When she raises a warning hand, I halt. "I thought we were divorced but there was a clerical error. Aisley's taking advantage of it to renegotiate our divorce settlement. She wants everything."

"If she's taking you to the cleaners, how did you plan on paying for top-notch investigators to clear my name?"

"I said Aisley *wants* everything. She's not getting it."

"Congratulations. You screwed over another woman." Erica moves toward the doorway, but I seize her arm to stop her. She does not glance at me. "If you think I'm like her, why are you helping me?"

"You are nothing like her. I know it."

"You talked me into a fling," she says, her voice strained and unsteady. "You said all those sweet things to me. And the first night at the bed-and-breakfast, you made love to me." She throws me a sidelong look. "It wasn't just hot sex. You *made love* to me."

My fingers tighten on her arm because, aye, she's right. I had made love to her in the truest sense of the phrase. I'd worshiped her, body and soul.

She searches my face, but seems not to find what she wants to see in me. "You led me on, Lachlan. You used my body and broke my heart."

I release her arm and brush the backs of my fingers over her cheek. "These weeks with you were the best of my life. But you're better off without me." I let my hand drop to my side. "I've nothing left to give, except money."

"You are a bastard."

"Aye."

What else can I say? Nothing that matters. I brush past her and hurry out of the kitchen. As I race out the front door, slamming it shut behind me, I know only one thing for certain.

I will love Erica Teague for the rest of my life.

<h1 style="text-align:center">Chapter Twenty-Eight</h1>

I fly home three hours after I walked away from Erica. Every airline is booked up for today, so I can't get a commercial ticket back to Scotland. I don't want to wait until tomorrow. Staying in America after shattering Erica's heart seems…unkind. Even if she will never know I didn't leave immediately. I suppose that's my guilt talking. Whatever the cause of my need to flee as quickly as possible, I charter a private jet to get myself home today. I pay hefty fees to make that happen, but I don't care about money.

Being alone in a Gulfstream jet for seven hours leaves me with nothing to do except think about Erica. I see her face in my mind, over and over, wrenched with agony when I'd told her I couldn't stay. Her words echo in my mind.

Don't leave me, Lachlan. I love you.

I grip the arms of my seat hard enough to make my knuckles hurt. Do I love her? Of course I do, but I hadn't realized that until after I walked out the door. Maybe I should have turned around and run back into the house to throw my arms around her and say those three words. But I couldn't do it. Not after everything I'd said and done.

You're a liar. Erica said that, and it's true. Not in the way she meant it, though. I couldn't bring myself to tell her how much I love her and implied I didn't want to stay with her. Those were lies, of a sort. I misled her, for certain.

Why did you call me your woman? Why tell me I'm more than a fling, I'm your gràidh? What the hell was all that about?

I'd meant every sweet word I ever whispered to her. I meant it when I made love to her at the bed-and-breakfast. Why else would I care so much about making her feel better and helping her with her legal problems? I've been in love with her for a while, possibly since the night we met. But Aisley had inflicted too many wounds, and I couldn't see past the pain and humiliation to recognize it when I had a good woman in front of me, a lass who loves me as I am, wounds and all.

Do you want to be with me? Do you love me?

When Erica asked me that, she hadn't sounded angry. Her voice had overflowed with the same sort of pain and fear I've lived with ever since the day I married Aisley. The question is no longer whether I love Erica, but whether she can ever love me again.

I lean forward, resting my elbows on my knees, and bury my face in my upraised palms. I suck in shaky breaths, but I can't erase from my mind the image of Erica's anguished expression the last time I'd looked at her.

My mobile rings.

Slumping back in my chair, I fish the mobile out of my pocket. "What is it now, Rory?"

"Are you all right, Lachlan? You sound…rough."

Because I just walked away from the only woman I've ever really loved, and now she hates me.

I groan. "Do you want something? Or is this a harassment call?"

"You haven't responded to my text. Did you receive it?"

"Aye."

"That's your only response? Aye?" Rory sighs, and I can picture him sitting at his desk in his office in his castle, frowning at me. "We need to formulate a response."

"I know exactly how to respond. Tell that slag she can rot in hell because she will not get one shilling of my money."

Rory falls silent for a moment, then he speaks carefully. "What has happened? You don't sound like yourself."

"I've gone off my head, that's what happened."

"Chicago didn't agree with you?"

Grunting, I push up out of my chair and begin to pace the aisle that separates the two sides of the jet. "You don't want to know what I've done, Rory. But it boils down to this. I met a bonnie, sweet lass who loves me, and then I broke her heart."

"I see. Do you love her?"

Do you want to be with me? Do you love me? Erica's plea resounds through my mind. I stop in the middle of the aisle and stare into space. "Aye, Rory. I love her."

"Then get her back."

"Why is the Ogre of Loch Fairbairn ordering me to get Erica back? You think marriage is rubbish, and I'm fair certain I shouldn't take advice from a man who's been divorced three times."

Rory growls softly, like a true ogre. "I may not want to marry again or date or—Well, you know what I'm like. But you are not me, Lachlan. You want to share a life with a good woman, so don't cock up your last chance at happiness."

My last chance? He seems to be implying I will never find another woman who will put up with me. Maybe I never will. Erica agreed to my barmy rules and lived with my secrets, then was willing to give it another go even after I told her I couldn't stay. She shared more of herself with me than I had shared with her, but still, she stayed with me. And begged me to do the same.

Bloody hell. I am a damn eejit.

"You're right, Rory," I say. "But I don't know if Erica can ever forgive me for what I've done."

"How will you know if you don't try?"

"I just do." I should give Erica time, shouldn't I? I can't waltz back into her life ten minutes after crushing her heart. And I need time too—so I can sort my life. But I also made her a promise, one I intend to keep. "I need your help to get her back, Rory. Erica is about to go on trial for a crime her ex-lover committed. I promised to fix this for her. Please, I need my solicitor's help."

"We will fix it. You have my word on that." A shuffling noise follows, as if Rory is searching through papers to find what he needs. "I'll call my investigator immediately and get the ball rolling. Now, tell me everything about Erica's legal troubles."

For the next fifteen minutes, I do just that.

And for two days, I focus on figuring out how to prove to Erica that I love her and will never abandon her again. I've never tried to win a woman back. With Rory on the job, I know I don't need to do anything except pay the bills for however many investigators, lawyers, and whoever else my brother needs to hire to save Erica from a false conviction. That leaves me with the even more difficult task of getting her back.

The answer comes to me on the day after I abandoned Erica. I need Rory's help again, but only to find me a telephone number this time. He does it without asking why. That's how MacTaggarts are. We stand by each other no matter what, and that's especially true of my immediate family—my parents, my two brothers, and my three sisters.

So now, I'm sitting in the living room of my house in Inverness holding a piece of paper in one hand and my mobile in the other, trying to summon the nerve to make the call. I stare at those digits for several minutes, until my vision blurs. Blinking to clear the haze, I sit up straighter and dial the number.

"Hello," a cheery woman's voice says.

"Ah, hello, Mrs. Teague. My name is Lachlan MacTaggart." I wince and scratch my neck. "I'm, ah, Erica's friend. We spoke on the phone once."

"Oh yes, I remember. What can I do for you, sweetie?"

Sweetie? I suppose Erica hasn't told her parents about the way we ended things.

"I'm worried about Erica," I say. "She's in trouble and needs you. I know I'm a stranger, and you have no reason to believe what I say, but I'm not exaggerating. Erica is in trouble. Please go to her. She shouldn't be alone right now."

"Aren't you with her?"

"No, I—" Fucked it up so badly I can't face her yet, and besides, she'll probably skelp me with a caber when she sees me. "I wish I could be there, but we had a falling out. I don't think she'll want to see me, not yet. She needs you."

"I'm putting you on speaker, Lachlan. Frank, come over here."

Shuffling noises follow, then a man's voice comes on the line. "What's going on, Deb?"

"Lachlan MacTaggart is on the phone. I've got him on speaker, honey, so you can talk to him too. He says Erica is in trouble."

"What have you done to my little girl?" Frank Teague demands.

"I haven't rung you to talk about my relationship with Erica. As I told your wife, Erica is in serious legal trouble, and she needs you both. Please, you must go to Chicago. I will pay for your airline tickets. Say you'll do this—for Erica, not for me."

"A strange man calls and orders us to do stuff for him," Frank says. "Yeah, that's not suspicious at all."

"Please, Mr. Teague. I willnae hang up until you both agree to go to Erica. I'll pay for you to fly first class."

"First class?" Deb says. "We can't say no to that. Can we, Frank? Besides, if there's even a sliver of a chance that Erica really is in trouble, we can't not go."

"Guess not. Okay, Lachlan, buy us those plane tickets."

"I'll ring you back as soon as I've arranged for your flight."

We say goodbye, and relief rushes through me so powerfully that I drop onto the nearest chair and let out the breath I hadn't realized I'd been holding. Erica won't be alone. At least I've done that much for her.

How long do I need to wait for Erica to recover from what I've done to her?

Mrs. Teague texts me the next morning to let me know they have arrived in Chicago. Erica will have someone there to support her through her ordeal. Rory rings me that afternoon with assurances that Erica's legal problems are solvable and he and his associates are working on it. Rory has no employees, but he's cultivated a network of professionals who help each other on tough cases. He even knows a bloke at the Home Office.

A few days after Erica's parents arrived in Chicago, I get an email from FedEx informing me that my package has been delivered to Erica. Will she even open the envelope? It has my name in the return address, after all. Maybe I should've written something poetic and full of emotional rubbish, but I couldn't make myself do that. It's too soon, isn't it? I kept my message short and to the point.

I'm sorry, it said.

My note had been accompanied by a sprig of bell heather—*Erica cinerea*. I hope she remembers the flower's name and understands its meaning. Though I want to know that she understood, it's still too soon to ring her or email her or show up on her doorstep.

But heaven help me, I want to do that so badly that restraining the impulse hurts deep inside me.

A few hours later, Deb Teague rings me.

"How is Erica?" I ask before she can speak.

"She's doing all right, considering. Your note and flower made her cry."

"I shouldn't have sent it. Sorry. I'm no good at figuring out what women want."

Mrs. Teague laughs, but it's an affectionate sound. "Crying means she loved it, Lachlan. Trust me. If she hated your guts, she would've burned the flower and the note, then poured holy water on the ashes."

"I see." No, I don't, but it would be impolite to question her statement. At least Erica doesn't despise me, apparently. "Thank you for calling to let me know, Mrs. Teague."

"Call me Deb. Though I have a feeling you'll be calling me Mom before long."

"Not sure about that. Erica shouldn't forgive me, even if she wants to."

"Unless you framed her for a crime, you deserve forgiveness for whatever happened between you two." She pauses as if she's deciding how to phrase her next words. "Erica loves you, Lachlan. Anyone can see that. Just give it time."

"I'm trying to do that."

"Good. In the meantime, you can call me and Frank anytime for Erica updates or just to talk."

"Would every day be too often?"

She laughs again. "Call us five times a day, I don't mind. Frank might give up after a while and go watch TV, but I'd love to listen to your voice all day long."

I can't help chuckling. "Thank you, Deb. You and Frank have been kinder to me than you should, but I appreciate it."

We chat a bit more, then say goodbye. As the days flow onward, one melting into the next, I develop a routine of ringing Erica's parents every morning to check on things. All right, it's to check on Erica, and Deb and Frank know that. They humor me, though. And I think Frank might be warming up to me. He hadn't been rude before now, but at first, he didn't say much during our daily calls. Deb did most of the talking, and bloody hell, can that woman blether. I need a lie-down after every phone call, but I don't mind. I like Erica's parents very much, and I'm starting to feel like they're my family too.

Rory keeps me apprised of everything to do with Erica's court case. I speak with her attorney, Doretta Harper, multiple times. The woman doesn't seem to mind, and she clearly knows the law inside and out, which gives me hope that with Rory's help, she can save Erica from going to prison. Doretta also informs me of the date for the hearing where she will argue for a complete dismissal of the charges against Erica.

For two days, I try to talk myself out of going to America so I can be there to witness Erica's exoneration. I pace and back and forth in my living room so often and for so long that I think I must've worn a path in the wood floor. I haven't, of course. Finally, I can't hold myself back any longer. I fly to Chicago.

I arrive just in time for the hearing and sneak into the courtroom, sitting in the back row, near the corner, where Erica will be unlikely to see me. She must not want to, anyway. Since I'm meant to be giving her time to heal, I shouldn't have come to court. But I need to see her again, after all these uncounted days without her.

Erica wears a plain pantsuit, dark blue, appropriately somber for the courtroom. Even dressed that way, though, she is the sexiest woman in the world.

Perched on the edge of my chair, I listen intently as the judge issues his decision.

All charges dismissed. Erica is free.

Doretta drags Erica in for a big hug, and they both start laughing. Tears stream down Erica's cheeks, but this time, they're tears of joy. Her grin seems to light up the entire courtroom. That's barmy, but it's how I feel when I see that expression on her face. The only other time I've seen her smile like that was when I pretended to battle with a giant statue of Paul Bunyan.

My chest aches. My throat constricts. I want to go over there, pull Erica into my arms, and kiss her senseless. But I can't. Not yet.

Erica scans the courtroom with her gaze as if she's searching for someone. Her focus veers in my direction.

I hurry out of the courtroom, fairly certain she didn't see me. I wish she had. If she did see me, she doesn't run after me. Does that mean she still hasn't recovered from how badly I hurt her?

After leaving the courthouse, I make one stop on my way to the airport. All right, it's not quite on the way. Erica's house is in the precisely opposite direction from the airport, but I go there anyway to leave a gift on her doorstep. Maybe I shouldn't do that. I tried to talk myself out of it at least fifty times, but my heart overruled logic. I set the glass vase of flowers on her doorstep.

A handful of bell heather nestles among a dozen pink roses.

I haven't left a note. Not sure what I could've said. I hope she understands this is my way of congratulating her on the court decision and wishing her every good thing she deserves.

The next day, while I'm home in Scotland, another gift I chose for Erica is delivered to her home. While I waited in the Chicago airport for my flight to start boarding, an idea had struck me. I placed an order over the internet, choosing overnight shipping. She has received a bottle of Talisker and a note from me that says, "To celebrate your freedom. Congratulations, *gràidh*."

Not long after Erica's victory, I realize I need to make some changes in my life if I want to prove to Erica that I am committed to winning her back. My life hasn't been satisfying for a long time, and even my job doesn't fulfill me the way it once had. How can I promise Erica a happy life with me if I'm not happy? I won't be truly happy again until she's with me, but I can implement changes to start my journey to recovery. Aisley did more damage than I've wanted to admit—until that day in Erica's kitchen when I confessed everything. No one else on earth knows about the hell Aisley put me through or how I let her beat me down with her words and actions.

No more.

My plan is simple—finalize my divorce, rid myself of the past, and then beg Erica to take me back.

Rory laughs when I tell him that, but he's not being an ersehole. He thinks it's amusing that I've made a plan to win back the woman I love. Cannae see what's funny about it, but younger brothers can be strange and bloody irritating.

I sell my business. I sell my house in Inverness. I give up the lease on my Edinburgh apartment. Since I filed for divorce with adultery as the grounds for the dissolution of our marriage, I had to prove Aisley cheated. Rory's investigator found ample proof of that. I hadn't wanted to tell anyone about the adultery, but I needed to give grounds for the divorce and so I'd told Rory back when I first filed, though I asked him not to press the issue unless it became necessary. With the evidence the investigator found, we had more than enough leverage to stop my wife from stealing everything I own. Aisley will receive the proceeds from selling the Inverness house, and I gave her the lease for the Edinburgh flat.

She gave up on trying to get her greedy hands on the money I earned from my business. Even Aisley didn't want to go to court to explain why she cheated on me so many times, more than even I'd known.

Now, I am divorced. Officially and forever.

For the moment, I'm living with Rory in his castle, Dùndubhan. Aye, my younger brother owns a medieval castle not far from Ballachulish, where we both grew up. The nearest village to Rory's home is Loch Fairbairn, where he has his office. Rory doesn't like visitors, as a rule, but he volunteers to take me in once I tell him my plan to divest myself of everything that reminds me of my old life.

When I tell him about my latest gift to Erica, Rory laughs even harder.

I scowl at him while we're sitting at the dining-room table enjoying a bloody good meal prepared by his housekeeper, Mrs. Darroch. "Why are you laughing, Rory?"

"Because you think arranging a job for Erica will make her love you. She might be slightly annoyed when she finds out. Or she might batter you with a blunt object."

"Why? I've done this to help her. That *cacan* Presley Cichon comes from a powerful family, and they might blacklist her or…something."

Rory shrugs and goes back to eating his meal.

I call Deb Teague later that evening, and she informs me Erica turned down the job—but not because I arranged it for her. "She doesn't want to be an accountant anymore."

"That's not surprising. She told me it wasn't her dream job. What does she want to do now? I can help—"

"Give it time, Lachlan. She's been through a lot. Let the girl decompress before you pull more strings to find a new career for her."

"Sorry. I know you're right."

A few weeks later, Deb rings me with shocking news. "I thought you'd want to know. Erica went to see Presley Cichon today. He was arrested for the crime he tried to frame Erica for, and now that he's out on bond, he asked if she would visit him at home."

"What did the scunner want?"

"To apologize. His parents have taken away his trust fund, and he's now living with his sister and her children. Presley's parents are paying Erica a settlement to compensate her for everything he did to her. Not that money can change that."

I wince. That's what I've been doing, isn't it? Trying to buy her forgiveness with lawyers and gifts and bloody stupid notes. None of that matters, does it? The answer is no. I need to tell her how I feel, face to face.

Eight weeks is long enough to wait.

"Thank you for letting me know, Deb," I say. "But I need to say goodbye so I can make arrangements to fly to America."

"About damn time." She says those words with affection. "Get your butt over here, Lachlan. You two have sulked for long enough."

"Aye, we have. It's time for action."

"Good boy."

Three hours later, I'm on a jet and in the air, flying to Erica.

Chapter Twenty-Nine

The next morning, at ten o'clock Chicago time, I walk up the concrete path to Erica's door. I'd arrived in America at seven o'clock UK time, but that meant it was one a.m. local time, so I had to wait until I knew Erica would be awake. Aye, she would've woken up well before ten, but I wasted a ridiculous amount of time deciding what to wear and what to say once I see her. The clothing I sorted. As for what to say…

I haven't got a bloody clue.

Casey starts barking on the other side of the door, but it sounds like a happy bark, not the way he snarled at the *cacan* Presley. Casey's barking becomes whimpering and then he gives a little chuff like he can't wait for his mistress to open the door.

It swings inward, and I see Erica for the first time in two months. Watching her from afar in the courtroom didn't count.

She smiles, but it's a bland expression she might give to a stranger. She stands straight as a board, her shoulders back.

I'm standing the same way, but it's anxiety tightening my whole body. My pulse beats so fast I feel slightly weak in the knees, and I have to remind myself to breathe. Despite her impersonal demeanor, the sight of Erica makes me want to pull her into my arms and kiss her while spewing romantic nonsense about how much I love her.

She says nothing. Just gazes at me with dispassion.

I ball my hands into fists, then flex my fingers in an attempt to relax. "Good morning."

That's all I can manage to say.

"What do you want?" she asks.

Never have I heard Erica sound so…cool and unaffected.

It's bollocks. I know that. Still, my shoulders slump, and I shove a hand through my hair. "Please, Erica, let me talk to you. Please."

She wrenches the doorknob, fingers tight, the knob clicking with each half revolution, back and forth, back and forth. *Click, click, click.* She gnaws on the inside of her lip.

Casey pushes between us to leap up on me.

Well, at least the pup is glad to see me. Since Erica is still gnawing on her lip, I know her cool composure is an act. She must feel as anxious and confused as I do. I scratch behind Casey's ears, but it's a half-hearted reflex. The pup scampers back into the house and straight to the sofa where he jumps onto the cushions and plants his chin on the sofa's back, observing us.

Is that blood I see on her lip? I reach out to touch it, and my thumb comes away spotted with red. "You're bleeding."

"It's nothing."

My throat tightens as I run my thumb over her mouth. "Why are you chewing on your lip like this?" Suddenly, I realize the reason why she bites her lip so hard her teeth break the skin. "It's me."

Frozen, she stares up at me for several seconds without speaking. Then she utters three words. "Go away, Lachlan."

"Please, *gràidh.*" I stroke my thumb over her lip twice more. "Don't hurt yourself because of me."

She barks out a harsh laugh. "Hurt myself? I don't need to. You've done a rather spectacular job of it for me."

Can't speak. Can't move. *Go away, Lachlan,* she said. Although the words had stung like a physical slap, I hadn't gone icy cold until she told me I'd hurt her more than she could ever hurt herself. But I won't give up. There will be no more running away. I will not leave Chicago unless Erica goes with me, and whatever it takes, I will prove to her I will never cause her pain again.

She squeezes her eyes shut to stave off the tears pooling in her eyes. Her lip trembles under my thumb.

I move closer until our faces are inches apart and whisper, "Don't cry."

Erica cracks her lids open.

For eight weeks, I've stayed a literal ocean away from her. To be so close to her but not hold her in my arms hurts in a way that I've never experienced before, like I've found a lost treasure after decades of searching but I can't keep it.

With both hands, I cup her face as I gaze into her eyes and pray she recognizes the pain in mine that matches her own, the anguish I'm responsible for causing. I slide my hands into her hair, massaging her scalp with my fingers. "I made a horrible mistake, and I've regretted it every day since, more than you could possibly know." My voice broke, but I don't care. And I don't give a fuck that tears are gathering in my eyes, burning like acid. "I know I broke your heart but—"

"Broke my heart?" She sniffles, her tone no longer cool but racked with pain. "You destroyed me, Lachlan."

My chin drops to my chest. What else can I say? I've destroyed us both, but there must be a way to make things right.

Her body slants toward me.

I bend closer, my mouth millimeters from her ear. "Please give me a few minutes to explain why I treated you so terribly. I need you to understand."

"Your ex-wife's a raging bitch. I get it." Her voice has evened out, though tears still shine in her eyes.

"I was afraid, I admit it. What I feel for you is so strong, I can't control it." My hands find her upper arms, though I had no conscious thought to touch her, and my fingers knead her flesh gently. "I thought I needed control, to protect myself from being tricked again. But I was wrong. I don't want to be without you any-more, you're everything that's good in my life. I need you, *gràidh*."

"Stop calling me that." She shakes free of my hands, stumbling backward a step. "It's too late. Go back to Scotland and move on."

"I can't do that." Rolling my shoulders back, I straighten and fix my gaze on hers. "I won't pester you, but I'm not leaving town without you. I'll be staying at The Langham. You can reach me there or call my mobile."

"Don't hold your breath." She squints at me. "The Langham, huh? Guess you're done slumming it out here in the burbs."

I know she's insulting me only as a means of scaring me away, but it won't work. "I would've preferred to stay with Gil and Jayne, my good friends, but I didn't want to crowd you."

"Instead, you're hanging around to stalk me."

"Erica." I scrub a hand over my face, sighing. "I told you I won't both-er you."

"But you're not leaving town without me." She scrutinizes me for a mo-ment, her sharp gaze making my skin itch. "Go home, Lachlan."

"I am home." I capture a loose lock of her hair between my fingers, tuck-ing it behind her ear. "You are my home. I'll spend the rest of my life making up for what I did, making you happy—if you'll let me."

She says nothing, though she rubs her arms as if she's cold.

I trail a fingertip down her cheek. "I've waited two months, *mo leannan*, the worst months of my entire life. I'm not leaving you again. Not ever."

Her chest heaves as she inhales a ragged breath. "It's not enough. I can't—I won't—"

The time has come to prove to her I mean every word I've said, and I will do whatever it takes to convince her—even expose every raw nerve to her.

I fall to my knees at her feet, tipping my head forward until my forehead meets her belly. Then I grasp her hips to hold her to me with my face crushed against her body. "Give me one more chance. I don't deserve it, but I'm begging you, please. I won't bollocks it up this time. I swear to God, I will be the kind of man you need, the kind you deserve."

Her breaths come fast and shallow, audible to me even from down here. She sounds like she's about to cry. I tilt my head back until our gazes collide. She's holding a hand to her mouth while short breaths hiccup out of her.

I surge to my feet and pull her into my arms like I've dreamed of doing for eight weeks, then I bury my face in her hair, loving the sweet, familiar scent of her.

She sags into me briefly, then wrestles free of my embrace while swiping tears from her face. "No."

Though I had expected that response, it still hurts like a sword driven through my heart. I nod, my shoulders collapsing, and rub the heel of my hand on my chest. My words come out as a monotone. "If you want me, you know where I am."

I turn to leave and hear the door shut behind me. Aye, she rejected me. And aye, it hurts like hell. But I haven't flown thousands of miles across an ocean to give up now.

No matter what it takes, I will win back her trust.

Chapter Thirty

While I wait to find out if Erica will change her mind about us, I continue making plans for my new life—our new life, I hope. What else can I do? I have to keep a positive attitude and assume she will forgive me, eventually. In the meantime, I still have something to wrap up. That means I need to call Rory, but before I can do that, my youngest brother, Aidan, rings me.

"What's Chicago like?" he asks.

"It's fine."

"Maybe I should go there sometime. Must be lots of sexy girls there if you loved it so much you had to go for another holiday."

I groan because I know Aidan is being sarcastic. Mostly. "Not sure if I like it here. Depends on what happens next."

"Oh, you mean the lass you met there. If she takes you back, you'll stay. If not, you'll come home with your tail between your legs. Aye?"

"No." I hold the phone away from my face just long enough to frown at it as if Aidan might see that and decide to behave. Then I realize what his sarcasm means. "How do you know I met a lass?"

He chuckles. "Everyone thinks I'm the one who can't keep a secret, but it was Rory who let that piece of information slip. I asked him what you were doing in Chicago, and he… Well, he didn't exactly tell me everything, but I read between the lines."

I groan again. "Who did you tell?"

"No one. My lips are sealed, Lachie."

"How many times have I told you never to call me that?"

Aidan chuckles again. "Too many to count. Might as well give up trying, eh?"

"I have important…things to take care of. I'll talk to you later, Aidan."

"Give your mysterious lass a big kiss from me."

I hang up without responding to his suggestion. Aidan is fifteen years younger than I am, but he's still a grown man who should behave like an adult. He won't, though. Aidan loves tormenting the rest of us too much.

Now that I've hung up on my youngest brother, I ring Rory.

He answers with a growl. "What do ye want? It's two o'clock in the morning, Lachlan."

"Sorry. It's important. I need to know the status of that purchase. Please, Rory, I need to know now."

"I meant to ring you in the morning." Rustling sounds indicate my brother is getting out of bed or at least sitting up. He yawns. "The sale was finalized this afternoon. You know this. You signed the documents digitally."

"And you're sure? It's mine now?"

"*Bod an Donais.* Of course I'm sure. You won't be haunting my castle without any trousers on anymore."

"I did that once. Thought you were in your office in the village."

"Good night, Lachlan." Rory hangs up on me.

And I haunt my suite at The Langham with no trousers on, though nobody cares because no one sees me. When room service brings my meals, I wear trousers.

Two days after Erica sent me away, I'm just getting dressed after a shower when I hear something that makes me stop breathing, sure I must've hallucinated it.

"Lachlan? Are you in here?"

Erica's voice. I must be off my head so completely that I think I hear her voice when I know I couldn't have. I'd given the concierge instructions to bring her to my suite immediately if she turned up at the hotel asking for me. But that day on her porch, Erica essentially told me to sod off.

Has she finally forgiven me?

I yank my clothes on, then walk out of the bedroom and pull the door shut behind me, hurrying down the hallway toward the living room. It's no surprise she didn't knock considering my explicit instructions to the concierge. I slow my pace as I approach the living room, not wanting Erica to think I'm so desperate to see her that I'm racing down the hall. I suppose that's manly pride, which I've displayed too much of since the day I met Erica.

I cross through the foyer into the living room.

And she's there. Waiting for me. She looks as bonnie as ever in her white peasant blouse and blue jeans, and though I want to kiss her right now, I know I need to wait. She might be here strictly to inform me that she's obtained a court order to keep me away from her.

She's leaning against one of the two curved sofas in the living room, just past a pair of nested black tables. The sunshine beaming in through the floor-to-ceiling windows casts a heavenly glow on her skin and hair. Aye, she is an angel.

And I clipped her wings.

She pushes away from the sofa, barring her arms over her chest and lifting her chin.

Defiance looks good on her.

Seeing the lass again triggers a wave of elation so powerful that I can't stop myself from grinning at her like an eejit. "Erica, I'm so glad you're here."

I take a step toward her.

She stumbles backward, holding up a hand, palm out. "No. You stay over there."

My elation crumbles away. I'd known I would probably need to grovel again, but I hadn't expected her to refuse to come near me. This is part of my penance, and I will do whatever is necessary to prove my sincerity—even if that means standing ten feet away from her.

Hugging herself, she backs up another step and shoves her hands under her arms as if she's cold. Her face has a faint pallor that I hadn't noticed until I came closer.

"Are you ill?" I ask.

"No." Her legs quiver enough that I can see it, and her knees start to buckle, though she doesn't fall down. "I'm f—"

I start to move closer, needing to touch her, but I halt with one hand outstretched, suspended in midair between us. "Erica?"

She straightens and waves at the surroundings, speaking in a breezy tone that's not believable at all. "Thought you had simple tastes."

"I do." Lowering my hand slowly, I consider what this suite, the most expensive one in the most expensive hotel in Chicago, must seem like to her. "There are two conventions in town and baseball games too. This was the only room I could get."

"Poor you, stuck in this hovel."

My lips curve up at the corners. "You almost smiled. Teasing me is a good sign, I hope."

She hunches her shoulders, focusing on my chest instead of my face. "I saw Presley a few days ago."

I'd already known that since her mother informed me the other day. Ever since, I've wondered what on earth could've possessed her. I lock my arms over my chest and frown at her. "Why the bloody hell would you do that? After what he did to you."

She says nothing for a moment, but finally, she lifts her gaze to my face. "You thought Presley was doing to me what your wife did to you. That's why you attacked him repeatedly, why you would never speak his name, and why you're so upset I went to see him."

"Aye. Wasn't it obvious months ago?"

She flaps her arms and huffs. "No, not to me. If you wanted me to understand that, you should've told me, for heaven's sake. I'm not telepathic."

I bite into my upper lip, my shoulders flagging. "Aye, you're right. My fault."

"Good. We agree on one thing, anyway."

Though I bunch my shoulders, I try to remain calm. "I would like to know why you went to him. If you'll tell me. Please."

She swings her arms several times, then stuffs her hands into her jeans pockets. "He asked to see me, and I decided I should put that demon to rest." She kicks at the floor with the toe of her shoe while staring down at the beige carpeting. "He's out on bond, and his parents have taken away all his toys. He's broke." She hauls in a long breath, releasing it slowly as she raises her gaze to mine. "He apologized for framing me. Says he always loved me and he hopes I have a good life."

Every muscle in my body stiffens, and I compress my lips. "Does he."

"Yep." She rubs her arms. "Men are apologizing to me right and left these days."

I sit down on the opposite end of the sofa from her, slouching forward to brace my elbows on my knees, my focus nailed to her. "You must think I'm just like him. Insincere, lying, uncaring."

"Actually, I think Presley was being genuine."

"What about me?"

"I'm sure you mean everything you've said."

"But?"

She spins on her heels to face the wall of windows, then sucks in a big breath, releasing it little by little. With her hands still shoved into her jeans pockets, she regards the cityscape. "I've never thought you were like Presley. He abused my trust and didn't see the error of his ways until he got caught. You figured out you'd screwed up without needing to be arrested. Plus, you told me from the start you couldn't give me more than a fling."

Mhac na galla. I wish I had never spoken those words to her. *Be my American fling.* What a bloody stupid ersehole I am.

I push off the sofa and come up behind her, gazing at our reflections in the window, though I keep a small gap between us. "From the moment I saw you in the club, I wanted to give you more, give you everything. The second I left your house that day, I realized what a terrible mistake I'd made, but I hurt you too badly to run back inside and beg your forgiveness. Giving you time seemed like the best choice, the only choice. Erica, you are *mo leannan.*"

She turns around, her face level with my upper chest, standing no more than an arm's length away. Her gaze wanders over my entire body, and her tongue darts out to moisten her lips. She coughs and scuffles backward, smacking into the glass, then lays a hand over her collarbone. "You never told me what *mo leannan* means."

Though I reach out to touch her, I hover my fingers near her cheek only to withdraw my hand and curl my fingers into my palm. "It means my sweetheart."

She swings her gaze up to mine. "All this time you've been calling me your sweetheart? Why wouldn't you tell me?"

I lift a hand to her face, trailing my fingertips down the line of her jaw while excitement tingles over my skin simply because I'm touching her. "Didn't intend to call you *mo leannan*, or *gràidh*. Those words came out before I realized what I'd said. By then it was too late, and I couldn't keep from saying them over and over." I feather my fingertips over her lips before pulling them away. "I want to give you more than sweet words, though. I want to give you everything."

"I just… Not sure…"

She sways slightly, her face going pale—and her knees buckle.

I catch her before she hits the floor.

Her purse tumbles off her shoulder to drop onto the carpeting.

I sweep her up in my arms, the way I've wanted to do since the day I fell to my knees at her feet, and carry her out of the living room. Her eyes drift shut while her head lolls against my shoulder.

Christ, she must be ill. Why else would she pass out?

When I lay her down on the bed without bothering to pull the covers back, she mumbles so softly I almost don't hear it. I can't tell if she's asleep. Though I'm reluctant to move even one foot away from her, I hurry to the bathroom and get a cool cloth for her, then brace one knee on the bed while trying not to jostle her too much. Leaning over her, I place a hand on her forehead to check for a fever. She feels normal, not warm. Thank God for that. I settle the cool, damp cloth over her forehead. Will that help? I have no idea, but it's all I can think of to do for her.

She opens her eyes a sliver to gaze up at me.

I brush the back of my hand across her cheek. "Erica, sweet, how do you feel? I should call for a doctor."

"Uh-uh." She pulls in a deep breath. "I'm fine. Besides, doctors don't come running when you call."

"If I pay enough, one will."

"Please don't. I didn't eat enough breakfast, that's all."

I adjust the cloth on her forehead, then comb my fingers through her hair. "Passing out is not the sign of a well woman."

"I must have the flu."

"Hmm." I frown because that doesn't fit what I've seen. I sit beside her, my hip pressing against her thigh, and brace myself with one arm on the opposite side of her body. "You don't have a fever."

"Stop fussing, I'm perfectly fine."

"Fine?" I shake my head, though I can't help smiling a little. "Is that why you're flat on your back in bed?"

"How much does a suite like this go for?" she asks, glancing around at the posh bedroom.

I'm fair certain she asks that only to avoid explaining why she passed out. And I feel a touch anxious when I think about telling her. But I do owe her honesty from now on, so I avert my gaze and answer her question. "Six a night."

"Six hundred?"

I give a curt shake of my head, helpless to stop myself from cinching my face up into a pained expression. Peripherally, I can see her reaction.

Erica's eyebrows shoot up. "Six thousand? Dollars?"

"Ah...yes."

"You said you had enough money to be comfortable, but you neglected to mention you're filthy rich."

I rub the back of my neck, though I force myself to look at her. "Does it matter?"

"No. I'm surprised, that's all." She yawns. "Money doesn't impress me."

"You told me that before."

"Did I?"

"Aye, but never mind." I study her, unable to figure out the answer to why she came here, so I decide to ask. "Not that I'm complaining, but why are you here? I thought you wanted me gone."

"I came here to—um, talk."

"Let's talk, then." I arch one brow. "What did you want to discuss?"

"Uh..." She groans, pressing a hand to the cloth on her forehead. "Can't think."

"Rest here for a bit." I get up and tug the blanket over her, letting my hand linger on her arm while I caress her skin with my fingers, drawing slow circles there.

Her lids flutter closed.

I move to leave.

"Wait," she says, pushing up on her elbows. The cloth slides off her forehead onto the bed.

Sitting back down, I angle toward her.

Her face bumps into my chest as the weight of my body depresses the mattress. Tilting her head back, she meets my gaze. "Stay with me. Please."

My lips curve up in a shaky smile, and I let out the breath I hadn't realized I was holding. "Of course I will."

I climb over her body to lie down beside her. Though I long to hold her, I don't try to put my arm around her or snuggle her body against me. Summoning all the willpower I have, I simply lie here a few inches away from the woman I adore.

Erica tosses the cloth onto the bedside table and settles into the plush mattress beneath the silk sheets.

And she falls asleep.

I close my eyes, intending to relax and wait for her to wake up, but before long I drift off too. Sometime later, I feel the bed jostling just enough to half rouse me. Is Erica awake? Mired in the fog of sleep, I can't hold on to the thought. Then I hear her voice whispering to me.

"I forgive you."

Sleep pulls me down into that mire again without giving my mind a chance to grasp the meaning of what I heard. When I finally wake up, I discover I'm lying in bed alone. Erica still can't forgive me. That's why she skulked out while I was asleep. No, I heard her say, "I forgive you." Didn't I? Maybe I'd imagined it because I want her to say those words more than I've ever wanted anything.

Sliding my legs off the bed, I stand up to yawn and stretch. My gaze lands on an object that lies on the bedside table. It's a folded piece of paper. I snatch up the sheet and unfold it.

I'm going home, the note says. *I'm fine. Need time to think, that's all, so please just wait for me to contact you.* She signed the note with only her first name. Had I expected her to sign it "love, Erica"? Since I'm a bloody stupid ersehole, I sort of did expect, or at least hope, she might end her note with a more personal sign-off.

I'm to wait for her to contact me. Pushing a hand through my hair, I sit down on the bed again. Waiting is torture, but for Erica, I will do anything. She needs time, so I will give it to her. All the plans I've made mean nothing unless Erica comes back to me.

The next day, I get my answer when she texts me with an invitation.

"Meet me at Dance Ardor," her message says. "Tonight, eight o'clock. I've made my decision, Lachlan."

"Cannae ye tell me now?" I type. I feel nauseous just hearing that she's decided my fate, and waiting one second more to find out what it is feels like torture.

"Please wait until tonight. You'll find me at the bar."

That's all she says. But I'd told her before that I would do anything for her.

And so, I wait.

Chapter Thirty-One

At seven fifty-nine, I walk into Dance Ardor, heading down the dark-ened entryway into the club proper. Erica told me she'd be at the bar, and I spot a woman seated there. Though she's facing away from me, I know it's Erica. Her chestnut hair falls over her shoulders in lush waves, and the emerald dress I'd bought her months ago highlights every dip and swell on her sensual body. The stiletto heels of her shoes are hooked over the rungs of her stool. As I watch, the bartender brings her a glass of clear liquid. I wonder why she doesn't drink brandy like she had on the night we met.

I suddenly realize I've stopped moving. Why? The woman I love is right over there waiting for me, so I should be running to her. Instead, I'm stand-ing here like a ruddy statue, gazing at the backside of Erica Teague, wonder-ing what her decision will be.

Should I take it as a good sign that she wanted to see me at the site of our first meeting? It must mean something that she chose this venue. Aye, it probably means she'll tell me to sod off and find another woman in the crowd of people on the dance floor.

But she's wearing the dress I bought for her.

While I stand frozen, a bloke dressed in an expensive suit without the jacket sits down on the stool beside Erica. He skims his gaze over her body, his face lighting up when his attention lands on her breasts.

I inch closer to them, but stop again when I hear the man speak.

The *cacan*'s mouth curves into a lascivious smile as he strokes his shadow beard, still focused on Erica's bosom. "Hey, beautiful. Can I buy you a real drink?"

Real drink? I'd said the same thing to Erica on the night we met. Will she accept the smooth-talker's invitation? She let me buy her a glass of whisky, but she won't fall for the slimy *cacan*'s line. Will she?

"Well?" the bastard says, finally raising his focus to her face.

"Thank you," she says, "but I'm not drinking alcohol these days."

Not drinking? Erica never does drink much, but I can't help wondering why she's not having a cocktail tonight. The clear liquid in her glass must be water. Sparkling water, I'd wager.

The *cacan* looks surprised and mildly disappointed. "What, are you Mormon or something?"

"No." She hesitates, wriggling on her stool. "I'm a health nut. My body is a temple."

The sedate music that had been playing fades away, replaced by loud electronic music with a bass beat that pulsates through the club. Erica swallows the rest of her sparkling water, gesturing to the bartender for more.

No more procrastinating, ye numpty. Go and get her.

I saunter up behind her, slightly to the side, so she can see me if she turns this way. "May I worship at your temple, *gràidh?*"

Erica spins around on her stool, her dress snagging on it and riding up her thigh. Her mouth drops open, but her lips kink up in a surprised smile.

I grin like an eejit while she rakes her gaze over me from head to toe. Well, I am wearing my kilt and the same black T-shirt I'd worn on the night we met, along with the same black boots.

The *cacan* beside her bristles. "She's with me, jackass."

"No, I'm not," Erica declares.

My pulse accelerates when she says that. Whatever else might happen tonight, at least I know she'd rather talk to me than that slimy *bod ceann*.

Erica tries to step off her stool, but her stiletto heels get caught on the rungs. She loses her balance as her right heel slips out from under her, careening her body toward me.

I catch her, savoring the feel of her body pinned to mine.

She tips her head back to gaze up at me, her expression somewhat dazed.

Is she all right? She'd seemed to get dizzy for a moment, which caused her to stumble into me.

"Relax, I'm just clumsy," she says, as if she read my thoughts. She sounds a touch breathless. "Feeling much better today, actually."

"Glad to hear it." One corner of my mouth ticks up. "You do have a tendency to swoon into my arms."

I'd loved it every time she did that. But she only swooned into my arms twice, I think. Or maybe this is the third time.

The *cacan* seems peeved that we're ignoring him and jumps off his stool. "This douche bothering you?"

"Not at all," Erica says while gazing up at me, not blinking, seeming as entranced by my eyes as I am by hers. Her tongue slips out to moisten her lips. "I'm with the Highlander."

I grin again, but this time I have no doubts my desire for her shows on my face. It's more than lust, though. I want all of her, not just her beautiful body. I need Erica in my life for good, but she still hasn't told me her decision.

She wraps her arms around my neck and hoists her legs up to encircle my waist, locking her ankles behind my erse. Heedless of the crowd around us, she crushes her mouth to mine.

Ahmno worrying about the bloody crowd either. Erica is kissing me, and I donnae give a toss about anything else right now. Our lips fuse in a messy and desperate kiss, and I grind my lips against hers with a fervor beyond anything we've ever shared before. Two months without feeling her mouth on mine, hearing her soft wee moans of pleasure, reveling in the heat of her body and the way her tits mound against my chest... I thrust my tongue inside her mouth, and she claws her fingers into my hair like she cannae control her passion. Who cares about control? The flavor of her drives me mad, and when she lashes my tongue in greedy strokes, I lose any scraps of my inhibition that hadn't already been demolished by our kiss.

The *cacan* mutters, "You weren't the hottest chick in here, anyway."

By the time I set Erica down on her feet, the erse who had propositioned her has disappeared. Blinking rapidly, I try to stem the wetness gathering in my eyes. Crying? Me? I'd been on the verge of tears on the day Erica had slammed the door in my face when I'd turned up at her house. Humiliation doesn't matter to me anymore. I will do anything to convince Erica she can trust me again.

I place one hand on her cheek. "That eejit's wrong. You are the hottest chick in this place."

She clasps her hand over mine. "I was afraid you might not come. I mean, I know how much you hate this place."

"I will always come for you." I shift my hand, cupping her nape. "Always."

She bites her upper lip, searching my face with her gaze. "I miss you. I want to make this work, but we need to talk about a few things first."

I'm fair certain I'm gawping at her like a dafty. Did she just say... I need to be sure. So I speak slowly, my tone measured. "Are you sure that's what you want?"

Donnae get your hopes up.

"Positive," Erica says. She brushes her lips over mine, murmuring against them. "Can't deny the truth anymore. I love you. I want to be with you, for as long as you'll have me."

"As long as I'll have you?" I shake my head. "I'll be having ye for the rest of our lives and whatever comes after. Ye'll not be getting away from me again."

"I wasn't sure if you were sick of my angst."

I shake my head again. "Don't be daft, lass. I'll never get sick of you."

My hand still rests on her hip. I glide it up her back, over her shoulder, grazing my palm across her collarbone and up her throat, letting it settle on her cheek. Her hazel eyes glint in the flashing strobe lights, setting off golden sparks within her irises.

She clears her throat. "The real question is, are you sure?"

I sling my arms around her and hold on like I'll never give her up, which I never will do. "I've let go of the past, once and for all. Losing you woke me up and forced me to see what I'd done to myself—to you. All I know is I can't abide a future without you in it."

Her breasts rise and fall, a sure sign she's breathing harder. Her lips struggle to form a smile, quivering with emotion as deep as what I'm feeling right now. My throat has constricted, and the moisture in my eyes has come back. She wants me. She loves me. I duck my head close to hers, but just when I start to speak, the music crescendoes to deafening levels and drowns out what I'd meant to say.

Erica cups a hand over her ear, shouting her words. "What? I can't hear you."

I pull in a deep breath, and at the instant the song ends, I holler, "I love you."

Everyone in the club turns to stare at us. Some look baffled, others amused, and still more glare at us like we've committed a heinous crime by interrupting their hip-thrusting dance moves. Fuck what anyone else thinks. I care only about Erica's opinion.

Tears stream down her cheeks. She staggers backward, turning away from me.

I come up behind her, caressing her shoulders with my hands. "I love you, Erica. Did ye not hear me?"

"People on Jupiter heard you." She clenches her fingers in the fabric of her dress, but I can't see her expression.

I slide my hands down her inner arms. When I graze the insides of her elbows, she shivers faintly. I skate my hands down, past her wrists, and fit my palms into hers, lacing our fingers and tugging her into me. When I bend my head to whisper in her ear, she shuts her eyes and sags into me.

My lips flutter over her earlobe. "What's wrong, *gràidh*? You said you wanted to talk, but now you're pulling away."

"Sorry. I do want to talk, but I'm—I'm afraid you won't like what I have to say."

I tighten my fingers around her hands. "Nothing you might say will change how I feel. I love you, and I swear I will never leave you again."

She squeezes my fingers.

But before she can speak, the music starts up again. Bass beats thump through the floor as a woman's sensual voice purrs lyrics about desire unheeded. I slip one arm around her waist to hug her close, my cheek pressed to hers. My hand drifts down to her lower belly, and I swirl my fingers over the silky fabric of her dress.

"Please, Erica." I raise our joined hands to my lips, feathering kisses over her knuckles. "Trust me to love you no matter what."

She nods. Her voice is constricted by emotion when she says, "I reserved a private booth."

I hustle her around the dance floor's perimeter, past the heathens who writhe and thrust and flail their arms as if they're engaged in a sex ritual meant to summon the devil himself into this hedonist club. I grasp Erica's hand tighter, tug her close to me, and lay a protective arm around her shoulders. I shoot a dark glare at a man whose gaze flies to Erica's half-exposed cleavage as we pass him.

The man cringes and swings his attention to the dance floor.

My initial impression of this club hasn't changed. It's not for me. I don't think it's Erica's style either. I'd noticed the private booths the last time we were here, so I usher her out of the main club area and around a half wall to the hallway that houses booths, each hidden behind plum-colored velvet curtains. Lavender light showers down from bulbs recessed in the ceiling, but even the strange lighting can't diminish Erica's beauty. The walls dull the urgent beat of the music, so I no longer feel as if I've entered the first level of Hell.

She points toward the third booth. "That one."

Halting in front of it, I sweep the curtains aside with one hand while I place the other on the small of her back. With gentle pressure, I urge her to enter the booth. A U-shaped sofa sits tucked behind an oval table with a single lamp on the tabletop, its light bathing the space in a muted, intimate glow. When Erica scoots across the sofa, her dress catches on the purple velvet upholstery and rides up her thighs.

I stifle a groan. *Bod an Donais*, I haven't seen this much of her body since our time at the bed-and-breakfast. My mouth waters just looking at her creamy skin.

By the time I tear my focus away from her thighs, she's trying to yank the hem of her dress down, but it won't budge. The velvet holds it fast. She seems to realize she won't fix her dress unless she stands, so she gives up the fight.

I lower my body onto the sofa beside her, one arm draped across the back behind her shoulders. I settle my other hand onto her bare thigh. "You still drive me mad, without even trying to."

"Ditto." She half stifles a gasp when I push my fingers down to stroke her inner thigh. "I should be more circumspect about this, but I lose my mind whenever I'm close to you."

"I know the feeling."

Two months without touching her has left me starved for the feel of her. I can't resist petting her flesh with my fingers, loving the way she sucks in a breath. I slant toward her, my lips close enough to hers that I could kiss her. "What did you need to say?"

"Guh…"

"Still afraid?" I drop kisses along her jaw, lightly teasing her. "You can tell me anything, Erica."

She lays a hand over her belly.

"I'll go first," I say, pulling back a little. "I'm divorced, finally and forever. I made certain of that."

"Congratulations." She wriggles in place when I massage her shoulders with my fingers, then rests her hands on her knees.

"Not looking for congratulations."

"What, then?"

"I want what you promised me yesterday when you thought I couldn't hear. I want—I need for you to say it now."

She aims her lustrous hazel eyes at me. "Okay."

My hand on her thigh tenses, and I curl my fingers. Will she say it?

"I forgive you, Lachlan."

Chapter Thirty-Two

Erica forgives me. I feel light-headed when she says that, and for a few seconds, I wonder if I actually heard the words or if I just imagined I did. That day in my hotel suite, I hadn't been sure I'd heard her either. Tonight, with Erica gazing at me lovingly, I know she spoke those words—and she means them.

I lean in again, my breaths reflecting off her lips. "I took the last two months to clear out my life. Finalize the divorce. Sell my company." I withdraw my hand from her thigh, clenching it on my lap. "And to work out my, ah…fears."

She turns her face toward me, bringing us eye to eye, our mouths skimming each other. "Why sell your business?"

"Because I don't need the income anymore, and I've lost my taste for helping avaricious elites stuff their coffers with more money than they'll ever spend."

Her brows lift. "Were all your clients that bad?"

"No, most were good folk. But I'd had enough of the few greedy ones." I scratch my jaw. "I want a better life. I want to build a family, but I'm missing the keystone."

"And what's that?"

I drop my voice to a whisper. "You, Erica. You are the keystone, and the life I want will fall down around me without you."

"Oh." She opens her mouth as if to speak, then shuts it.

All I can do is watch her and wait. Forgiveness doesn't mean she wants to spend the rest of her life with me. I move closer until our bodies collide and her mouth hovers so near to mine that not kissing her takes all my willpower. "I made a mistake. I will spend the rest of my life making it up to you. I love you, lass, with all that I am. My life will be meaningless without you in it."

She searches my face again, like she's waiting to see something there.

The time has come to risk everything. Win or lose, I need to do this.

I reach into the breast pocket of my T-shirt and take hold of the small object hidden in there. With it concealed in my palm, I close my fingers over the object and offer her my hand. "This is yours, whether you take me back or not. It's a token of my love and respect for you, both of which will never die. I'm yours forever, my sweet Erica, my *gràidh*, the bonniest, sexiest lass ever to grace this earth and the cleverest, strongest woman I've ever known."

She holds perfectly still, not even blinking.

The moment of truth has arrived. My face has started to tingle, probably because I've stopped breathing. I won't catch my breath until I know her answer, so I spread my fingers, revealing the object in my palm.

Erica stares at the diamond ring.

My first impulse had been to buy the most expensive ring I could find, but that's not Erica's style. We both want a simple life, so I bought her a simple ring. A single glittering diamond tops the plain gold band. I'm praying she'll think it's tastefully beautiful, not a rubbish excuse for an engagement ring. The diamond isn't enormous, but it's not small either. When I'd bought the ring, the stone had seemed like the perfect size for her hand.

Erica jerks her head up, and our gazes intersect.

Maybe I've gone off my head for good, but I swear a bond snaps tight between us when she looks into my eyes. I crook a finger under her chin. "Will you marry me?"

Her gaze flits to the ring, then back to me. She raises a trembling hand to her throat. "Remember on our road trip, the first night we stayed in the bed-and-breakfast?"

Why is she talking about that? "Yes. I upset you, though I didn't understand why at the time."

"Now you do?"

I nod. "I was still pretending I could walk away from you and feel nothing about it."

"It's all in the past." She folds her arms over her belly. "Do you remember what happened after I threw my boots at you?"

I flash her a grin. "I made love to you, and after, you were very relaxed."

"Uh-huh." She falls silent for a moment, her gaze trained on me.

And I still have no bloody clue where this conversation is going.

She clears her throat. "We forgot something."

"I don't follow you, sweet. You'll need to be a wee bit more specific in what you're trying to say."

Her gaze darts away from me again, then back to my face. "No condom."

I arch one brow at her, still unsure of what she's getting at. But I let my mind travel back in time to that moment in the bed-and-breakfast. Several moments, actually. I'd made love to Erica, worshiping her body because I couldn't bring myself to admit I'd developed deeper feelings for her. The memory doesn't shed any light on Erica's strange obsession with that experience. Is she worried I'll be angry that she forgot to remind me to use a condom?

Brushing my lips over her cheek, I pat her naked thigh. "Hardly matters now."

"You don't understand." She winces, wringing her hands on her lap. "I'm pregnant."

I'm fair certain my eyes bulge. The best smile I can manage is a fragile one that tugs at my lips, faltering in repeated attempts to take hold, until at last a grin overpowers me. "We're having a bairn?"

She grunts and nods, but I imagine she's as stunned by the news as I am. "It's my fault."

"Your fault? Is this what you were afraid to tell me? Did you think I'd be angry?"

Erica hunches her shoulders and hugs herself. "Should've reminded you. About, you know, the condom."

"I seduced you that night." I sigh, nuzzling her neck. "It was my responsibility to remember a condom. I got so caught up in needing to wipe that frown off your face, I forgot everything else. It's my fault."

"Are you sorry it happened?"

"I'm sorry I was so careless with you." I let my hand drift higher, so close to her mound that I can feel how wet she is, even through her knickers. Aye, we still crave each other anytime we're close, even when we're in the midst of a serious conversation. I drag my lips down her throat, then angle my face up to hers. "But I could never regret making a bairn with you."

She slumps into the sofa, her expression full of love. "Neither could I."

Erica nods while tears fill her eyes, as if she can't summon words but hopes her nodding conveys what she can't say. Somehow, it does. Neither of us could ever regret what happened that night.

I splay a hand over her cheek.

She startles, glancing down at the ring I still have hooked over one finger.

Forgot about that. She hasn't answered the question I asked earlier.

Grasping my hand, Erica draws it to her chest and holds it over her heart. She plucks the ring off my fingertip. "Yes."

"What?"

"Are you deaf? The answer is yes. I would love to marry you, Lachlan."

Laughter rushes out of me, and a reckless grin stretches my lips wide. "Thank you, *gràidh*. Thank God for creating a treasure like you and, heaven almighty, thank you for giving me another chance." I pepper kisses over her cheeks, her jaw, her chin. "You will never regret it, I swear on my life."

Half crying, half giggling, Erica glances at the ring. "Are you going to put this thing on my finger or what?"

"Och, yes."

I haul her onto my lap and shimmy down the sofa to its end. Rising, I deposit her on the sofa with her feet hanging off it. Her dress has ridden up even higher to crumple around her waist, and black lace knickers peek out from under the fabric.

Black lace? She must be trying to give me a heart attack as punishment for my bad behavior. I don't care. She can torture me as long as she wants, provided she never leaves me. I will never leave her again, that's a certainty.

I kneel before her on one knee. My gaze flicks down to her knickers, and I scrub a hand over my mouth, blinking furiously, then I lift my gaze to her face. Taking hold of the ring, I raise it between us. "You are the center of my universe, Erica Teague, and I'm blessed to have you for my wife."

"My goodness, I've never heard you babble before tonight." She grins despite the tears flowing down her cheeks. "You really are a changed man."

I slip the ring onto her finger, head bowed, and turn my eyes up to look at her. "Don't care if I sound like an eejit. Best get used to my babbling because I intend to let you know every single day how much I cherish you." Dropping my head, I press my puckered lips to her belly. "And our bairn. Which I'm certain will be a bonnie wee lassie just like you."

When I tilt my head back to smile at her, she bends to rest her forehead on mine. "I think it'll be a boy. Braw and handsome like his father."

"Hmm. Maybe we should have several bairns, to make sure we get a boy and a girl."

"How about dozens of little MacTaggarts running around in the heather?"

"Dozens, aye."

A smile of unrestrained joy breaks across my face. Never in my life have I been this happy before. Through half-closed eyes, I drink in the vision of her, from her slender ankles to her perfect breasts and higher to her beautiful face. Cannae help that my gaze stalls at her bosom for a heartbeat. Everything about her body is spectacular, and I'm imagining every possible way I can make her come for me tonight, over and over and over. When I meet her gaze, I capture her face in my hands and let my lips tease hers as I sketch the outline of her mouth with my tongue in swift licks. She thrusts her hands into my hair, dragging me in for a kiss that scorches me through and through, our hungry tongues wrestling while our mouths muffle each other's moans and groans.

Suddenly, she breaks away.

I pull her tight against me, certain she can feel my erection. "Not done with you."

"Oh, Lachlan."

I shove my fingers inside her knickers, down into her cleft. "You're so wet."

"Please, wait—" Erica shudders when I rub my fingers up and down her flesh in slow, relentless circles. She throws her head back, exposing her throat to me. I lick and nip and kiss a path up from her collarbone to her ear, suckling the lobe while I torment her nub with my fingers. She gasps. "Not here. Please."

I freeze with my fingers resting on the damp hairs between her thighs. "Where?"

"Can't go to my place. My parents are there."

"My hotel," I growl, and sweep her up into my arms while I surge to my feet.

"Hurry."

I manage to yank her dress down to cover her thighs without letting go of her, a feat I can pull off only because she fits snugly in one arm. Aye, she is perfect for me in every way. She snatches her small purse off the table an instant before I stride out of the booth, the curtains billowing around us, and storm down the hallway into the club proper. Erica padlocks her arms around my neck. I march straight across the dance floor, ignoring the couples who scatter to get out of our way. People stare at us in disbelief, but everyone steps aside.

Once we've exited the building, I pause. "Where's your car?"

"There." She points across the parking lot. The cool night air raises goosebumps on her skin, but she'll warm up soon enough once I've got her alone and naked in my hotel suite. She wraps her arms around me more snugly while I rush across the pavement to her car and set her down beside the passenger door.

"Keys," I command.

She digs them out of her purse and hands them to me. "I see we're back to monosyllabic Lachlan."

I grunt, unlock the door, and hurl it open. "Not capable of conversation right now. All I can think about is stripping you naked and ravishing you until sunrise."

"Well, in that case…" She climbs into the car and—on purpose this time, I'm sure—lets her skirt hike up. "Get a move on."

Chapter Thirty-Three

On a sunny Wednesday morning, I stand in a field of heather, hand in hand with Erica as we speak our vows before our gathered families. Erica looks bonnier than ever in her elegantly simple white dress that's trimmed in lace, its full skirt fluttering faintly in the warm breeze that whispers around us. She is more than beautiful, though. My soon-to-be-wife is a vision of angelic grace. When Erica had first seen me as she and her entourage strolled up the hill toward me and my groomsmen, who are my brothers Rory and Aidan, she had grinned at me. Well, I am wearing the kilt I know she loves, but instead of a black T-shirt, I've chosen the top half of a suit—a shirt, tie, and jacket.

Now I stand amid the heather on a tree-cloaked hillside that slopes up behind us while a gentle grade extends down behind us to our new house, and beyond that, the glassy waters of Loch Leven with its smattering of islands. The village of Ballachulish nestles along the loch's shores, hemmed in by mountains. The shadows of those peaks stretch over the village, but not a single cloud mars the azure sky, and a disk of pure sunshine lights up the village as if Mother Nature herself wants to give us the perfect view today.

A certain golden retriever dances around amid the guests as far as his retractable leash will allow. Frank Teague holds tight to the leash's handle, but no one seems fashed by Casey's exuberance. Just as the ceremony starts, the pup sits down and falls silent, as if he understands the importance of this moment.

The minister recites the usual spiel, and Erica and I say the requisite words, but I can't focus on the vows or anything except her shimmering golden eyes. How did I get this lucky? I cocked it up so badly and so often with her that I can't imagine why she took me back. But she did, and I'm more grateful than I could ever express that I'm standing on this hillside, binding my life to hers forever.

When I slip the wedding band onto her finger, tears roll down Erica's cheeks, but I know they're tears of joy. She gazes at me with rapt adoration, and I know I'm looking at her the same way. My smile trembles as she places the ring on my finger, and my eyes glisten too, though I manage not to cry. I wouldn't care if I did shed a few tears. The happiness I thought I would never know had found me in the last place I would've ever expected—in an underground club in Chicago—and despite the odds stacked against us, Erica and I have found our fairy-tale ending.

After the ceremony, Erica's father claps me on the shoulder and says, "Glad I didn't have to shoot you."

I arch one brow. What is he on about? Shoot me? Over the past few months, when I talked to Erica's parents on the phone every day, I learned Frank Teague has a strange sense of humor. That means he'll fit right in with my family.

With a sheepish shrug, Erica tells me, "The possibility may have been discussed at one point. Weeks ago."

Her father grins. "I offered, but Erica said 'nah, don't bother.'"

"Frank," Deb Teague says in the indulgent tone I've often heard her use when she's speaking to her husband, "don't scare the poor boy. We decided we like him, remember? Offing your new son-in-law is rude."

"I'd only wing him," Frank insists.

Erica had warned me about the Teague family's favorite pastime of harassing friends and relatives with strange sarcasm, assuring me that "it means we love you, honey." I informed her that she might need a similar warning before she meets the MacTaggart clan.

Now Deb envelops me in a bear hug while Frank grasps my hand to shake it vigorously. I aim a bemused smile at my wife.

"Okay, okay," Erica says, pushing her parents away from me and linking her hands around my arm. "There will be no winging Lachlan today."

"Today?" I ask, eying her askance but with a slight smirk.

"I need some way to keep you in line." Erica raises onto her tiptoes to peck a kiss on my lips. "Can I have my own sword?"

"We'll see."

My brothers approach us then, with sly grins lighting up their faces. Even Rory is beaming today, having set aside his reputation as the Ogre of Loch Fairbairn for this happy occasion. I know Rory has issues he doesn't want to discuss with anyone, not even our cousin Jack, who's a psychologist. I hope Rory can recover from his past the way I've done, and I'm glad to see him smiling today.

Rory and Aidan both slap me on the back.

As the youngest brother, Aidan always feels it's his duty to harass me. So naturally, he winks and says, "Picked a hot one there, Lachie. When do I get to kiss the bride?"

"Never," I reply in a dead-calm voice. "Don Juan MacTaggart does not get to practice on my wife. And don't call me Lachie unless you're wanting to get skelped."

"So sensitive," Rory says, as he sidles around Aidan to get closer to my wife. "Welcome to the family, Erica. Best get used to Lachie being a humbug. He's a boring, humorless man."

I'm humorless? The Ogre of Loch Fairbairn outdoes me in terms of stoicism and curtness. Well, usually. But not today.

"Oh, don't worry," Erica assures Rory while snuggling closer to me. "My husband is exciting and entertaining for me. Maybe he just doesn't like you two scunners."

Aidan and Rory burst out laughing.

I shake my head at them as a slight smile curves my mouth.

"She's already taking to our language," Rory says. "Better watch your wife, Lachlan, or she'll be a true Scottish lassie before you know it, cursing at you in Gaelic."

"Let me help her along," Aidan announces, his expression full of mock innocence while he clasps Erica's shoulder with one hand. "Now, just say *an toir thu dhomh pòg.*"

Aidan, you bloody cacan. You'll pay for this, mark my words.

I slap a hand on Aidan's chest and shove him away. My brother stumbles backward, laughing so hard his eyes water.

"What?" Erica asks, glancing between me and Aidan.

My brother loves to joke, and I can't stop my lips from twisting into a half-restrained smile. "*An toir thu dhomh pòg* means will you give me a kiss."

Done harassing me, Aidan and Rory wander off to mingle with the other guests.

My parents come over to congratulate me and Erica, which of course involves hugging. My father, who has never been much of a hugger, throws his arms around me and thumps me on the back.

"This time it'll stick," he whispers to me.

Niall MacTaggart has already started to teach Frank Teague how to play shinty, so I don't need to worry about how everyone will get on. Aye, my family will fit in very well with Erica's. They're all barmy.

Gradually, the wedding guests head down the hill to their cars parked in front of our house, so they can drive into the village for the reception. And aye, holding the wedding festivities in the village was my idea. I'd planned to sneak off to our house for a private party, which meant I needed to get rid of our families and friends so I can make Erica scream my name as loud as she wants and we won't disturb anyone. Our parents, the last guests to leave, stop to say goodbye before the MacTaggarts drive the Teagues into town for the reception.

Casey bounds around us with his tongue lolling and flapping. Casey will stay with Erica's parents tonight, though he will come home in the morning. I think he'll enjoy his new life as a Scottish farm dog.

Deb hugs Erica and whispers something I can't hear, something that makes Erica blush.

My father whispers to me too, though I don't blush when he says, "Do us all proud, laddie, and shag Erica until dawn the way I did with Sorcha on our wedding night."

I did not need to know about that, and I have no idea how to respond. Fortunately, our parents leave and spare me the agony of discussing sex with my father.

But aye, I'm planning to shag my wife all night long.

As the last taillights of the last guests recede into the night, I hoist my wife into my arms and carry her over the threshold of our new home—*our* farm in the Highlands, where we will raise as many bairns as Erica wants, whether that's one or half a dozen. I'd worried I might never break free of Aisley and that even if I did, the damage I'd let her do to me would never heal enough that I could find the life I'd always wanted. But I'd been wrong. Though I wouldn't have admitted it at the time, I fell for Erica the first time I saw her tending the roses outside her house. I'm still falling, a little more every day, and I won't ever stop.

I set my wife down, shut the door, and smile. "Welcome home, Erica MacTaggart."

"It's so beautiful, Lachlan."

I hold up one finger. "Got another surprise for you."

"You know how I love your surprises."

Trotting into the living room, I grab the item and return to Erica.

Her hand flies to her chest, and her eyes flare wide for an instant. "I thought you were kidding when you said—"

"A Scotsman doesn't joke about these things." I spread my legs wide and raise the sword in front of my chest. "Like my claymore?"

"Oh, yes."

I brandish the five-foot-long sword with both hands. "Better run for yer life, lassie, 'cause ahm coming fer ye."

Erica sprints for the bedroom, giggling all the way while I race after her. When we reach the bedroom, she lets me catch her. I toss the sword onto the floor and sweep her up into my waiting arms. "Time to pay the tithe."

"Tithe?"

"Aye," I tell her with sarcastic solemnity. "Every Highland wife must pay her husband a tax on the wedding night."

She rolls her eyes. "You've got way more money than I do. Want the five bucks I still have in my purse?"

"Not money, *gràidh*." I heave her onto the bed, making her yelp while she whumps down on the lush bedding, her erse sinking into it. I give her a wicked grin, infusing it with all the lust she inspires in me. "I had another kind of tithe in mind."

"Hmm, in that case..." She stretches her entire body, the movement lifting her breasts high enough that they almost spill out of her dress. "I'll pay up gladly."

I strip off my clothes faster than ever and sprawl on top of her. Thrusting a hand under her, I fumble for the buttons on her dress but can't quite grasp any of them. My lips tighten, my jaw aches from clenching my teeth, and I feel like my cock will explode before I ever get this ruddy dress off her. After about thirty seconds of jostling and struggling, I spring to my knees and throw my arms up. "Bloody hell, woman, what kind of contraption have you got holding you in that thing?"

"Buttons." She pushes up into a sitting position, her face aligned with my waving erection, and bats her eyelashes at me, her face the picture of false innocence. "Is there a problem, my lord and master?"

My mouth puckers again, but this time because I'm trying not to laugh. Never in a thousand lifetimes would Erica obey my every whim and command, and I don't want her to, anyway. I love her fiery spirit. "Careful. I might take you up on the lord-and-master bit."

She gets to her knees, shuffling around until her back faces me, then she glances over her shoulder. "Surely a powerful warrior such as yourself can handle a few buttons."

A challenge? Oh, she's in for it now.

I growl low in my throat, seize her dress, and rip the buttons open with one jerk of my hands. Buttons go flying, but ahmno paying attention to that. With Erica's back exposed to me, all I can think about is the many ways I plan to fuck her tonight. So I flatten my hands on her back, running them down to her waist and up again until I meet the barrier of her bra. Unhooking the tiny clasps, I drag my tongue down her skin, tracing a slick path along her spine, dancing my tongue over each vertebra while she shivers and sucks in a ragged breath. Then I shove the dress off her shoulders.

With my mouth now on her neck, I murmur, "*Tha gaol agam ort.*"

"I don't speak Gaelic yet."

But I mean to teach her, with a special focus on dirty Gaelic.

I push the fabric over her hips, and the dress pools around her knees. I dispatch her bra, sending it fluttering to the floor. She reaches behind her to slide her fingers into my hair. I clasp her around the waist with both hands to heft her up and out of the dress, spin her around, and lay her across the bed flat on her back. Finally, I tear her knickers off.

She smiles, biting her lip.

"*Tha gaol agam ort* means I love you," I tell her while I lower my body onto her with my hard cock trapped between our bodies. "Forever, *mo leannan.*"

"I love you too. Forever and ever." She wriggles, which makes me suck in a breath. "You're mine, Lachlan MacTaggart. *Gràidh.*"

Cradling her head in my hands, I gaze deeply into her eyes. "I love the way you say *gràidh*. You pronounce it perfectly."

"Is it my pronunciation you're interested in at the moment?" She locks one leg around mine, rubbing my body into her slick, swollen cleft.

The sensation of her naked body beneath me and the scent of her cream makes me so randy I almost choke on my own saliva. "Couldnae give a fuck about yer pronunciation right now."

Wrapping her arms around me, she rakes her nails up and down my back. "Show me what you *are* thinking about."

I slant my mouth over hers in a hard kiss, full of heat and tangling tongues, groaning into her mouth because she feels and tastes so bloody wonderful. When I pull away, she gazes up at me with raw hunger burning in her eyes and coloring her cheeks.

"Now," she begs, arching her hips into me. "Please."

"Anything for you, *gràidh*." I drive into her with one long, powerful thrust, my eyes half-closed because she feels so perfect wrapped around me. Erica cries out, her back bowing. I take her with leisurely strokes, reveling in every sensation while she claws at my back and pleads for release, only to beg me never to stop with her very next breath. I want this moment to last forever, but I need to come inside her body even more. So I brace myself on my straight arms, grunting and shouting her name while my chest heaves and I pump harder and faster until the slapping of flesh on flesh fills the room. Sweat sheaths my body and drips off my chest onto her where it mingles with her perspiration. I want to lick up every last drop of moisture on her body, from the sweat glistening on her tits to her cream that coats my cock.

Her body convulses as she comes with a whimpering scream, clutching at me until her fingers dig into my upper arms. The feel of her body milking my cock does me in. I explode inside her with a sharp, hoarse shout. After a few more thrusts, I'm done, and I collapse beside her, breathing as hard as she is. For a few minutes, all I can do is struggle to catch my breath and wait for my pulse to slow down. Making love to Erica always drives me wild with lust, but it calms me too. The contradiction makes perfect sense to me.

I pull her onto her side, tucked against my body with her head nestled on my shoulder. "Are you happy, sweet?"

She props her chin on my chest to aim her lustrous gaze at me. "You know I am. A few months ago, I thought I was going to prison. Just a few weeks ago, I thought I'd never have what I really want." She snuggles into me, brushing her fingers over my cheek. "Now I have everything. With you."

I capture her hand, enclosing it in mine. "You've given me more than I ever dreamed I'd have. Nothing will ever take me away from you, Erica."

"I'm not going anywhere. This is where I belong." She clears her throat and says, *"An toir thu dhomh pòg?"*

A breath blusters out through my nostrils. I hug her tighter, my passion for her suffusing my voice. "Keep speaking Gaelic."

"Why?"

I flip us both over, with her body beneath me and my quickly rousing cock trapped between us. "Because hearing you speak Gaelic will keep me going all night."

"Promises, promises."

"A guarantee."

For the rest of the night, I prove to her that I will always keep my promises. Sometime in the wee hours, we curl up under the sheets, exhausted in the best way, and fall asleep in each other's arms, content in our life together.

At long last, I've found bliss. *Thank you, mo leannan.*

Epilogue

Nine months later

Brothers are a trial, for certain. In the year since I first met Erica, my life has changed beyond recognition—and that's a good thing, since my old life had, as my wife would say, "sucked big time." Now that I'm happy, with a wife and a new bairn, I want my siblings to find the same joy Erica has given me. Erica suggested I should give them each a push in the right direction, but I will not meddle in their lives. It would be impolite.

Erica laughed when I said that. "Like you MacTaggarts ever worry about being rude to each other. It's a family pastime, though you guys do it with love and affection, not nastiness. So go on, meddle in the lives of your brothers and sisters. I'll help."

"No, you bloody will not. And I bloody will not either."

"Okay, okay. Calm down, honey, it was just a suggestion."

I gave up on discussing the topic with Erica after that, since she has barmy ideas about meddling, ideas only a woman would dream up. Though my sisters seem happy enough, my two brothers are not. Rory survived three failed marriages, though none of us knows exactly what caused those relationships to fail. It must've been awful, that's all I know. A few months ago, Rory informed everyone, at a family gathering, that he will never marry again.

He really should know better than to say that in front of the women in our family.

Naturally, my mother and sisters have decided to play matchmaker and help Rory find a wife.

I might be on board with that plan if they weren't so blatant about it. Ma keeps arranging for Rory to "accidentally" bump into eligible lasses whenever he leaves his castle to venture into Loch Fairbairn or Ballachulish. Those are the only places he wants to visit these days, and he doesn't leave the castle compound very often.

As for Aidan… Well, he suffered a major setback six months ago, but I'm sure he will bounce back soon. My youngest brother has never been married, though he loves to flirt with the lasses. That's why everyone calls him Don Juan MacTaggart. I know the incident six months ago has changed him, but I don't realize how far off his head he's gone until the day he comes to visit me and Erica at our farm.

Aye, we're growing vegetables, and we have dairy cows too.

Getting back to Aidan, the eejit announces his ridiculous plan while Erica and I are enjoying lunch with him in our kitchen.

"I need a holiday," he says. "Thought I'd go to America. Chicago, to be precise."

"Chicago?" I say, probably sounding more shocked than I intended. "Why the bloody hell would you want to go there? You hate the city, any city. I remember when you graduated university and declared you would never leave the Highlands again because three years in Edinburgh was too much."

"I'm older and wiser now, aren't I?"

"Like hell you are." I bar my arms over my chest and aim my sternest glare at him. "You're twenty-eight, Aidan. That's not old enough to be wise. What is the real reason you want to take a holiday in Chicago?"

He squirms and contorts his mouth, as if he's sitting on the sharp tip of a rusty nail. "Well, ah, I sort of thought…"

When he trails off, I huff. "Spit it out, laddie."

"Donnae be calling me laddie, unless you're wanting me to shout 'Lachie is a cradle robber' in the middle of the village." He winks at Erica. "You're much closer to my age than to this old man's."

"Haud yer wheesht, Aidan," I all but growl.

"If you want me to explain my plan, I cannae shut up. Aye?" He smirks when I roll my eyes. "Now, about my plan. You found a bonnie, sweet wife in Chicago, and I'm so much sexier and more entertaining than you. I'm thinking I can find a wife there too."

"Chicago has millions of people in it. The biggest city you've ever seen was Edinburgh, which has half a million."

"Aye. That's why I know I can find a wife in America."

Eying my brother with suspicion, I squint at him. "Is there more to your daft plan?"

"Of course." He grins. "I plan to visit the same club where you met Erica."

"What? No, you will not."

"Ah, I see. It's good enough for you, but not for me." Aidan clucks his tongue. "Uptight and a hypocrite. Careful, Lachie, you're almost turning into Rory."

Though our conversation continues after that, I give up on trying to talk Aidan out of his brilliant plan. He called it brilliant, not me. I think his recent calamity has knocked him off his axis, and he's desperate to find his equilibrium again. Can't blame him for that. Maybe a trip to America will help him move on.

So I agree to lend him the jet Rory and I recently bought, so he can fly to Chicago without having to deal with airlines and security checkpoints and all that rubbish. If my brother means to take a holiday across the pond, I will do whatever I can to ensure he doesn't get in too much trouble. But I've given up on convincing him not to visit Dance Ardor.

Instead, I decide to do to him what he often does to me—play a wee joke on him.

While we stand on the tarmac at the Inverness airport, beside the jet, I clap Aidan on the shoulder and tell him, "There's something you should know about that club. Every Friday is kilt night at Dance Ardor."

"Really? The lasses love me in a kilt."

Ah, the young are so gullible. After all the grief he's caused me, I've earned a touch of payback. Besides, I know he will go to the club no matter what I say. I wish I could see the look on his face when he realizes no one else is wearing a kilt, but I'll settle for hearing about it after the fact.

"Oh aye, American women love kilts," I tell him. "You'll be a hit for certain."

"When I come home, I will have a wife. Care to wager on it?"

"No, I do not."

Erica and I watch Aidan climb up the stairs to board the jet, then we wander back to the parking lot. Just as I've turned the key in the ignition to start up our new Land Rover, my wife turns to me.

"Why did you tell Aidan every Friday is kilt night at Dance Ardor?" she asks.

I chuckle. "Payback, *mo leannan*. It's the currency of brothers."

"Only to the MacTaggarts." She leans over the center console to kiss my cheek. "Now, since you're in a meddling mood, let's talk about Rory."

"No, Erica. You women are doing him enough 'favors' already." I shift the car into drive and back out of the parking space. "I'd much rather talk about what we're going to do tonight after our son falls asleep."

"Get naked and play Highland lord and master again, of course."

"You are the naughtiest Highland lassie of them all."

And I love that about her. I love her, full stop. I wouldn't change a thing about my life.

I've just steered the car onto the highway when my wife speaks up.

"Since we have time on the three-hour drive to get home," she says, "let's talk about how we can help your sisters and brothers find their soul mates."

I groan. "Can we stop for a wee piece first? I'm famished."

"Sure thing, honey. I live to serve my lord and master."

For the rest of the day and all night, I forget about the rest of the world. Maybe I do want my siblings to find love and start families of their own, but meddling is not the answer.

How will Aidan fare in Chicago?

Only those American lasses know the answer.

Want more of Aidan MacTaggart? Experience his story in *Aidan in a Kilt*, book two in The Ballachulish Trilogy.

Did you miss the original version of this story told from Erica's viewpoint? *Dangerous in a Kilt* is available now everywhere.

Anna Durand is a bestselling, multi-award-winning author of contemporary and paranormal romance. Her books have earned bestseller status on every major retailer and wonderful reviews from readers around the world. But that's the boring spiel. Here are the really cool things you want to know about Anna!

Born on Lackland Air Force Base in Texas, Anna grew up moving here, there, and everywhere thanks to her dad's job as an instructor pilot. She's lived in Texas (twice), Mississippi, California (twice), Michigan (twice), and Alaska—and now Ohio.

As for her writing, Anna has always made up stories in her head, but she didn't write them down until her teen years. Those first awful books went into the trash can a few years later, though she learned a lot from those stories. Eventually, she would pen her first romance novel, the paranormal romance *Willpower*, and she's never looked back since.

Want even more details about Anna? Get access to her extended bio when you subscribe to her newsletter and download the free bonus ebook, *Hot Scots Confidential*. You'll also get hot deleted scenes, character interviews, fun facts, and more! Plus you'll receive the short story *Tempted by a Kiss* and mutliple bonus chapters in both ebook and audiobook formats.

Visit AnnaDurand.com to sign up.